Going to Patchogue

Thomas McGonigle

GOING TO PATCHOGUE

Dalkey Archive Press

BEWARE
It's all true.
It's all made up.
—The Mayor of the Mascot Dock

© 1992 Thomas McGonigle

Library of Congress Cataloging-in-Publication Data
McGonigle, Thomas.
  Going to Patchogue / by Thomas McGonigle.
  1. Patchogue (N.Y.)—History—Fiction.   I. Title.
PS3563.C3644G65   1991   91-13068
813'.54—dc20
ISBN 0-916583-87-2

First Edition

Partially funded by a grant from The Illinois Arts Council.

Dalkey Archive Press
1817 North 79th Avenue
Elmwood Park, IL 60635 USA

Printed on permanent/durable acid-free paper and bound in the United States of America.

FOR the instruction of the alien residents within the foreign enclave in Patchogue:
Barbara, Helen, Mike, Maria, Johan, Ilse, Eugene, Hilary, Geoffrey, Christian,
Anne, Eddie, Philip, Audrey, John, Harritena, Giovanni, Marina, Susan, Nuala,
Anne Marie, Todor, Julián.
May the waters not harm them too much.

Perhaps mazes
of structures to transmit dust.
—Gil Orlovitz

The pale Usher—threadbare in coat, heart, body, and brain dusts his old lexicons and grammars, with a queer handkerchief, mockingly embellished with all the gray flags of all the known nations of the world. He loved to dust his old grammars and memories; it somehow mildly reminded him of his mortality.

It will be seen that this mere painstaking burrower and grubworm of a poor devil of a Sub-Sub appears to have gone through the long Vaticans and street-stalls of the earth picking up whatever random allusions to Patchogue. Therefore you must not, in every case at least, take the higgledy-piggledy statements, however authentic, in these extracts, for veritable gospel. Far from it. As touching the ancient authors generally, as well as the poets here appearing, these extracts are solely valuable or entertaining, as affording a glancing bird's-eye view of what has been promiscuously said, thought, fancied and sung.

So fare thee well, poor devil of a Sub-Sub, whose commentator I am. Thou belongest to that hopeless, sallow tribe which no wine of this world will ever warm; and for whom even Pale Thundering Sherry would be too rosy-strong; but with whom one sometimes loves to sit in the cool oasis, and feel poor-devilish, too; and grow convivial upon tears; and say to them bluntly, with full eyes and empty glasses, and in not altogether unpleasant sadness—Give it up, Sub-Subs! For by how much the more pains ye take to please the world, by so much the more shall ye for ever go thankless!

Here ye strike but splintered hearts together—there, ye shall strike unsplinterable glasses!

—H. Malgrad

The word *Patchogue* without the capital *P*, in Old Finnish, is the adjective used to describe the quality of light given off by the setting sun when seen through a stand of white birch trees.

Rice-growing is not an occupation in Patchogue.
   The lace mill has been closed for some time.
   Steel tapes are manufactured in Patchogue.
   Coastal steamers are no longer constructed in Patchogue though clamboats are still built and repaired on the Patchogue River.
   There is a small movie industry and a literary circle meets once a month.

Dad talks of the first winter. On the morning when the bay froze over for the first time I went down to the beach and walked out on the ice. Sea gulls had been trapped in the ice. Some of them were still alive. I hit them over the head with a piece of drift lumber. Then I took my penknife and cut the bodies off at the first joint of the leg. I left behind a little forest of bloody stumps. We had a lot of sea gull soup that first winter.

PATCHOGUE INVITES YOU
ON GREAT SOUTH BAY
THE METROPOLIS OF LONG ISLAND
ON THE SUNRISE TRAIL
OFFERS YOU EVERYTHING THE VACATIONIST
COULD ASK FOR
FINE STORES
FINE HOTELS
NATURE'S PLAYGROUND
FOR PARTICULARS APPLY
PATCHOGUE
CHAMBER OF COMMERCE

It was never conclusively proven but it has been long believed that those new French people who moved into the Pellogrino place on Cedar Avenue mixed ground-up glass into the bowls of fresh dog food and placed them along the property lines. People said this was the way foreign people must announce their arrival in a new village in Europe: dogs hemorrhaging in kitchens all over the neighborhood.

The population of Patchogue varies. Each year a number of people die and a number of people find themselves born in the village.

Yip, Yip, Yaphank, the Irving Berlin show that included the hit song, "Oh, How I Hate to Get Up in the Morning," had its pre-Broadway tryout in 1917 at the Star Palace Theater in Patchogue. The building, at 8 West Main Street, now houses the Main Street Press, among other businesses. Stationed at nearby Camp Upton in Yaphank during World War I, Mr. Berlin returned there in 1942 to prepare the musical, "This is the Army." While at an earlier date, P. G. Wodehouse was writing about a bungalow in Patchogue.

The Patchogue River has been fenced in and trespassers are advised to use caution.

from the eyes of God drops of semen flowed forming a divided humanity of blonde women dressed in white brassieres and black panties while men walked along with penises so big they had to carry them on stainless steel Breslow Wheelbarrows . . . such was the scrap of writing left behind by the assistant pastor of St. Francis de Sales Church when he was transferred back to the City where altar boys liked to have cigarettes stubbed out on the backs of their hands; they were tough in the City. The priest was said to be writing a learned article, "On Awful Fairness," having seen and been struck by the well-known symbol of justice up on a shelf behind the back of the judge in police court where he was protesting a ticket for a broken right rear light on his 1958 Dodge on the grounds of clerical immunity.

The Bulgarian with the new orange hair was telling Brad Walbauer, the Village Gutter Stream Cleaner, that she had thought her husband was English but he turned out to be American via Ireland when she first met him in Sofia.

Her husband had a penguin walk and liked blonde girls just like husbands do all over the world. However, unlike husbands in Bulgaria, he did not beat his wife or eat more than his share of the *mousaka.*

Bob C. (last name ending in a vowel, Mr. Furman noted) was arrested for selling Italian ices made out of donkey piss. Bob was taken before a Patchogue Village justice of the peace who said he would have to be sent to undergo a psychiatric examination as to his sanity before he could stand trial. Bob C. (probably afraid of offending the civil rights of that organization that doesn't exist, Miss Fisher replied to Mr. Furman) told the judge that he would be better advised to commit to an institution the man or person who would have to decide whether selling ice cream made of donkey piss was insane or not.

Bob C. asked that his last name not be printed in the newspapers as his daughter was competing in the Third Annual Freestyle Ballet Competition in Varna, People's Republic of Bulgaria, *and* whoever heard of confusing Italian ices with ice cream?

4

your mother threw me a fuck and then your old man put a fuck into her while a bunch of guys at the Oasis were going on about your sister who's a piece of meat every nigger in Africa on Rider Avenue had a go at after the Fourth of July parade your mother doesn't use the leg of a chair to comb hair   no matter what people say   she washes her head in the toilet bowl and doesn't comb her hair   your mother uses cut up pieces of sheet when she got the curse and uses the blood for fingernail polish   your mother sits on the Mascot dock stuffing crabs up her snatch   (a note found in the parking lot behind the junior high school on South Ocean Avenue, November 1958)

In 1942 old man Nellis was breeding yellow cats behind his shack on Furman Lane. The Village Board had asked him to do this so they would have objects to hang at the annual Fourth of July parade as an example of what they expected their boys to do to the Nip bastards.
   In 1950 old man Nellis was again raising yellow cats.
   He died in 1963 so he made no contribution to the Vietnam War effort.

PATCHOGUE, 56.2m. (7,147 pop.) has been something of an industrial center for two centuries. Three small streams in the vicinity were dammed for lumber and gristmills probably before 1750. By 1800 the Union Twine Mill, third of its kind in the United States and the first to supply cotton carpet warp, was in operation. Later capital turned to the manufacture of lace, which now provides employment for about 800. The population includes a considerable number of Italians and Poles. Lakeview Cemetery (L), State 27 near Waverly Ave., embraces the site of the former Hart's Tavern, visited by Washington in 1790, and contains the grave of Seba Smith, who wrote under the pen name of "Major Jack Downey," an early philosopher of the Sam Slick and Mr. Dooley fraternity. With him is interred his wife, Elizabeth Oakes Smith, writer of many books and short stories, and a pioneer in the agitation for equal suffrage for women. East of Patchogue is a dwarf pine and oak country, through which the route hugs the Long Island Railroad.

Little girls used to wear in Patchogue little boy's underwear all the time. But there was a time when little boys caught a terrible time of it when they were had in sixth grade St. Francis de Sales gym class wearing little girls' underwear. But it was later said that everything was okay most of the time afterwards because little girls turn on/off like water faucets or opening/closing icebox doors.

Coach Joe Agostinello in hygiene class told the boys that when you picked it, swallow it and don't put it under the desk where you guys keep the chewing gum. Good eating habits begin with good picking habits.

A friend of André Breton mentions in a letter that he drove out to Patchogue from New York City with Breton during World War II, or at least drove toward *Pas de Chos,* never wanting to actually reach such a place, though happy pronouncing it aloud each to the other, because this friend and Breton had done it so many times at this other place near Paris—though then they did not have highway signs announcing Patchogue in forty, thirty, twenty, ten miles.

Ortel's was a bucket of blood sort of place when it was full of people who for the most part believed if you put a horsehair in a glass of water it would turn into a worm. On a busy night the buckets had to be emptied three or four times and there was a danger the lima-bean plants would rot in the ground from overwatering. Ed Nowiki said, you don't want to know what happens when people had a bad time of it. Just for beginners, blonde girls get locked up in closets and . . .

O, Carol Lynley on the cover of the paperback of *Blue Denim* (1961) in W. T. Grant's store on Main Street. You have a teenage problem, *that one,* caused by Brandon de Wilde, later as a kissed stranger you come out of the surf with a speargun not killing the kid but the beachball because it's on your beach and you have to get ready to upstage Larry Olivier in a drunken English pub. In spite of film buff disapproval of your thunder thighs I look forward to eating meals out of your cookbook and looking at your paintings because in the midst of a busy schedule you are becoming a painter as well as being a writer, an actress and a mother to a child from a guy who was a real dipshit. Ah, Carol, your blonde hair lashes the insides of my eyeballs.

City People were not allowed to use the municipal swimming pool because they'd piss and even shit in the water. With the passage of time village residents were known to piss and shit in the pool. There was talk of issuing nose- and mouth-guards to swimmers but no one wanted to be the first to suggest such a step.

It was a night on the town. They had been to Bastille: The Cell Block of Rock and were on their way to the Cro-Magnon Club when the car went out of control. It was a closed-coffin funeral. The undertaker did not give the girl's sweatshirt to her mother. It was just too icky, the girl's sister told her mother. The mother was very upset. The sweatshirt was printed with the only photograph of the mother's first grandchild. That child wasn't much more than a puddle when they got it out of the wreck, that night. It was a shame. If the accident had happened only a year ago they could have printed a picture of the girl and her boyfriend on the IN MEMORY page of the *Record,* the yearbook of Patchogue Senior High School.

In 1960 the "Swedish handjob" was popular. Girls and advanced boys went to this new place on Bay Avenue and had their fingers filed down to the size of the pinky. Someone had read that sharp edges were then popular in Sweden, a state in

Scandinavia. If you go to the Oasis Bar on South Ocean Avenue, you can meet people from that time. They are still real sharp.

Brick Bolger was the last independent trustee on the Village Board and he was disgusted.

City People, I know, have a right to come out here and use their homes off of Cedar Avenue, mark you, that bungalow colony should never have been built, during the summer right! But something's got to be done, I don't know, maybe along an educational line, that come September, they can't leave their pets and abortions scattered all over the village. It's unhealthy, unsafe, and rude of these people. They take up these defenseless kittens and puppies in June, play with them all summer, and come the weekend after Labor Day, back to the City they scoot, leaving behind these pathetic creatures that have to be collected and disposed of by Hal Johnson. And the abortions: I know a lot of them have doctors in the family and those sorts of people can't resist turning a quick buck, I just don't understand why they can't use their clinics in the City or even the rooms of the Cedar Grove Motel—it's beyond me why they get these poor women to squat and leave these puddles of flesh in the far corners of the backyards, attracting vermin, dogs, and even human perverts from Bellport, who, it's said, use these fleshy stains in pagan rituals tolerated by the Unitarian Church. An urgent education campaign is called for and while I no longer complain of these City People monopolizing the tennis courts on Rider Avenue, there are limits, because sexual relations aren't just another sort of sport.

Victor had a bayonet with real dried Jap blood on it that his father got in the war. Victor had a friend who lived up in Africa near Rider Avenue even though he wasn't colored like most of the people there. Victor and he used to go to the wholesale meat market on East Main Street and because they were white the Jewman never watched them. Victor and his friend always came home with a smoked beef tongue because it fits nicely under the armpit. Victor's neighbors looked down at him because they didn't steal parts.

The vets are sitting in the Oasis on South Ocean Avenue the day before the checks arrive; got enough money between them so three can drink and two get enough to piss, still talking about Paula P. who got knocked up on the night of the Senior Prom, scratched a brilliant career at Suffolk Community College, in Communication Arts, still talking about Jack when he got his draft notice followed the railroad tracks into the City because he couldn't figure out the timetable and hard to believe that Barbara G. ended up in Berlin playing Moroccan music when the clock in the belly of Miss Rheingold has been stopped for . . .

A judgment restraining three owners of property on Furman Lane, Patchogue, from obstructing the narrow twelve-foot road which is the only access drive for a number of homesteads in the southern portion of the village, was handed down recently in Supreme Court by Justice Peter M. Daly.

Litigants in the latest skirmish of what has been an intermittent battle for the past twenty years were Mr. and Mrs. John McSweeney, plaintiffs, and Bertha E. Evans of 297 Cedar Avenue, Patchogue, and Mr. and Mrs. Antonio Buttoglione of of Coram, defendants. Mr. McSweeney, a New York attorney who is a summer resident of Furman Lane, acted as his own counsel in the case. The defendants were represented by Charles T. Koop, Patchogue attorney.

Judge Daly's decree restrains Miss Evans and the Buttogliones from "interfering with the free and uninterrupted use of said Furman Lane . . . by the plantiffs . : . for the purpose of ingress to and egress from their property . . ." and further orders that the defendants pay the plaintiffs' costs in the action, amounting to $156.50.

As kids we had the idea that older boys and girls filled up these rubber things with stuff they didn't want after they were done and tossed them out of the car windows, down where they parked at the Sandspit, as a precaution against becoming scumbags later on in life.

The Stick with Patchogue Committee and the Merchants Division of the Chamber of Commerce announced Thursday the existence of a potential parking lot gap.

Patchogue is first in Suffolk County in the number of parking spaces in the downtown area but unless immediate steps are taken, that position will come under attack and Patchogue will be in danger of being no longer Number ONE in parking spaces. "Without our spacious parking lots," Bill Roe, committee chairperson, said, "Patchogue would be just another bump on the Long Island Railroad. As it is, Patchogue is known to the four corners [laughter from the audience] of Suffolk County as the Number One parking lot of Long Island. And that is something to be proud of.

"The life and blood of our Main Street," Mr. Roe continued, "is in our parking lots. Without a parking space a potential customer is scared away. And in a lighter vein, where else are our young people going to learn the facts of life? In the gutter? Answer me that!"

A reception will be held at Felice's to draw attention to this crisis as part of the Stick with Patchogue Committee's campaign. Patchogue Always on the Move. A new slogan will be unveiled:

PAVE IT TO SAVE IT

Then: Stoffel Brinckerhoff was a man of few words, but prompt actions—one of your straightgoing officers who march directly forward, and do their orders without making any parade about it. He used no extraordinary speed in his movements, but trudged steadily on, through Nineveh and Babylon, and Jericho and Patchog, and the mighty town of Quag, and various other renowned cities of yore, which have, by some unaccountable witchcraft of the Yankees, been strangely transplanted to Long

Island, until he arrived in the neighborhood of Oyster Bay. Later: But when the British warriors found by the tenor of his reply that he set their power at defiance, they forthwith dispatched recruiting officers to Jamaica and Jericho, and Nineveh, and Quag, and Patchog, and all those redoubtable towns which had been subdued of yore by the immortal Stoffel Brinckerhoff, stirring up the valiant progeny of Preserved Fish, and Determined Cock, and those other illustrious squatters, to assail the city of New Amsterdam by land. In the mean while the hostile ships made awful preparation to commence a vehement assault by water.

Richie Kaler and Ed Brown used to take Sharon Lang into the swamp and do things to her.

Sharon grew up and moved away to become the wife of a young congressman from North Dakota.

Ed Brown disappeared.

Richie got his charging a machine-gun nest in Vietnam.

Only recently have I heard again the sounds they all made in the swamps of Patchogue: von Webern's Five Movements for String Quartet, op. 5.

He heard there's a real-estate agent in Harlem who keeps a list of black as they come colored people who you could call up and get to bust a block if you had your mind set on doing so: carefully screened out all of them lightskinned ones who sadly what a pity thought themselves, as a nice Jewish woman once said, to be white . . . not any sense in biting off more than you could chew or handle . . . and ain't nobody about to set up another Gordon Heights in Patchogue or North Bellport for that matter.

When Harold "Bud" Rooney died in the City from (cause never disclosed to this day) the sports editor from the *Advance* wrote the obituary and said that Buddy the Instrument was a triple-threat athlete.

Seventh Grade. St. Francis de Sales School. Marty Zimmerman is saying, "Some people die just when you want them to."

We were walking back from our teacher Miss Gorman's funeral. Her penalty for messing around was the writing of the sentence in blocks of 100s, 500s, 1,000s:

OBEDIENCE IS THE VIRTUE THAT DISPOSES US
TO DO THE WILL OF OUR SUPERIORS.

Marty owed her 1,500 Obediences. I owed her 300.

Miss Gorman's father was crying at the funeral, "I'll put the car in the garage."

The Loyal Lodge of Scumbag Hunters was formed at a dinner held at Felice's on the Bay last Thursday night.

Patchogue is a village.
　Henry David Thoreau was a visitor.
　Jeffrey MacDonald supposedly learned his knife tricks on South Ocean Avenue.
　Troy Donahue was a problem child in the village next door to Patchogue.
　Phyllis A. Whitney was once a writer living in Patchogue.
　Philip Evergood lived in East Patchogue and taught Melinda's mother about painting.
　William Patterson, a classmate of Jeff MacDonald, was convicted of shooting his wife in the neck while she watched television. He claimed he didn't do it and was sent away for twenty-five years.

In bathtubs all over the village, little boys are sitting in the water dreaming of the day when a young woman will come, wrap straw about the grown penis and set it on fire to light the way for . . . or another version had it that Jim Bohuslaw saw his mother washing out the pieces of sheet she used once a month when her body leaked Red Indian water and so spent summers, year after year, over at Leja Beach, lapping at organs that did not bleed . . . while many always thought that the mayor should have banned, once and for all time, inner tubes after the O'Neill twins drowned in the Patchogue River when their tubes sprung a leak and like good Irish children they went straight to the bottom never having learned to swim: quicker to fly on to their reward.

Hugh McGonigle of Patchogue phoned to say that there is a steel apron leading into Patchogue River which is available to anyone. He noted that quite a few outboard enthusiasts use it. Plenty of parking facilities are also available at the scene. Hugh said the apron is next to the slip for the Davis Park ferries. It is near the foot of Bridgewater St., on what is called the "sandspit."

Next to the Rendezvous Bar & Grill (Family Dining & Drinking at Its Best) which featured the first indirect lighting in the village was a small shop: We Love 'em All, Inc., specializing in war souvenirs and relics. Last time I looked they had in the window: a shrunken Japanese head from Guadalcanal, a German thigh bone from Stalingrad, a string of Viet Cong ears, a petrified Indian donkey dick with the guaranteed teeth marks of Lord Mountbatten, and nine Filipino fingers collected by H. T. X. Dickey, who served under in more ways than one Douglas MacArthur in 1942. Three doors the other way from the Rendezvous is the clubhouse of the Patchogue Porkers, a chapter of the Loyal Order of Pork, whose slogan is: *Boils and Clits: we'll suck on anything.* The next regular meeting features a reading by Dean Gwin from *The Education of Henry Adams,* followed by a slide show of Jim Slavitt's visits to the clapshacks of Connecticut.

He gave up everything: the cold water artistic apartment on East Third Street in the City, the job Uptown, being historian of the Patchogue Lions Club, honorary member of the Patchogue Latin Sports Club, his unofficial obligation to taste the first clam of the season, all, all, so as to say, with his head on the death pillow of the spit-encrusted bar rail of the Oasis, that one word, as last said, M e l i n d a.

colored people live in africa over on rider avenue, spics live 7 in a room 'cause they don't like the cold weather, polacks get their own polack speaking priest for confession, wops got their own church 'cause they like gaudy statues and spaghetti dinners. micks eat green potatoes, drink green beer and puke green vomit on st. patrick's day in the k of c hall. jews served coke in the temple social hall to the kids who get at least 10 gold stars in the reading circle at the public library. and those other guys own the whole fucking village. don't let anybody kid you.

By 1958 the German Army in the Patchogue Sector was reduced to bicycles and wooden weapons.

    F. Hilley was cut down in the second-to-last assault by heavy machine-gun fire and a twisted toenail.

    T. Whitney Rommel in a daffodil patch fell forward dead by his own hand rather than in disgrace.

    The famous communiqué went out, All Quiet Finally Near the Great South Bay.

Bumper jumping is a whole other bag of fish, like the time only one head popped up out of the backseat.

A couple of guys were standing in front of the convent for St. Francis de Sales School in early summer, 1957.

    Do you know what the strongest race in the world is? Ed asked.

    The German, Gene replied.

    No.

    The Jewish?

    No.

    The White Race?

    No.

    The Chinks?

    No.

    I give up.

    The race to get laid.

    That's old hat.

    So what?

The nail of his big toe curved over the toe itself providing a yellow helmet for that appendage. The man was hunched over himself, sitting in front of the broken-into Roe Family mausoleum in the Protestant cemetery on West Main Street, behind the memorial to the guys who died out in the camp at Montauk Point coming back from the Spanish-American War. He was trying to suck himself off and not able to, asked if he could use mine to calm the thirst in his throat. He did not have blonde hair and had creases on his face as deep as the bay in the middle. There are no blonde girls waiting in the cemetery. Blonde girls only allow colored boys to fuck them in the cemetery.

Roger Kennedy, sitting around with Whitey Leavandosky, was suddenly gripped with a reminiscence and pulled out a clipping from the May 25, 1956, *Patchogue Advance*. "This kept us in stitches, you could say, back then," Kennedy said.

"Walter 'Wally' Morrow, 41, of 37 Amity Street, Patchogue, was charged May 13th with the first degree murder of his pregnant wife, Rachel, 21, of the same address. Police reported that the accused repeatedly stabbed his wife in the face with a pair of kitchen scissors, and tore open her stomach. There was evidence of careful planning, police said, and Morrow was believed to have sodomized the 7-month-old fetus, but at press time it was not known if the fetus was alive or dead at the time of the assault."

Whitey was impressed and said, "Things just aren't like that today in Patchogue, but you never know, do you, what could happen and now we do have those bio-degradable stitches."

Since it was the last meeting of the year Tuesday's Village Board meeting had a wandering quality to it. After hearing reports from the housing and sanitation committees Chuck Roe declared, we won't stand for any more phony imitations in the village. He was seconded on this by Rick "Tiny" Nemsick who said he was tired of all action and no words. However, there was an interjection from the floor by Craig Crabtree who said, you got to work on your past if you expected to have a future.

When this family moved into the house next door on Furman Lane where I grew up, people came to visit my parents.

Aren't you upset, they asked my father, about those colored people moving in next door?

Why should I be, he replied. They're a lot cleaner than most of the white people in Patchogue.

woptalking scumbags with arms used to listenlaugh at Paddyjokes of Pat and Mike back from the City and Mike asking six months later if when you Pat went with that woman did she put a raincoat on your thing to make sure you wouldn't want me to get a little Rita now would you and Pat said she did and Mike asked do you think I can take my raincoat off now?

Some complaints and compliments were heard after the First Annual Polish Luau was held by the Ladies Auxiliary of the Knights of Columbus, in their hall on Railroad Avenue, the other night.

The kielbasa in the pineapple jello wasn't fresh, Frank Wietkiewicz said, and my wife, Lucy, didn't like the shredded carrots in the cherry jello; she believed celery would have been a better choice. However, Frank Lombardi did put in a word for the strawberry marshmallow syrup though he thought there were too many hot Mexican jumping bean candies and not enough sliced canned peaches, but who knows, I ain't a chef [laughter/applause]. And Hank "the Duke" Rossi stated that the Hawaiian Punch and vodka was very exotic and hit the spot in as many ways as you can.

"Guess you could say it was just one of those things that got by us," Bill "Hitch" Rogers said replying to a question from the audience at the La Bonne Ville Residents Association. Later in the evening he explained that they thought they were getting an extension to the Social Security regional office but it turned out that Patchogue was earmarked as the site for the second national leprosarium in the United States.

"These things happen," Hitch Rogers said. "You know how it is, but we got to look at the positive side of things. A nice bunch of jobs will be created and these lepers don't go around dropping off parts of themselves anymore, what with progress in science and technology."

FIRST SEE AMERICA is the slogan of Jack "Sweet as a Chocolate Kiss" Hershey's Boat Station. This year, he organized the first annual coastal boat excursion to Delray Beach where seventy-nine Patchogians witnessed and took part in Florida's "Execution Week," an annual event designed to cut the intolerable length of the waiting list for aspirant official witnesses at state executions.

"Execution Week" is when the state of Florida gets to try out new and innovative methods of capital punishment. This year, Patchogians witnessed what was described by one person as "Whamo." Convicted murderers are strapped to the fronts of 1959 Chevy Impalas and by remote control these vehicles are sent from opposite ends of the large Delray Beach Civic Arena into predetermined head-on collisions resulting in two debts to society being paid.

The group returned to Patchogue Thursday looking forward to next year's "Execution Week" when the theme will be "Creative Repression: Solving the Problem of Runaway Children." A clambake and raffle will be held at a date to be announced.

Patchogue NY   Probably from an Indian tribe, whose name may have been derived from the Algonquian term discussed under *Pachaug.*

Pachaug   Algonquian "turning-place." Numerous names, especially in New England, contain the element, most commonly spelled *pach,* e.g., Pachade, Pachassett, Pachasuck, Pachatanage, Pachest, Pachgatgotch, Pachuach, Pachusett, Packachaug, Paskhommuck, Pauchaug, Putchaug. The meaning is tied up with the idea of turning, dividing, or forming a boundary, but the significance is not clear, and may have varied in different names. The term may indicate a point at which a trail turned, or a boundary (necessitating a turning-back) between tribes or between the English and the Indians.

*PATCHOGUE, Village; Suffolk County; Pop. 11,300; Area Code 516; Zip Code 11772; on S. shore of Long Island, on Great South Bay 53m.E of N.Y. in SE N.Y.; three small streams in the vicinity were dammed for lumber and gristmills probably before 1750. By 1800 the Union Twine Mill, third of its kind in the United States and the first to supply cotton carpet warp, was in operation.

   Industry/Mfg.—Plastics, boats
   Mayor—Franklin "Whitey" Leavandosky 475-4300
   Chamber of Commerce—15 N. Ocean Ave.

PATCHOGUE [pætʃɔ'g], a village in Suffolk Co., in southeastern New York, on the south side of Long Island, 50 miles east of New York City. There is a deep-water channel to the Atlantic Ocean at Fire Island Inlet, 15 miles southwest. Blue Point with the famous oyster beds, is 2 miles southwest. Patchogue is a popular summer and fishing resort and a shopping and trading center for a large part of Suffolk County. It is governed by a mayor and trustees. Brookhaven National Laboratory of the Atomic Energy Commission is nearby. Patchogue is served by the Long Island Railroad. Ferries provide service to bathing beaches. Manufactures include knitwear, plastics, aluminum products, steel tapes, coin meters, and electronic equipment. Pop. 1970, 11582.

PATCHOGUE. *Geog.* Ald. e los Estados Unidos, en el de Nueva York, condado de Suffolk; 3,824 h. según el censo de 1910, Está sit. á 55 milias al E. de Nueva York, en la costa de la Gran Bahía del Sur, Est. f.c. Residencía veraniega, con hermosos hoteles é iglesias, escuela de segunda enseñanza y biblioteca pública. Industrias de pesca, ostrícola, papel, hielo, etc. Tiene carácter de corporación desde 1893.

PATCHOGUE, pa-chog. village, New York, in Suffolk County, on the south shore of Long Island, on Great South Bay, and on the Long Island Railroad, about 50 miles east of New York. Here in 1800 the Union Twine Mill, third of its kind in the United States, and the first to turn out cotton carpet warp, was placed in operation. Since then the place has become an important center of lace manufacture. Lakeview Cemetery embraces the site of the former Hart's Tavern which George Washington visited in 1790. In the cemetery are the graves of Seba Smith who wrote under the

14

name of Major Jack Downing, and of his wife Elizabeth Oakes Smith also a writer. Pop. 11582.

PATCHOGUE / 'pách-,ōg'/. Village and summer resort Suffolk co., SE New York, on S shore of Long I., on Great South Bay 53m. E of New York; pop (1970c) 11,582.

The Paris-in-Patchogue Boutique, 38 South Ocean Avenue was struck by burglars at about 3:20 A.M. last Tuesday, according to police. A burglar alarm began to sound at the shop, which resulted in a police response moments later, but when officers arrived they found only a shattered front window. The shop's proprietor was called to the scene, and found that the intruder had taken an as yet undetermined amount of jewelry from a window display.

PATCHOGUE (pach'äg, -óg), village (1970 pop. 11582), Suffolk co. SE N.Y., on Long Island, on Great South Bay, inc. 1893. A resort area, it has some light manufacturing.

Police on patrol in downtown Patchogue arrested a man whom they spotted urinating in public. Officer Dunkirk witnessed the offense at 4:10 P.M. Wednesday, when the subject allegedly began to urinate in a parking lot at East Main Street and Rose Avenue, in front of several other people. Adam B. Wiener, 19, of 860 Greenbelt Parkway West, Holbrook was charged with exposure.

Brooklyn Daily Eagle Automobile Guide

WEST		EAST	
N.Y. City . . . . 58 miles		Westhampton . . . . 23 miles	
Brooklyn. . . . . 55 miles	Patchogue	Riverhead . . . . 34 miles	
Freeport . . . . 32 miles		Southampton. . . . . 40 miles	
Bay Shore . . . . 14 miles		Montauk. . . . . 69 miles	

"The Metropolis of the South Shore," as it is locally known, is one of the largest villages on Long Island. PATCHOGUE is a busy town as well as a popular summer resort, and its hotels are among the finest on the Island. The village has lately completed the finest high school on Long Island at a cost of over $600,000, and is now building a $165,000 grade school. The Elks of Patchogue have a beautiful $250,000 clubhouse, which the motorist will note at the east of the village. All the conveniences of a large city can be found in PATCHOGUE, a fact which has greatly added to its popularity as a summer resort and a stopping place for motorists. Ocean Ave. and Bay Ave., handsome boulevards, lead directly from the main road to the Shore. At the foot of Bay Ave. the spacious lawns connected with the Cliffton Hotel, and the magnificent view of the Bay, constitute one of the show places of Long Island. Here will be found every facility, for boating, yachting, bathing and fishing.

At the foot of Ocean Ave., connected with the Mascot Hotel, is one of the largest swimming pools on the South Bay. Also concrete pier for boat landing. The name PATCHOGUE is derived from the Patchoag tribe of Indians which had its principal village here, the territory of the tribe extending east as far as Eastport. Passenger ferries run to WATER ISLANDS and CHERRY GROVE from the foot of Ocean Avenue. On Medford Ave. in the east end of Patchogue starts the cross-island turnpike in the middle section of the Island. It passes through MEDFORD and CORAM and thence to PORT JEFFERSON (14m.). Motorists will find that a visit to the Long Island R.R. Demonstration Farm at MEDFORD will well repay the short run of 4 miles from PATCHOGUE.

PATCHOGUE (pa'chäg″, -chŏg″), resort and fishing village (pop. 7,361), Suffolk Co., SE N.Y. on S Long Isl., on Great South Bay, 30 mi., E of Freeport; mfg. of clothing, lace, hair preparations; wood, leather, and metal products; concrete blocks, lamp shades, floor coverings; boatbuilding. Nurseries. Inc. 1893.

PATCHOGUE HIGHLANDS, village (pop. 1,159), Suffolk co., SE N.Y.

To celebrate completion of Patchogue's million dollar parking lot plan and opening of the final field on Terry Street, village officials and representatives of the Chamber of Commerce officially cut a giant ribbon on the Four Corners. Shown holding mock giant scissors is Donald Schneider, village trustee acting for Mayor Waldbauer, and beside him is Abe Siegel, chairman of merchants division of Patchogue Chamber of Commerce acting for George C. Furman, president of Chamber. Young ladies from Four Sisters Community Center wear sashes inscribed "Miss Parking Lot" and later greeted visitors at the various entrances of Patchogue's four big fields.

Lord Patchogue will host a SALES EXTRAVAGANZA on November 6, 7, 8 at the Four Corners in Patchogue in conjunction with the Merchants Division of the Patchogue Chamber of Commerce, the French Ministry of Culture, the Agence Générale du Suicide (L'A.G.S.) and the Village of Patchogue Recreation Department.
The event will be in memory of Jacques Rigaut who gave so much to the people of Patchogue in his passing.
A large assortment of buttons and match boxes will be given away.
Everybody is invited to come early and often during this three day affair.
Music will be provided by Dru and the Rochelles of Oyster Bay.

Patchogue sordid? "Oh, not at all," said Village Clerk Rose Marie Berger. "I think of Patchogue as one of the most progressive villages on the South Shore of Long Island. We have a great waterfront with recreational facilities. We have a very dynamic business district. We have a terrific sewer system. In snowstorms, our streets are cleared. We have back door sanitation pickup so you don't have to put your garbage pails in front of the house. We were one of the first villages with a recycling program. Now that recycling is mandatory, everyone is jumping in."

TO PATCHOGUE

Each journey is the consequence of unbearable longing.
—Evan S. Connell

he had the scum of all kinds of authors fermenting in his pericranium
—Washington Irving

Cultivating the apprehension of my delightful anxieties
—Robert Pinget

To go to Patchogue in May.

To go out to Patchogue in May.

To go to Europe in August.

And to say Europe is to diminish, while to say Patchogue is to exaggerate.

There is no reason to go to either place. No woman, since I am a man, though I could, given this day, be looking for a man . . . no woman to marshal up my purpose and send me, urge me along, day by day. No seeking of revenge for a wrong done me, my family, or my own kind.

My father is dead.

My brother died before I was born.

No treasure to be sought and anyway one does not go east looking for fortune except for purposes of irony, given all the commands to go west, and to go west, I am fond of reminding, was the way soldiers described a comrade's death during the First World War.

Just another day like all the other days as they go on: one by one, right into

EVERY ITEM A BARGAIN

Is there any place, rhetorically, to travel to: not seen before, leaving that place called home, hook for the hat—seems almost reasonable to postpone the journey when, come to think about it, already know so much—delay until next year, by which time the itch to travel should have been dissipated.

SANS ISSUE

No one has done it for the last time.

A catalog of things not done.

Sit him in a bar drinking bitter lemon with ice, years after he had sat in bars with a bitter lemon and ice.

No more beginnings. Eugene is certain of that. In the moment it becomes too difficult and one is uncertain of the value or the lack of value. A desperate teasing out.

AVIS AUX VOYAGEURS

After twenty-two years he could imagine falling in love with Melinda, only, possibly, to strangle her at the moment.

Around in circles and hurrying about it.

The tale-tellers are lining up with: winter arrived, spring arrived, on a warm May morning.

Of course there are all the excuses of culture, appreciation, improvement, being able to come back and telling the people left behind: this is and this was what you missed and will continue to miss.

Going traveling: setting off with more baggage than I ever remember taking before.

> —and this one is a famous painting
> —i am tired of famous paintings

To live pushed into myself because there is no ear, while the constant insult of these streets, the voices, the people.

No adventure possible in travel—either age or not being alone. To travel together with another person is to live in constant accommodation to the other's mood. Bad enough to have to deal with one's self—but the other: growing callouses to pick at.

No way to escape what happened. Some throw away address books and hope to begin again with a whole new set of friends.

TO EXPLORE THE DYNAMICS OF CYNICISM

Ran against that wall so many times the gore serves as a sort of cushion.

To go away only to have to come back.

No one admits to missing anything anymore.

He had been talking to a mother who makes photocopier art; is preparing a show of the photocopied wrists of her daughter who ran a knife across those wrists to create jagged estuaries of the Amazon.

The roads are so full, these days, with people who do not know, who

have been struck, as if at the mint, dumb, deaf, and developing no
compensating sense.
I can imagine rooms with high ceilings and windows.
Once long ago, is how the passage would have to begin.
It is never quiet in this room.
When I was younger it did not matter.
Let us be   gone.

For twenty years I have carried her on my back from Patchogue to Europe,
back to Patchogue, again, away from Patchogue and back again and away,
as far away as possible and then back, so finally or at any rate, at the
moment: sixty miles away from Patchogue, I sit, three thousand miles
from Europe, I sit, and could rehearse for you a litany of Melinda and
Susan and Teresa and Susan and Barbara.
I have always wanted to be away from wherever I've been living.
Always away and when I do go away it is only after telling myself and
anyone who will listen, I am going away so the final moments when doubt
nearly stops me I have to go because I cannot face:
I thought you were going away.
On the station platform I have never been able to make up my mind:
is it better to be the person doing the sending
is it better to be the person who is being sent
maybe just stand there and watch all this coming and going
with the sort of eye, an eye I will never have, I know, that wonders why in
what: go, come, leave, return; always back here, stuck here.
Living in five rooms on Second Avenue and Fifth Street in New York
City. In the City, the city being the island of Manhattan. To live in
Brooklyn or Queens is not to live in the City of New York no matter what
the map says.
Some say travel is to get away from the self. Head hits the tabletop. A
cliché gives the reader a little confidence. The territory to be advanced
through won't be that strange. Pepsi machines at every corner; vets stand-
ing in front of **STOP** signs waiting for the colors to change.
Promise, what will be the promise of this journey?
Hesitation as to when I am to get myself into gear and get to Penn
Station or out to the airport.
I am to travel alone. I will not invent a companion. Not that I have not
traveled with someone, just, the challenge to do it alone—more reek of

the popular press. How these newspapers crawl into the brain and set up shop.

To say something by so going or not to say something by so going. Get the cleverness out of my system early on.

Starting and returning.

And the how long will the journey be. To count off the days until the return. To reduce the journey to the first and the last day.

Yeah, and not to simply say: let us say we went and don't go. Who will be the wiser and who will care. We can say the postcards must have gotten lost: you know the mail these days!

I would like to travel into your heart.

The fragility of these rooms sends me wanting to go away.

I would, I would try to get a move on because it does no good to allow moss to grow on your ankles.

To celebrate Furman Lane.

Patchogue: a place I come from, a place a person goes away from.

South Ocean Avenue
Ulitza Yordan Lutibrodski
Grandview Avenue
Grosvenor Square
Ely Place
rue d'Ormesson
Highlever Road
South Circular Road
Cedar Avenue
Amity Street
Rathgar Road

Alone here, my itching scalp, a sudden burst of traffic from the two-in-the-morning avenue, the right corner of my mouth is cracked and sore when I open wide, just to see if it still hurts as it did this morning when I woke up, had to open wide to see if it was still as cracked as it was when I went to sleep.

Get the physical details down. See what sort of wine gets poured into this five-and-dime glass.

Waiting. Not as in some play, or in the movies for the curtain to go up, or the train to come into the station, or the bus to come along the avenue.

Cockeyed, I must be, going on and no glass appears even though I have said there is wine to be poured.

Let the wine run out across the table forming puddles on the floor. The dog walks across the wine and does not realize what it has done. There is yelling from across the room: the dumbshit dog can't walk a straight line.

Have to get myself out of this hole in the wall and grow wings. Everyone can burst wings out of their shoulder blades and fly.

But no reason for this going away, beyond wanting to hear some joker say: **WHAT ARE YOU DOING HERE?**

I turn and look. Same as you.

You don't live here. I just saw you get off the train.

It's a free country ain't it.

It is if you got a ticket.

To go. To look. To come back, having forgotten what has been seen: stuck back here with the blindness necessary to walk about these streets. The man hunched into his rotting coat, head bent into the groove created by his knees drawn up. He is shivering in the cold. I walk by. Of course I walk by. This is none of my business, none of what I am supposed to see. If I did stop and look I should have a camera in hand and begin to take a series of photos I can mount up as an interesting series of lives on the street. They stalk these men on the streets of New York. Imprison them on film. They have no shame, these merchants of photography.

A truck goes by down there on the avenue and the building shudders.

Hours upon hours of sleep lost during travel. Here, if I close my eyes, the war begins again. The running, the mud through which I had to wade. The waiting for the bullet in the back. Or feel my flesh explode across the screen. Not enough to fill up a mess kit plate. No one even to get back at with my death in the bathtub. No one who will be bothered by the mess.

A hop, skip, jump.

And I am still in my room. Thought I could get myself out of this room and down to the avenue and onto the street and then to the train and out of this city.

But no, I am still here. To go is to be already on the way back. Sounds like two drunks in a bar arguing about the origin of zero. How the world lurched after the Arabs or was it the Chinese or give me two plus two equaling four: I am right with the world. The Arabs invented the zero and fell in.

I am impatient with myself. I want my body walking down South Ocean

Avenue. I want to walk past the Komsomol office and into the American Embassy on Aleksandr Stambolyski Boulevard in Sofia. I will have to be getting down South Ocean Avenue because I am told they are getting ready to urban-renew it, though Patchogue is not urban in the sense of being a city, just someone in the village office has figured out how to get money from Washington to get into the real estate game, *in a big way,* in that sort of big way a small village can involve itself. But the walls are still all about me. No door opening and a tall elegant blonde woman entering calling my name, to leave and be led by herself into the wilderness of Second Avenue.

Not even a postcard to tape to the page and turning to it, reminded not of what is depicted, but of the when and where the card itself was purchased.

We hope to run a ship free of complaint, free of any reason not to use our service at some future date.

I have always, until recently, traveled alone, made my own arrangements and come back with tales that grow shorter and duller with each telling. Lacking the imagination to embellish, I cannot make allowances for recently acquired listeners; only old friends need apply for these tales of travel in foreign places. Only they are prepared to grow old and used to each telling and retelling, to grow bored and jaded by the same twist and sharpened corner in the story: to expect at an earlier and earlier point in the story a foreshadowing, underlined with Woolworth mascara, the ending, the moral, the reversal.

Still on duty. I have not left my listening post. I have not sent out for a change of clothes; have not made my way into the night. I sit under the electric light and am visible to one and all. I have constructed a possible posture. No longer do I worry if my back will grow my nose down to the ground. There are no enemies, that I know of, gunning for me. Assassins I carry within myself. My central nervous system has closed my fingers to your touch; the gash across your throat is only of aesthetic interest to my eyes.

He does go on but no more so than the next guy on the block. An argument easily rejected as it was in the sixth grade when learning about companions, evil companions, and how do I know they are bad and evil until I have developed that sense, that caution as you would for a stranger coming down the lane in the middle of the night, dressed all in brown.

The luggage we cart along even before going on a journey. When we travel, at least some of it gets left behind. There is only so much two hands can carry, two shoulders. These little carts added to our burden but usually can't find the one with the large wheels so the small wheels and a frame not large enough to support the suitcases which must be taken, breaks down before the end . . .

Travel is an agent of aging: propelling us onto the ladder in the charnel house. How slippery, because of memories it creates and then the desire to go see how it is, is it still, and the harder we look the more we see and the more we didn't see and wondering did we see anything the first time around and then back home to wonder if we have to go again to just see, one more time, if it is/was/will be . . .

Caught, probably, finally, on the deathbed or for a moment, like Dad, in the middle of a parking lot: have to come back and see what I saw or am seeing: is this all there is/was, could I have lied to myself with such consistency and polish?

Just have to act and hope the reasons catch up with the bus. Have to believe the clerk when she says, the baggage will catch up with you before you notice it's missing. Mark my words, if you get the chance, but I have nothing to worry about because you ain't coming back, all that way, just to pass out stars, red demerits, or an encouraging scrawl across the bottom of the page.

Just here or there, if this was to take a path—no, I am not of that mettle. To get out of this room, to Patchogue, to Europe. Should be the easiest thing imaginable.

Sixty miles out there or three thousand miles from here: my hands about my own throat at the thought but it is impossible to squeeze myself into the next world. Too much hesitation. To drive, be driven down those roads out there across on the other side of the river is to be led down those roads for the first time. A first time every time, as the jingle goes.

Back and forth and now here in the City, facing defeat because out in Patchogue it is believed people in the City live in the hope of one day being able to leave the City and it is only something—cowardice, fear, sloth, laziness—that stops them from leaving. In my case it was the fear of the black void between the lighted houses at night, or something like that, while, God, at such a late date, can I still be using the mind of Patchogue for a reasoning machine when it comes to where I am supposed to be?

Once it was the correct form when doing a biography to go back as far as you could tracing out the family of the subject and then around chapter five slip the kid into the world at a time in the early morning hours, with Dad at the door and Mom worn out; into the world and five hundred pages later slip him out of the world, or her out of the world or it.

I heap up my corpses before departing for the country. Before I set out on my travels to Patchogue, to Europe.

My mother died at home in her own bed. She was not used to the bed in which she died. When they moved back east from the heartland they sold their marriage furniture for a receipt acknowledging a donation to Goodwill Industries. The stuff was old and they were tired of it and wasn't it time for a change and why should they pay to move such junk. In the long run, not so long after all, it would pay to get new furniture when they bought the house in Saugerties.

So, I got the mother dead. The father dead. I was almost dead once upon a time, seven years ago. But that passed in a couple of days.

John Currier is dead.

No, I will not begin a Litany for the Dead. I am getting ready to go forth. I must have my wits about me and there is merriment to be heard. I will not have the sackcloth, ashes, holy water and oils, salad greens, donkeys to bear us forth into the . . . caught up in the drift of language and not wanting to think about John Currier or Melinda so off to Europe in the evening, out from Kennedy having to fly Aer Lingus this time because all the other flights were booked. To Ireland. In Europe. Just barely and now Ireland, part of the EEC complete with expense-account whores in Dublin and

and what?

I am still in New York City on Second Avenue on the Jewish Rialto if I am to believe the WPA guide, just republished with a modern introduction noting that John Cheever before he became Mr. John Cheever was one of the guys who helped put this thing together to earn a room, heat, and three squares a day during the time of the depression, economic, mind you, unlike the one people seem to be walking through at the moment down there on the avenue, walking just waiting for someone to question their qualifications for walking on the street:

just cross me motherfucker and you won't live to see
just cross me motherfucker

THIS IS NOT COMPLICATED

Nothing is ever to be that complicated. The Negro breasts of John Currier's wife, now widow, upon the gray sheets of the room in the Earle and then we walked across a field behind a church in southern England, in the trees: crows, ravens or rooks as in the trees, this winter in Vienna, those black omens of good fortune or bad depending on the mood of the eyes seeing them . . . Denise from Trinidad . . . failure of nerve, to say the least or lack of interest or distance or both of us came equipped with the smell of the grave: Denise staying on in Gloucester for a while and now back to Trinidad . . . why ever am I doing this to myself for in all that . . . for whatever reason . . . is it just to escape my fate of going back to Patchogue and finding of course, I have not changed.

Nothing has changed in the village. Houses are torn down, streets are rerouted, new shops open and the old ones are long gone. A face is seen that reminds me . . . it is not. In how many years of going out to Patchogue —I have yet to run into a person I have known from years gone by.

Those large Negro breasts. Those large blonde breasts. How's that for contrast, basic contrast, not comparison and something for all who seek the common desired touch. Well, if you are a man, as any woman could point out to any other woman or man; this pathetic male fantasy. Can't the boys grow up and find something just a little different to latch onto, something other than these bags of fat dangling from a woman's chest. Don't these men see how painful it is to have these globs of matter hanging from the front of your shoulders, pulling you down to the earth, to the mud of the day to day, stuck you are, walking ever so slowly, not able to walk right along, there, smartly, without every male eyeball getting itself connected to some part of the male anatomy which issues forth with the strangest sounds.

I was just going off to Patchogue with my heart going off to Europe. In Patchogue my heart was torn, nipped at, chewed over, while in Europe I realized I had been born, and being born is the only problem.

I haven't packed my bags yet or bag if I am only going to Patchogue. There is the debate as to which books to take along, how am I to see these places through which I am to travel. I took Goethe's *Italian Journey* to my high school reunion. And to Europe I went with *The Death of Virgil* and didn't get through the book, saving it until another time, always another time, maybe. Different sorts of books are needed when travel is undergone: those long serious books, to be dipped into, always planning to be read but never getting around to, *The Decline of the West,* for instance, and I have traveled with Julien Green, at different times, and cried, yes I did, coming back on a plane from Europe, a failure, returning to the United States. I had not carved out a ledge upon the mountainside of Europe. I was thrown back to the swamps, to the *just back here.* Probably, I thought then, where I belong, because I didn't have what it takes.

But there are people all over the world who would give their eyeteeth for the chance to come to this country. And I know what they mean. I too would give my eyeteeth to come to this country.

This country doesn't exist. This country has never existed. It didn't exist when my great something got off the boat, one after the *Mayflower* if I can believe the family story . . . well, some of it I have to believe, rotting there in a Marlboro, New York, cemetery, with the name of the character out of Tennessee Williams.

Never existed, I am sure, for those other children, though a person of twelve then wasn't thought to be a child other than when an old woman would lean forward from her chair and say, Child, what is the matter with you, dropping the bowl of soup into the master's lap, whatever is the matter with you, child. Children they were in Philadelphia, servants to work off the passage from Ireland to the new world, arriving with debts to climb out from under only to go under when they were done out of their shops by another immigrant from Ireland who had another idea, another way of doing things, I guess: bigger is best and the more you can cram under a roof the more the Americans will like it and giving them always a feeling of space—after all, the only thing this country has going for it—this feeling of space, more and more of it planted with rotting automobiles, skeletons of murdered children: O, a-hunting we will go; the children are never missed because after awhile the parents get used to the silence and realize that . . . never a new country, to echo the poets.

Running around in a corner, dog with can tied to its tail, cat with scotch-tape on end of tail, my past running around and unable to say, just give me a moment, please, while I collect my thoughts and I will hold forth on the question you raised, as a form of cross upon a hill of skulls though in Patchogue on South Ocean Avenue we called it Dead Man's Hill: a Cape Cod with garage wings was placed on that lot after it was bulldozed down and the earth carted away.

Not trusting the little bit of life given to me to live through. Have to run off at the mouth about this whole fucking country and its place in the world at large. Three hundred years this show has been around, a blink of time, if you stop . . . give the kid another beer, we got ourselves a real intellectual here in our midst. Send for the professors from Suffolk Community College, over there you have a real powerhouse of the intellect. And that is no sneer.

I am not out there, yet.

I have not left the comfort of my bookcases, the street, down there, the Deli Stop across the way with its DELI sign projecting out from the building and a neon arrow whipping around the edge directing the eye and hopefully the body into the restaurant. In the morning I look out from my window and the light is still flashing, the arrow urging passersby into the DELI and I am still up here wondering how I ended up here, knowing there is never a reason, never a final understanding for why something has happened.

Even with this last journey to Europe or the one that will eventually be made to Patchogue: when did I decide to go away? What was the reason for going away? Why did I persist in the reason for going away?

And yet I go away, come back, sit and wonder when I'll be going away again.

Always away and there is no way back to:

Saturday, Sept. 4, 1965

Dear Tom,

I only wish I could express ——— But..

Be very careful

I love you,
Melinda

Then going away and no way to escape going away. Just one of those things and like all of those things called "just one of those things."

Here we are pages later and not a single character has made the scene; there has been no conflict laid into the story, there is no motor installed in the locomotive of plot, no sex to grease the wheels of the pages. Still sitting. Stuck you could say at the thought: to go on is to leave behind and to have been left behind by other people.

Strange it is that people who I thought had everything—and hold on for a second before I list this everything—are the ones to persist in their friendship for me. Who seek me out. No one writes or calls to find out why I have not written to them. A cause to wonder at. For a moment anyway. On with the tale of going to Patchogue, off to Europe.

The train back from Patchogue, the last train before a five-hour wait for the first one in the morning. The conductor moves down the aisle punching tickets. He carries a nightstick suspended from his belt. A can of mace on the belt. He is prepared for the night air and the damage. Things ain't getting any better. One of these days they'll issue us guns and wonder why they waited so long. You can never be too careful. Does a tragedy have to happen before they wake up. I wouldn't want to carry a gun right now, not unless they gave us some training.

On that train in from Patchogue, so late at night, the feeling: one is at the end of the earth; every mile being discovered anew by the light of the locomotive, as if a train just ahead was laying down the track, not even the faintest possibility of such a feeling to be had on a train, say, in the suburbs of Vienna or Paris: yes, a wit like Metternich can say the Balkans begin at Landstrasse or that the South begins at some name the suburb of Paris but that is very different from imagining a land without a track, without a road. No road on this island is more than four hundred years old. Most are no more than one hundred and you would have to stretch the idea of a road to include the paths beat into the sand by the first settlers.

(((((OF COURSE the Indians were here on this island but they are now just two pockets of people, kept alive with transfusions of Negro blood, they're dark anyway; to think of an Indian on Long Island requires such concentration you might as well be thinking about climbing the sheer face of Everest)))))

Out there. With every step I was not crushing bones.

I was walking in the New World. A lot of potential, a lot of space to fill up with bone, not like the streets of Paris, built upon the bonemeal of centuries—what purpose, little child! When you die, they will use your bones to prop up, to fill in a slight dip in the road, down there, even on Furman Lane, after every rainstorm there are always new ruts and your bones will help to even out the road, what a reason to grow big and strong, to know you have been of some purpose.

For a young man, you are certainly morbid, so they do say, but at least I have not carved out an estuary for the Amazon upon my wrists. I have preferred the smell of death, the sound of it in my mouth as it is formed of words.

I'm supposed to be getting ready to go on a journey.

This is getting my house in order.

You can't leave a mess behind. Get the girly magazines and blonde pussy pictures in order and file them under: Further Research.

In my father's wallet, I found a page from *Playboy,* carefully folded, of a large-breasted brown-haired woman. It was the most brutal thing I ever did to my father, discovering this picture.

How to retain some secrets.

Setting out, things are always left behind, to be construed. To be found out. Not to go too far into this. He is dead and left behind this folded clipping and a series of strip photos of a woman taking off her clothes in the bushes to end up sitting with head between hands as if crying or in shame. It can mean anything. Or something just left behind.

This going away.

A list of the motives for travel should be given. Beyond the one that says a person can set out with no motive at all: a spring day, a winter day, putting one foot in front of the next, greed, lust, adventure, aesthetic, religious.

And all of them mixed up together and none separated out as being the predominant motor for the story. However, it smacks all so much of this life being lived in this room. Should be some, even if very tiny, movement, difference. Closed down at the thought.

He turns his back to the street. Closes his eyes. Feet are up on wooden chair. The ache in his leg ceases. Cars pass down there on the avenue. Water moves through pipes as the guy upstairs takes a shower. The woman next door changes channels; the news is announced at eleven o'clock. That was two hours ago. The movie is still on. Halfway through this life. Give or take whatever number of years depending on degree of optimism to be displayed. Modifying genetic inheritance of a short lifespan, with the fact of being born in 1944 and all the usual benefits said to accrue and not smoking and no longer drinking. Four wisdom teeth missing and other teeth moving into candidature for removal. Obscure pains, aches, really, just to remind: don't get too comfortable, you never know when . . . John Currier has been well chewed by the worms, rot and as well, his own mother and father out there in the sand on Long Island . . . he sits and knows at the moment of his death all of these memories spun off into what am I going to do with all this stuff: who will be looking on, or will he have disposed of most of it . . . or most of it will have long been lost and he will be over there in the White House with the other men—well, upstairs in the morning when the colored guy comes to hose down the room: call the meat wagon, got another one, third this week, must be the new moon or old weather or just my luck and nothing in his pockets, must have been picked over by the rats, not a tooth in his head, not even the chance to pry out a couple of teeth for the sparks of gold. Not worth the effort for the silver content, the compounds they use these days. Once a couple specks of gold was worth the time and bother.

Too much romance in all of this. Have seen too many movies or not enough so I can: walking by the guys who stand in front of the White House. I watch the ones who are not drinking, who are not drunk. They have ended up. Looking for pointers.

I have been away. Don't worry I can tell you the story of when I had to sit on a train in northern Yugoslavia for twelve hours so you can tell me about losing all your baggage in Mexico and finding yourself without even the proverbial dime in Kansas City and on the other hand there is always the fog bearing down on the airport in Ankara and not getting away to Samsun today and Jim will have to go back to Bafra and wait another day for my arrival in the middle of the night, it will seem, though he will have just gone out for a late night dinner with the military governor, since he is an honored guest, there teaching English in a high school for the Peace Corps—a nice way to spend the years 1966-68.

or

or

FROM NEW YORK, BROOKLYN AND JAMAICA						
MONDAY TO FRIDAY, EXCEPT HOLIDAYS						
Leave				Arrive		
New York	Brook-lyn	Ja-maica	Baby-lon	Say-ville	Patch-ogue	
AM	AM	AM	AM	AM	AM	
12:40	12:40	1:03	1:40	2:02	2:09	C
1:40	1:40	2:12	2:56	3:26	3:35	C
6:21	6:21	6:42	7:40	8:02	8:10	ZB
7:43	7:43	8:02	8:56	9:15	9:22	ZB
8:40	8:39	9:02	9:43	10:07	10:16	C
9:32	9:31	9:51	10:26	10:50	10:57	ZB
11:32	11:31	11:51	12:26	12:48	12:55	ZB
1:32	1:31	1:51	2:28	—	2:50	ZB
1:40	1:40	2:02	2:43	3:07	3:14	C
3:23	3:23	3:44	4:26	4:50	4:57	ZB
3:45	3:48	4:09	4:53	5:17	5:24	ZB
4:20	4:19	4:50		5:48	5:57	C
4:41	4:40	5:05	5:48	6:14	6:23	C
5:09	5:10	5:34	6:14	6:40	6:49	C
5:51	5:49	6:17	6:59	7:25	7:34	C
6:23	6:22	6:43	7:26	7:51	7:58	ZB
▲6:49	▲6:48	▲7:10		8:09	8:18	C
7:32	7:24	7:51	8:26	8:51	8:58	ZB
8:32	8:31	8:51	9:26	9:51	10:03	ZB
10:32	10:31	10:51	11:26	11:50	11:59	ZB
PM	PM	PM	PM	PM	PM	
SATURDAY, SUNDAY & HOLIDAYS						
AM	AM	AM	AM	AM	AM	
12:39	12:40	1:03	1:40	2:02	2:09	C
2:42	2:43	3:05	3:44	4:06	4:13	C
7:35	7:33	7:54	8:27	8:55	9:02	ZB
7:55	8:00	8:24			9:25	C
8:09	8:00	8:33	9:08	9:34	9:41	C
9:39	9:30	10:00	10:36	11:04	11:11	C
10:06	10:08	10:29	11:22	11:43	11:50	ZB
10:12	10:08	10:34			11:40	C
11:34	11:33	11:54	12:27	12:55	1:04	ZB
11:59	11:59	12:25		—	1:25	C
1:34	1:33	1:54	2:27	2:53	3:00	ZB
1:58	2:00	2:24	2:57	3:16	3:25	C
2:33	2:33	2:54	3:27	3:53	4:00	ZB
4:33	4:33	4:54	5:27	5:53	6:00	ZB
6:00	6:03	6:26	7:02	7:28	7:35	C
6:39	6:30	6:58	7:55	—	8:17	ZB
7:08	7:08	7:30	8:06	8:32	8:39	C
7:56	7:56	8:17	9:14	9:33	9:40	ZB
T 8:02	T 7:56	T 8:27	—	—	9:23	C
9:00	9:00	9:21	10:14	10:38	10:45	ZB
Y 9:00	Y 9:00	Y 9:25			10:24	C
10:47	10:47	11:08	11:43	12:09	12:18	C
PM	PM	PM	PM	AM	AM	

PROBLEMS, COMPLAINTS 9am–5pm WEEKDAYS
PUBLIC AFFAIRS (212) 526-6020
LOST & FOUND (212) 526-0020 or (516) 742-3900
MAIN SWBD. (212) 526-0900 or (516) 742-3900

BY 16

TO JAMAICA, BROOKLYN AND NEW YORK						
MONDAY TO FRIDAY, EXCEPT HOLIDAYS						
Leave		Arrive				
Patch-ogue	Say-ville	Baby-lon	Ja-maica	Brook-lyn	New York	
AM	AM	AM	AM	AM	AM	
3:18	3:26	3:51	4:29	4:51	4:51	C
5:04	5:12	5:40	6:26	6:57	6:46	ZB
5:56	6:04		7:11	7:30	7:37	C
6:35	6:43	7:15			8:18	Z
6:53	7:01	7:31	8:17	8:38	8:38	C
7:34	7:42	8:10	8:51	9:11	9:11	C
7:55	8:03	8:33	9:15	9:41	9:35	ZB
9:40	9:48	10:06	10:59	11:19	11:20	ZB
11:23		11:46	12:27	12:48	12:52	C
11:32	11:40	12:04	12:38	12:56	12:59	ZB
1:33	1:41	2:04	2:39	3:17	2:59	ZB
3:23	3:31	3:57	4:35	4:54	4:57	ZB
4:00	4:08	4:32	5:08	5:27	5:35	ZB
5:06	5:14	5:37	6:10	6:29	6:32	C
6:58	7:06	7:31	8:07	8:27	8:26	ZB
8:32	8:40	9:04	9:39	9:58	9:57	ZB
9:19	9:27	9:51	10:29	10:50	10:49	C
10:35	10:43	11:07	11:58	12:20	12:16	ZB
+11:18	+11:26	+11:45	12:24	12:51	12:51	C
PM	PM	PM	AM	AM	AM	
SATURDAY, SUNDAY & HOLIDAYS						
AM	AM	AM	AM	AM	AM	
3:18	3:26	3:51	4:30	5:01	5:01	C
5:50	5:58	6:25	7:01	7:22	7:24	C
7:11	7:19	7:45	8:19	8:50	8:39	ZB
8:31	8:39	9:06	9:43	10:07	10:09	C
9:56	10:04	10:31	11:08	11:31	11:31	C
10:41	10:49	11:15	11:47	12:07	12:09	ZB
12:41	12:49	1:15	1:47	2:07	2:09	ZB
1:32	1:40	2:00	2:35	2:55	2:57	C
2:41	2:49	3:15	3:47	4:07	4:09	ZB
3:41	3:49	4:15	4:47	5:07	5:07	ZB
5:09	5:18	5:43	6:14	6:35	6:35	C
5:33			6:30	6:53	6:54	C
6:09	6:18	6:38	7:13	7:33	7:33	C
6:55			7:52	8:14	8:14	C
7:09	7:18	7:45	8:17	8:37	8:37	ZB
8:05	8:14	8:34	9:06	9:33	9:25	ZB
8:55			9:52	10:14	10:14	C
9:09	9:18	9:45	10:17	10:37	10:37	ZB
10:05	10:14	10:35	11:30	11:30	11:31	ZB
■10:56			11:53	12:16	12:10	C
11:31	11:39	12:03	12:37	1:02	1:03	C
PM	PM	AM	AM	AM	AM	

BY 16

or

or

But there is no one I must leave these rooms to see, right now. All of them are far away. And have always been far away. When met it takes days to—what do you call it—get over the fact of having been apart and how strange it feels: just like there hasn't been this long separation of years and miles. Just seems like yesterday we were planning to meet in Hagia Sophia, wasn't it: Susan? and Dickie who says, of course I remember as if he were actually hoping I would forget, finally, allow him his decent retreat into the provinces. When you postpone, the provinces welcome you with that special venom reserved for people who should be in the capital but because of circumstances, the decision was postponed, the axe taken up too late, the just-what-to-do never appearing. So to the provinces with the sense of being left off, left there, stuck down midst all that space, all that darkness, all the going to bed early, rising early and seemingly about one's task, because if not, talk is shaped up into: he's a queer one, ain't he?

I have been out to Patchogue. I have been to Europe and that is understood or at any rate it should be understood. I have been away. I will go away once again and I am going away. Please do not comment: he is really away as it is. I have heard that before.

How to hold all of these items in my hands. How to keep the horizon from rising up and crushing me with its possibilities. A second there, please. I have not set forth to ride into the setting sun or greet the returning sun with morning. I have not seen myself against a background of bruised sky.

There are limits.

The arrow whipping around the edge of the DELI sign is not whipping around the edge of the DELI sign. It seems stuck or one of the parts of the light is undone. There is a shuddering in the light.

During this night no one calls. No one has ever called this late at night. No one has ever felt a need to call me at this late hour to see if I am still alive, and finding out, know they are alive. Is this an impossible sort of wish: to have someone call? Of course certain names are behind this wish: Melinda, Barbara, Denise . . . I could go on.

I am aware of my rotting body. Of the teeth that will not be replaced, of hair that will only reappear in my final, boxed form; of aches that do not go away, of books that will never be read, of the smell of blonde women never to engulf my nose, the brush of hair against the side of my face.

Everything and nothing.

No one.

If I could imagine lust.

A room with screens off which insects bounce all through the darkness before the morning and the asking of names and where to for the rest of the day until the evening when both can get lost from each other to find another . . . an electric kitchen clock in the shape of a cat with eyes moving back/forth, along with tail moving with each tick until the hour announced with a mechanical meow, just to be cute. When I go to the kitchen to get a couple cans of beer for the last moments before the eyes click off into the next morning when the accident of the person sitting next to me on the airplane . . . sharing a taxi in from the airport . . . meeting in a pub when she asks if he knows where . . . flattered that she took him for being a native and he also thinking she must be pretty stupid or unobservant that she didn't see he also was from Patchogue . . . to think three thousand miles from home, three miles from each other back there and meeting in this place . . . getting very strange to say the least.

Must remember he has never ——— a girl from Patchogue or been ——— by a girl from Patchogue or ——— and or a boy for that matter, just to show I am aware of what goes on just down the block from where I am sitting at this moment.

No bounce to the step. A slowing down. Am I coming down with something or do I just want to go down on someone.

Out to Patchogue and driving around the Sandspit. They still sit two to the frontseat: the two-headed monster of driver education class—two heads into the windshield: not a pretty picture. No bumperjumping to see what pops up out of the backseat. It's daylight and we're getting on to forty, the hair ain't on top of the head. No longer a kid but a dirty old man trying to get his rocks off seeing what the kids are doing. All over the world they are doing these things. Buckets of semen flow across marble steps. Mountains of blonde hair pile up. Fishhooks are inserted into my eyelids and my eyes are open in a banal way.

On the go. Always on the go because. If he only knew. As is said so many times in this story of going away and coming back if he only knew but when and finally or always where, and before he had talked of going to Finland. He had longed to go to Finland as a way of saying he longed to go to Sweden, so as to avoid all the easy associations that the word *Sweden* brings up, in particular if you are a man mouthing that word *Sweden,* and had an audience of male ears hearing that word *Sweden* . . . so Finland, in the winter when it is more dark than light for much of the day, when the sun is a rumor, when the doorkeeper counts the number of places in Urho's Pub and when that number has been admitted locks the door until someone inside has drunk his fill and another can come in . . . and in that country he was staying in a high-ceilinged apartment in the center of the city, visiting a woman he had met in New York, visiting her in the midst of her family, having flown from London because he had gotten drunk on a trip to the country; fallen into a ditch and come up with a rash on his arms, nettle rash or some such, they say, sitting in a country kitchen in Ascot wondering why he was there . . . well, he was there because he had known these people, again, yes, that was the reason, because he had found these people again, the mice running about the chairs, the wine being drunk, the cognac was all gone; his trousers were dry and it was time to go back to London to wake up and get to the West End Air Terminal and get the next flight out to Helsinki, via Copenhagen, arriving in the dark. He should have called: but if he had called she might have said not to come and so he was in this apartment in the center of Helsinki; Russians lived on the two lower floors. Ilse's father had held on to the apartment after the war because he had done some favor for a Russian officer; something about respect for former enemies, though the father later showed us his Luger and invited us to imagine the number of Russians that didn't make their way back to Russia. Started early in the morning into the beer with Ilse's mother, in the kitchen and then to walk down to the harbor, up the steps of the Lutheran cathedral as if walking up into Limbo, in defiance of all the childhood stories as to where Limbo is located. Away in Helsinki in the middle of the winter, nothing worked out or it was as if I had . . . everybody was very polite, can't say they were not polite and later I met Maria, rather he met Maria who was just back from Canada because things hadn't worked out there for her mother . . . the place was too big, too many miles between . . . and always so many more miles to any place you might want to go.

True coldness in Helsinki. A poetic turn of phrase that might or might not mean something. A mind muddled by watching *The Robe* on television twenty-eight years after seeing it in the Patchogue Theatre. The final scene of Richard Burton and Jean Simmons being condemned to death: they walk, heads held high, walking to the archery field to be done to death and enter *their* kingdom. Though the scene that came back from the years ago: having laid there in storage, as it were, for all these years, to repeat myself, and saying, I remember, was Caligula walking into the throne room, up to where his throne is and swirling his cape about behind him, swirling it once again just before he sits . . . remembering how impressed we all were (I was) by Father Dunne's cape, brought back from France: how tall and elegant he looked. The only moment of elegance in twenty-some years in Patchogue: Father Dunne's black cape with the black silk lining—how I would like to line the cape with red silk . . . and why couldn't I line it with red silk? This is my tale. He is my priest, in my village, on my island, in my state, in my country, on my continent, in my world.

Not alone, the darkness to the sides of the houses and the darkness in front of the houses. I know there is grass planted. Probably a couple of patches of flowers, maybe even an iron man with white face. The courage is lacking to paint on a Negro face.

To be swallowed up by these lawns. How many have trod across lawns only to never reach the door where their heart lies upon the stoop.

He is sitting in the dark in the MG. Lights turned off after he turned into the street. Careful to coast down the street and park just out of the light cast from the porch lamps. He is hoping Melinda will walk across the picture window, well, behind the picture window, across the living room. He looks. He sits. He looks. He waits. She will never appear in the window. He will start the car, drive very slowly past the house, turn on the lights, and then at the end of the road make a U-turn, come back as if just passing through . . . he looks . . . she is not behind the window, never is she behind the window. He does not ask himself what he would do if he did see her. The problem never arises. It is all just a matter of wanting, wanting, wanting and everything and no body is excluded. His life is a daily humiliation. He is empty, given up to his love, yes, he does call it that. He will go away and write to her from Dublin. A couple of letters will be exchanged and he will return to Patchogue. He will call Melinda. They will walk to the movies. *The Train.* They will walk back from the movies. In a dark lane near her house they will kiss. He will hear his watch ticking. He knows what the watch ticking means: it will end and in less than two months it will have ended, have been ended. He will travel to Wisconsin; he will come back to New York City the following May. He will travel out to Patchogue. He will see Melinda. He will travel with her over to Mattituck; there will be a drunken scene: his fist bashed through a glass door. His arm is covered with blood and he will travel back to Patchogue, back to New York City, back across the country to Wisconsin, eventually to Los Angeles in preparation for going to Turkey. He will not go directly to Turkey but will have to get to Wisconsin, again, and then to Dublin and then to Turkey, then back to Dublin and finally to Sofia, then to Ireland, then to the United States and THERE for many years he will be

THERE in the United States—he will meet Melinda again, on Fifty-seventh Street, later will see her at her parents' house in Mattituck, she will be with her second husband.

Alone with the story of a ninety-year-old man who is sitting in a living room in New Jersey talking about his hearing gone, his eyesight gone: there was this old couple they were found sitting on a sofa with plastic bags over their heads. They were holding hands, suffocated, an easy death, but the old man can't really have any part of it because the goddamn sons of bitches insurance companies won't pay for a suicide and why didn't that couple tie a red/white/blue ribbon around their necks so they would be hailed as a couple of great patriotic goddamn American heroes.

Alone with this story, and having no insurance and no one to get at because he knows how quickly people forget, how easy death is to wash from the mind or at least to dilute the shock and well, life just has to move on, even if we don't, life just keeps going on and on like you are doing with this page of this reading, on and on: gone forth waiting.

Beatrice and Laura did not get out of their teen years . . . well, that is a bit crude: did a person back then have teen years during the time of Dante and Petrarch or was it all a long sigh before death.

Should work up the usual would you like to live in another time and there, over there, is a sneering old man . . . would you like to live back before anesthesia. You have the privilege of being contemporary; eyewitness to another one of those break ups and how this one is different from all the others and on and on. I should get going. I am on the case.

An admission: of failure to provide a psychology for Melinda, for the narrator, for Denise, for the man with the story of the woman he couldn't get his arms around (this is coming at a later moment).

A lack: of tension, character formation, clash of temperaments, beliefs. All of this stuff left out. To begin again.

Driving back and forth along the road in front of window behind which Melinda might appear was the longest journey I have ever taken. How to convince anyone of this. If I have to think about convincing someone of this . . . obviously, or is it, I have failed to, failed to what? I am stuck with this driving of an MG past a large, modern sort of house on a road in East Patchogue in the early 1960s.

Love beads almost make their appearance . . . 1960s, so to be more exact: drove that car, 1962-63-64, only in 1965 did I ever stop, park the car in the driveway, walk up to the front door, ring doorbell, wait, and how easy it all was. Come in while I get my coat or sweater and why don't we walk, it's such a nice night. Walked to the Patchogue Theatre for a movie . . . anyway, exact dates and just before the time usually referred to as THE SIXTIES . . . so not within range of those who are forming up THE SIXTIES into an ideological sledgehammer to be used to beat today's whoever into whatever mold is ———— more blanks, using blanks I am, at this late hour, afraid to shoot myself in the foot, not a very dignified way to proceed forth on my journey: self-inflicted foot wound due to obscure dilly-dally in the backwater of those grim weekly political newspapers.

There is a wanting to not go away. A wanting to stay exactly where I am at the moment.

God, in heaven or wherever, do I hunger my mouth to get a taste of those flesh-bearing bones.

AM I ON YOUR LIST, MARTY?

Relax vigilance for a moment and you don't know what is gonna come crawling in under the door and this ain't some sort of lurch into another genre.

Marty, and I am making no reference to the movie of the same name though I have seen it a number of times, have cried a number of times, difficult admission, worse than saying I used to fish out the bloody sanitary napkins of my mother and suck on them, out in the backyard under the white birch tree before it blew down in hurricane Carol, and doing the nosh under the weeping willow before that blew down in hurricane Alice . . . better to admit these acts than saying I gave a tear to *Marty* . . . though I can think to say I was just preparing to see Carol Lynley in *The Poseidon Adventure* with Ernest MARTY Borgnine, sensitive slob that he is.

Confusion, for a moment. Back on the path.

So, you got me crying in *Marty* not the first time around in the movie theater.

Marty, short for Martin Zimmerman, lived on Rider Avenue in Patchogue and was in the same class in St. Francis de Sales School, back before going to high school, and you ain't seen a movie set back before high school. Marty wrote with his left hand, had a pencil box with a built-in drawer. He moved, rather his family moved to Patchogue in the third or fourth grade. They had the largest house of any of the kids I hung around with. His father wore dark blue suits and gave the largest donation to the church on all the holidays and feast days for which they printed up a list of the people giving money. Marty wrote with his left hand and I tried to write with my left hand. With his left hand he made up lists of who his best friends were.

AM I ON YOUR LIST, MARTY?

The game was never to ask, so your mouth hurt so much from not asking —it wasn't a game, this was life, the life being lived and it did matter if

AM I ON YOUR LIST, MARTY?

Marty only smiled and his was the smile of someone who knew how to smile, knew the worth of a smile, knew a price was always attached to the smile. Marty wasn't my best friend. Frank was my best friend. Marty was something like Larry. Someone you hang around with all the time, like Joey Costello and Kevin Burnes . . . but he wasn't different from those guys and you weren't supposed to say "those guys"; who do you think you're trying to be, who do you want to think we think you want to be when you grow up . . . some sort of punk from the City who ends up in the river with cement overshoes because that's all you would be good for if all you can say is, those guys . . . they're your friends, am I not correct—your friends are not something called "those guys."

Marty said I could carry his pencil box home and show it to my mother, show it to your Mom, is how Marty put it because Marty was the sort of boy who had a mother and coming in from a hard day he was supposed to greet her: *MOTHER,* can you. Eventually, a pencil box was acquired but by then it was something you didn't carry to school with you and you didn't want to leave it in your desk . . . it was just a nuisance.

When are you getting on the road?

Before long you'll have us back into the womb with all of that.

To go anyplace requires . . .

These fucking pencil boxes didn't make room for compasses. How to carry a compass back/forth without it poking your leg, let alone being used as a weapon to attack the eyesight of . . . the man in the moon for all I care.

Just trying.

Gene had been saying something like that: just trying, just trying, and there can only be so much of just trying when you got to say I tried and it worked or it didn't work and then if it didn't work you got to remember what your father would have said, to save the fishing pole you got to cut bait. When I get pressed in class as to what something matters, means, I get lost and have to lean back on the old teacher dodge of let's discuss this and if there are any growls from the lion's pit it becomes a written assignment due yesterday which is what you got to say these days, due yesterday and the kids know what you're meaning; I guess they do because I haven't a clue what is going on in their heads, if anything. Some of them still got some brain cells left, not many, and those that are left are pretty strange. Of course we were strange back when we were kids, kids are always a mixed bag and always a big dumping ground for every cliché in the editorial notebook, as if they keep a little book of these pithy sayings by their typewriters and once a year wheel them about with as much predictability as City people coming out to Fire Island after Memorial Day . . .

Gene was in the third grade, I guess it was, and I was in the second grade and he ran me down with his bicycle and we became friends, for all the years of our lives, as we said back then . . . and it was all the years when you are making such friends. Only later to find myself in here in the City without a single friend of that sort.

Friends now take the form of appointments.

Gene was always tall and one year older. Eventually came a time when we could no longer be friends. Sometimes those years are weathered and if the two people live on in the same village, town, or city within a couple of blocks of each other it is possible to renew the friendship with years of talking about what had happened back then and in all the years in between.

Our fathers went into the City together on the train. I do not know what they talked about. Maybe it will come to me. It would come to me and . . . to find out your father was very uninteresting or that his son did not know how to make him interesting even with a sworn statement in favor of the ordinary universe. He is stuck with the absence of poetry: two men who take the 6:59 train from Patchogue into New York City and catch the 4:something back from the City to Patchogue, arriving at seven o'clock. Mom is waiting at the station with the car . . . waiting was hearing the train as it went through the crossing at River Avenue, whistle sounding, getting out of the car, walking to the platform, waiting, and Dad was on the steps of the train always with a little quick step down from the train before it stopped with the *Journal American* under arm turned to the comic page . . . he would get in at the driver's side and if it was Friday—it always seems like Friday in the moment of memory—we would go around the block to the liquor store where he would buy a bottle of Thunderbird . . . to drink from little jelly jar glasses to unwind from the week.

One Christmas all the needles fell off the Carrolls' Christmas tree. A strange sort of clothes tree with strings of Christmas lights, no miniature village under the tree, some crumpled-up white wrapping paper, more like tissue paper . . . the bare wood floor and to think, Dad would say, that man, Carroll, makes more money than I do and this is what happens to him . . . you just never know about some people and what can happen to them.

They were a source of some lesson-learning for one and all. To have parents like that who sit in the bars every weekend, leaving the kids either at home or dragging them around to sit in the car in the parking lots of bars for a fifteen-mile radius of the village; and that woman, those children, in spite of what they have to live with, are always so pleasant, always ready with a nice smile or a pleasant word, never a smirk like the Zimmerman children or those others I could name but wouldn't because I don't want them to even think I or we notice but your father and I have discussed them and they are just what we don't want you and your sister to turn out like . . . now, Gene is such a nice boy . . . not like . . . he doesn't probably get a decent home-cooked meal from one week to the next, if I know the Carrolls and how lucky you are.

I don't have to travel to Patchogue to be there. I am always in Patchogue.

Gene went away from Patchogue to play tennis for a college in Pennsylvania, met a woman there, had a child. She got some sort of cancer. They didn't have any more kids. They got divorced.

Patchogue is sixty miles from Manhattan.

Europe is three thousand miles from New York.

Both are as far away as you could want to go . . . of course there are some who will go to Tasmania to really get away from it all and if you live up on East Eighty-eighth Street just off of Park, coming down to this apartment on Second Avenue and Fifth Street is almost as far and requires as much thought and setting of schedules—

I miss Gene. All those years in between. No way to catch up or begin again. Probably some awful Latin poem about this problem. I miss Gene.

I miss a whole fucking lot of people. Most of them are not yet dead with the exception of John Currier. Most of them are still alive but they might as well be dead as far as it would be possible to begin again any sort of friendship. As if we have been carving out our coffins and are unwilling to make a little room: we get used to the wood shoulders, the feel of the wood at our feet, the soft padding at our backs and just don't want to make room at this late date . . . twenty . . . twenty-five years after the last time . . . or am I all wrong. Young people are only genitals at various stages of excitation and here is not that moment, those moments: all just imitations learned from the movies without the dissolves, fades, wipes, jump-cuts . . . now as if the wrong sound track got stuck within the mouth of this guy sitting here in the City.

Gene has a life to lead and be led by. So do I.

I am doing the traveling, at this moment.

Rita, to change the subject, sex, and degree of intimacy, lived on South Ocean Avenue and strange for a Catholic girl did not go to St. Francis de Sales . . . or I am jumping to a conclusion without doing whatever the logic demands? . . . she had an Italian last name . . . lived in a large white house, behind a thick, tended lawn. The house could have been a funeral parlor or a Mafia residence, foot-soldier level. But all this is thinking only to the point, Rita had an Italian last name, lost when she married and moved to Texas to take up the occupation of being a wife to a man who has a wife who is involved in their four children's education and does some volunteer work on the side. Airport supervision is her husband's field of work or he is about to go into the soft-drink line. Really thought she was going to end up somewhere. Well, we all end up somewhere, just no telling where that where is going to be. Far away from this room. I hope. All of this is far away.

Rita was editor of the high school yearbook, a cheerleader and a member of Phi Beta Kappa. She was never unfriendly to me. She did not have to ride the schoolbus. Pretty girls did not have to ride the schoolbus.

Can I make it a rule of human behavior in these United States: a pretty girl does not ride the schoolbus. How to explain to a person in Sofia, Bulgaria, what it means to ride a schoolbus or for that matter how to explain to Marina in Milan, a woman who is a translator, with a doctorate in English, what it means to ride the schoolbus . . .

Chopping myself up and losing the thread of what I am supposed to be doing. To ride a bus. A schoolbus when one is a teenager. The humiliation of being stuck in those seats with all those other kids. The thirty-minute ride, stopping and see you tomorrow, tomorrow as if it would be any different, on and on and not a second to compose yourself after the day of the classrooms and then the home.

If we could get the emergency door open we could throw who was it out the back door and no one, not even his parents, would miss him.

June of 1958 is clear in my head. I would be fourteen in October of that year. The next year or so is unclear. The metal feel of a gym locker against my cheek as my head is banged against it . . . standing in a gym in gym shorts, the heat turned off, standing, never so conscious of being so short, the coach took a certain pleasure in pitting the short guys against the tall ones for basketball.

In a Catholic high school, to be tall is to be closer to heaven. This was going on in Patchogue. Why should I be concerned that the heat was turned off? Why didn't the head against the locker happen earlier in the year? . . . something is off.

Florence. She changed her name to Flo when she was an adult and the mother of three kids. How appropriate, she said, her name, a nurse since she was a kid and the oldest of ten brothers and sisters . . . got into a convent after the eighth grade with the idea she wouldn't have to be in the kitchen all the time on her hands and knees cleaning up after the kids, but the convent was exchanging children for adults who had never grown up and were just as demanding, as petty, as foolish, and most of them were waiting to fall in love with her.

Flo, Florence, came back to Patchogue a year behind everyone else and was no longer . . . or she was already going out with the man, then a boy, who would later be her husband.

I delivered the *Long Island Press* to Florence's home, collected for it on Thursday. She smelled of baby powder. Once I saw her dancing with her sister in front of the television. It must have been to *American Bandstand.* I didn't like the kids on the show: all Italians, American Italians from Philadelphia: watched her dance and thought even then dancing was a thing of the past, for this kid. I had at one time been able to dance . . . did dance in St. Francis de Sales Hall for some sort of dance, I remember: *he's a real jitterbug*—with Cynthia McInerny; she went away to a convent. Her brother never wore a coat even during the winter. A coat made you soft and he didn't feel the cold and it's hot more months of the year than it's cold so wearing a coat gets you out of shape for the summer when you don't need to wear that much.

I would ride my bicycle past Florence's house on South Ocean Avenue, up to Laurel Street and then down Lee Avenue because you could see the back porch and I was thinking if I didn't see her in front of the house I would see her in the back.

Never did and I thought of this driving past Melinda's house. Always looking and not having the lyric gift; not living four hundred years ago— get myself reduced and dismissed into some psychological category.

All this writing is taking place (the radio says it right now) on a day called Thursday.

I have gone out to Patchogue and come back.

In the mail a change-of-address card from Norrköping, Sweden. I am still alive in Sweden. Or my life is still important in Sweden. They want me to know where they are moving to.

Francis finally got out of Patchogue . . . all the way to Bellport, via Florida and Texas.

I had known him since first grade. Maybe even before that in kindergarten . . . how I remember kindergarten: had a rubber knife and it was taken away from me by the teacher who made me sit under her desk as a sort of payment . . . Linda Hubel was in the class as was another blonde girl . . . this other blonde girl had two brothers . . . also blond and they are all lost . . . except I remember they had narrow faces—something like that . . . Francis? . . . he lived around the corner off Cedar Avenue. His father was a huge man, well over six foot six. There was a brother equally tall who went away and was eventually in the diplomatic service. Francis was shorter, or I am just . . . he was always fat. He cried in second grade when he was sentenced to wear eyeglasses. All of his classmates were looking to the future with no help from a glass lens.

Francis stayed on in Patchogue and was with me when I drove over to Mattituck that last time I saw Melinda. He must have helped me back to Patchogue. Left me off at the diner on Main Street. You were a real mess, he said later. A real mess.

Francis was almost married a number of times.

Francis has taught school.

Francis has collected tolls on the bridge going to Jones Beach.

Francis has played golf.

Francis manages the cold cuts department of a shop over in Port Jefferson.

Francis moved to Bellport after his mother died and his father remarried.

Francis hasn't seen his brother in many years.

Francis doesn't have anything to say to his brother who has lived all of his adult life outside of the United States.

Francis doesn't play ball anymore but should.

Francis and I used to play tennis all the time.

Francis was the manager of the basketball team at Patchogue High.

Francis twisted his toenail in the fifth grade and has been a minor legend ever since.

Francis and I played strip poker in the ruins of the old swimming pool down near the Mascot Dock. The guy who lost had to stand and be naked to the sky.

Francis and I rolled around in the water off the Sandspit Dock, when there was a beach there.

Francis and I didn't have any hair on our balls.

Francis and I felt warm together.

Francis and I have never talked about this, ever, and never will.

Francis and I: sounds like a title from *Christopher Street*.

Francis has never written to me.

Francis was one of those guys from the old home town who stays in the old town, who makes you feel like you have missed something in the old town, though you know you really haven't or, again, using the word *town* is always complicated out in Patchogue because Patchogue is an incorporated village within the town of Brookhaven, so it should be something like back in the old village.

Francis stayed except for the times when he was away, gone away, and always came back.

Francis is too young to move to Florida.

Florida is where people move to when they are fed up with the Island, with the village, with the winter, with all the shit moving out from the City.

Francis wasn't slow in a derogatory sense of the word and not even in regard to what was or was not inside his brainbox. Francis moved at his own speed. We all got our own speed and when I decide to do something, I do it and not until then, everything gets done, just don't rush me.

You're not like Francis, Mom would say, look how far you went away to school, all the way out there to Wisconsin, do you think anybody else in Patchogue went that far to college or had to go that far to college—you've done everything you have ever wanted to do . . .

I would ask Francis what had happened to Melinda, what had he heard
—she was engaged to Larry, she was married, she was divorced, she was
married again.

Melinda was engaged to the Mouse. Larry the Mouse. Now there is a
story somewhere in the midst of that.

Lost in this world because of that loss.

Well, you did get off to Bulgaria and meet Lilia . . .

Came back from Europe, later, crying, because it did not happen again.

plot

A man is living in the City. He takes the train to a village out on the Island. He
walks around the village. He meets a number of people. He comes back to the
City.

Nothing could be more straightforward. Nothing could be easier to follow.
Everybody likes to complete a journey.

plot

A man living in the City decides to go to Europe. He has been there before. He
lives in New York City. He goes to Europe but cannot decide which country he is
going to. He does not know if this matters. He is going to Europe. Possibly it
doesn't matter which country he goes to because it would needlessly complicate
the whole idea of going away . . . people just want to know you have been away
and to indicate the country . . . but then heaven forbid to go into details about the
country is to invite: more than I wanted to know and more than he knew he was
talking about . . . and who cares, really. Who cares. I'm going away next week,
anyway, and my version is just as good.

Everybody is alike these days . . . just get me to the postcard shops so I can buy
a postcard of what I have seen or not seen and should have seen—just say we have
seen it all and there was no reason to have gone . . . but we had to go otherwise we
would have lost our deposits and what would we have said to—

plot

A man is out in the village of his childhood. He is thinking of where he would like
to be. And is *there* at the same moment through the miracle of modern fiction. He
has no need for that dreary realism of one place at a time. Seems like a failure of
the imagination to expect me to stick to the itinerary of the writer: the Long
Island Railroad to Patchogue . . . to jump on the train at Penn Station might just as
easily be jumping on the train at Köln at two-thirty in the morning, having to

catch the train from Hamburg because I, he, wanted to get the train that hooks up
with the one to Calais so I can get to London in time for the early evening train to
Dublin via Holyhead because I want to be met at the station in Dublin in this
prose.

All aboard!
All abroad!
Marty, Gene, Frank, Melinda, and I should drag in Joe.
Joe stayed in Patchogue. He did not go away. He was to be a father
within a year of getting out of high school. He became a cop and eventually
got to wear a suit. He is good looking and looks good in a suit. He knows
and knew how to smile. He makes you feel you were part of the team,
even if there was no season or a sport. He knows when to leave a guy to the
getting on with what he has to do. Just one of those guys who got the knack
for getting on in the world: he knows how to dance, how to shake hands,
how to smile, how to say he is sorry when he hears your mother, father,
husband, wife has gone down for the count, down the tubes, up the creek,
or just belly up on you even when you were hoping . . . Joe was the sort of
guy girls get crushes on and the guys don't get pissed off at because he is
always just one of the guys . . . ' not one of the boys because he is never
really down there, muck on his hands, and no one expects him to be . . . he
has never left Patchogue.

How I do go on about these people. As if they cared. I do care a little about
them and worry about seeing their names in the *Advance* on the obit pages.
I have mostly stopped looking for their names on the marriage pages. . . .
How close they all are coming to the cut. That shudder. That shiver. No
ghost stories for me. It is all too close. Always has been.

JOSE JUAN MUNOZ

Jose Juan Munoz, "Rocky," 38, of Patchogue died September 29 at
Brookhaven Memorial Hospital. Born in the Bronx, Mr. Munoz was
a subcontracting administrator at Grumman Aerospace, and was a
veteran of the Viet Nam era.

Something about the long winters in Patchogue. Down there on
Furman Lane, that little street between the two avenues, Ocean and
Cedar, both going from the village, up there, to the bay—anyway, on the
lane with the kids next door sitting on the porch yelling at the speeding

cars going past

SLOW DOWN

but not during the winter when most of that part of the village is emptied
out and the only people there are the old people with no place else to go
. . . now, it is all changed of course. I was talking about thirty years ago.

Thirty years ago. Might as well be talking about the Middle Ages as far as a
lot of people are concerned . . . so far back it almost seems like another
what-have-you. Back before television. Imagine that! When there was a
little gap between what was going on in the City and what was going on in
the village . . . and how it really didn't matter what was going on in the
City . . . life was just as interesting in those streets of Patchogue . . . enough
was going on . . . there was no wider world.
    Sounds like a crank.
    Brains have sunk under your chair if you ask me.
    Where else to keep them on a day like this.
    AND I WAS STRUCK WITH THE IDEA: a walking tour of Long
Island . . . as if I were walking through the strangest part of the world . . .
but the reader would or should be getting this idea without being told it,
like this, right up front, as it were.
    A W A L K I N G T O U R first, about these five formerly Ukrainian
rooms. Then down the stairs, onto the street, then the avenue. No riveting
detail to grab the eye. Just walk along and say: Joe, how's it going?
    Fine as you can expect these days.

> First you fuck it up
> Then you tear it down

    Another time. Another day. You know how it is; how things are going,
these days, just like they always do.

New York, Woodside, Forest Hills, Kew Gardens, Jamaica, Locust
Manor, Laurelton, Rosedale, Valley Stream, Lynbrook, Baldwin, Free-
port, Merrick, Seaford, Massapequa, Massapequa Park, Amityville,
Copiague, Lindenhurst, Babylon, Bay Shore, Islip, Great River, Oakdale,
Sayville, Bay Port, Blue Point, Patchogue.

These people to the north of the house on Furman Lane: always renting and once there was a family who tried to buy the place but the man worked at one of the aircraft factories, the company lost its government contract; the man lost his job and the house. They were back in the City before you could catch your spit from the wind . . . not like your father, my mother would say, all these years with the American Can Company . . . why do you think he does it . . . not like these people . . . people don't understand how important it is to hold on, in spite of and in the face of, you got to hold on, because there'll come a day when you'll regret, you WILL REGRET, mark my words: like those people in that house to the north of the house where you spent your childhood, gathered the idea of your happy child-hood—living in the spiritual slums of the twentieth century. And now little bit more than a pot to piss in. Some people, some of my cousins, my sister Ronny, barely have a pot to pee in and it was all due to your mother's father that they even have a pot to pee in . . . an obscure family quarrel . . . brought back to life, way in the background to a young man driving his MG. I had the car for a month when I had an accident and it was back to the schoolbus for a month and the kids thinking the bank had taken the car back. Hot shit. Look at him. Looking at Melinda walking to a car with the center of the football team . . . the stubble of a beard, you could see the oil oozing from the pores on the backs of his hands . . . to sit in the schoolbus and watch her get into his car, a sports car. The way your shifting arm rests on the leather-covered armrest. The close smell of sun leather complete with temperamental carburetor. You had to open this bolt on the top and put in a couple of drops of oil, that was the trick in dealing with a moon-governed carburetor . . .

What happened: my luck, Irish luck, just feeding up some information so things will be clear later when . . . a spoiled kid can only soil other lives. It is expected of this person.

I do not add to myself at this moment of the writing by writing of Eddie Nowiki. I take a moment away from the moment. Should get out my tables of measurement: how to subtract a moment from a moment?

Eddie Nowiki's old man and my father did not get on with each other. Eddie's father saw my father as one of those men who went into the City, made their money there and were not dependent on what the neighbors thought. Nowiki had to kiss the ass presented to his lips for servicing. My father didn't say it. I wish he had. Dad was not a man with the words.

Oh, he had the words once in a while but I cannot drag them up on cue.

They came from the region known as after the moment, after the thought.

Isn't it always like that and him an Irishman—pardon, an Irish-American. His parents were born in Ireland, shipped out as teenagers to work as servants, met, opened a little shop in Brooklyn, eventually had three little shops . . . driven to the wall by James Liddy's old man, who died young and back in Ireland—James is using the silver instruments and the good china and cashing the bits of money from Morgan Guarantee Trust Company . . . and my father, the son of these two young and then old people: she lived on forever. She never wanted to go back to Ireland. What was there for her? Just a land to leave . . . to get away from, the land that hated its young because they reminded it of nature's promise and nature had always been an old whore, ridden with the syph, the clap, the drip, sores, the final paralysis . . . at least away from that here in America in spite of the hard knocks, are there any other kind, any life was better than in the green moldy place.

Toothless old men and women muttering about those of us who deserted the ship. Rats, they called us. Them's the rats just wanting to suck on our flesh. Let them gnaw on their own bones.

O, we will sing the songs, play the instruments, more to just get away from the fact: we are here and they are there, back there. How good the songs sound here: a full stomach and a warm room to sing them in and on. Back there you sang to forget the hunger, to forget the cold, but once the radio came people were contented to put the thing on and listen . . . I am listening to the radio. And do not disturb my listening.

Annie Marie McGonigle. Before that, Loughlin, I believe. Married a Hugh McGonigle . . . I think, though I am not sure. She is dead on October 1, 1962.

I was in Wisconsin, so didn't have to go to the funeral where her granddaughter, the nun, wanted to climb into the grave. She was held back and some said she was putting on a show because she thought it was expected of her, expected because she was a nun and knew people said she was a spoiled child . . . but that is how people talked in the family. . . . Annie Marie had a fine casket and a fine hole in the ground. Her sons were drunk and her daughters were drunk. She had a fine send-off.

Annie Marie was dead. Glad to be done with the world. Her son has sold her house and drank the money, or so it was said, when no money was found, not even the pair of goat horns this son had sent to his mother from the Far East, on his first trip there as a merchant seaman, wireless-radio operator. Everything was sold and there wouldn't have been a pot to piss in if the ghost of her husband came back to give a quick look round the house on Willoughby Avenue. Who would want to live there: the niggers moved in and are cooking who knows what or who in them pots: ain't safe to walk there even in the middle of the day, says many a person, the sun excites them to hatred for their own dark color and the fair hair of the white girl's arm; these people with knives and guns and gobs of spit.

Annie Marie just sat in her chair in the large basement kitchen of her house and it was said she had begun to forget who she was or where she was and who were all these strange creatures coming to visit her, always wanting something or just give me money, man, money is what I need, there is always a payment falling due.

Patchogue is sixty miles from these voices. The telephone is only used for emergencies. If you want to talk you know how to write: a letter is more welcome—a long-distance call announces a death.

Patchogue is just far enough away as to be too far; no one just drops by for a visit, just out for a drive and thought we'd stop in to see if you always keep the bathtub clean enough to see your face in the enamel.

Patchogue was to give us, the children, the country, to give us grass, the bay, the sand, and not the streets, what can be learned in the streets.

Annie Marie knew why her eldest son was out in Patchogue, of course, she knew. That is why we were out there. You moved, you cut bait, you got away.

There is never any reason to stay around when things have gone the way they always do. Not even a family curse to be summoned up. No one raped or sat on or killed . . . just things happen and you know a wall will not give way to the soft flesh of the top of the skull. You can bang all you want and if you meet these people in Ireland, you can see the result of too much banging the head against stone walls though there is many a person on the road who enjoys the feel and sounds of his or her head going against the stone wall, the cement forced between the stones, noting this detail, being one of the pleasures of this particular sport in the streets of Dublin, not that I ever spent any time in that pesthole, a village is bad enough in Ireland but to be stuck in the largest village in Ireland, with all of the features of village life magnified ten, a hundred times: a chorus every moment of your life as you stepped from the house: she has never lived, she does not know how to live, she does not want to live, and on and on putting words into your own mouth, they'd always be, because they're afraid you might have a thought of your own and what would that do to the whole shebang and these seeds were of course dragged across the ocean, allowed to germinate, when living in Philadelphia, another cesspit of boredom, if you ask me, a boredom not even released by it taking place in the largest city in the country, the boredom of a second-rate city, to have a good word for anything, I learned, very carefully, is to be suspect: you were on the payroll, even if you wouldn't admit it, you had to be had and had been more than once by him or her or any idea come walking down the road last day before the next one.

So they filled up the boats and stuffed us into them, not that it was unbearable: we were leaving that place and what more can anyone dream of who is born there.

Oh, the waste of it all. How do they continue to hold on to their lives. As simple, I will tell you, as the old man coming to the door and saying, try to strangle yourself with your own hands: it can't be done. That's why they stayed on and didn't all just pack it and themselves into the earth, the place truly longed for, eating from it three times a day with the potatoes which they would string as pearls if they had been small enough or if they themselves had been a bigger people. I do go into the realm of mockery but can anyone help it who has been born in that place. It is the sole consolation, the sole recreation, the sole religion of those fields, those hills, those streams, those latrines into which people pour themselves. Of course, I have no wish ever to go back. What is *there*, exactly? Can anyone tell me the truth? Can anyone name a single reason to go to Ireland that does not in some way involve a homage to futility, to self-sacrifice, to a denial of beauty and to hope?

Ireland is a fine antechamber to death, absolute death in spite of all the promises of the priests, all the beads of the nuns, all the relics of the church, all the dead children sent speeding on their way to eternal paradise. An antechamber to death and itself a long preparation for death alone— the learning how to say no even if the word is yes—in truth to say yes in Ireland is to lie down with one's throat exposed to the pigsticker himself who comes with polished accent, good manners, in most cases with a smile as broad as the ocean. A smile is a dangerous sea upon which to sail your fate. It can never be trusted. Always a knife lurks in the folds of the mouth. As sure as the rain comes down, as sure as Salzburg is in Austria, as the ocean is wide and every other cliché one can name off the grocery shelf.

But no one thinks that this place is any better. A place where each is afraid of the person with a skin color a shade darker than her own. But can any blame that person. The old rule is of experience.

Here one is allowed to get on with the business though no one is ever told what the business might be.

In Ireland every bit of slime on the road got an idea what the business is and is prepared to ram it down your throat if you pause for a second to catch your breath. It being almost impossible to talk continually without a breath. Once in a while, though many's the man who is practiced in the art of taking a breath when you're not looking and cutting out your heart, purse and all in the bargain. Here left alone to face the day and the night without the slightest clue. Probably better in the long run. I am stuck where they have placed me. Having outlived everyone, and not talking to the one or the two who might be said to be alive, alive in the technical sense of the word, still walking or shuffling about without six feet of earth piled on their chests to keep them down, there, where they have always wanted to be. Just look at their lives.

Can any man of you tell me: those are lives that want to be lived. Just hoping for one of those dark shades to come and zip zip, wondering, why they never called them shades; they are closer to that than some of the other names.

Gripped by a nightmare of being sent back to that place from this place, back there with them knowing something went wrong in the New World, as they curl their mouths about those words, *the New World,* you call it, sounds like the same old story, an old carny trick, just ramming it into your puss, day after day, that you are always born into the wrong century, the wrong country, the wrong universe and your true home is over the sun, or back of the moon, and generally up there—somewhere—where all the little babies are gone to, where the good are said to go while the bad are down there. The little ones that didn't get splashed with the priest's water are somewhere in the middle: neither fish nor fowl, as himself the priest said, once, and pass me the finest leg of the turkey, he did also say.

Here in Brooklyn and he would have me out to his house in Patchogue, so I imagine her thinking, but I know my place: he is to come to visit me and I'm to sit here waiting for . . . just that, waiting for . . . he comes here saying: it is not as nice as, to make himself feel more at ease out there, imagine, near the ocean, away from all of this, but of course, he is to be never away from all of this.

This is called: calling up the voice from the City or something like that—a listening to the voices floating about and giving a particular name to them.

I sit stuck down in this country with all the airports closed in, the seaports blocked, the borders to the north and south closed, not from any political reason but closed due to poverty. Remembering once sitting in Trieste, on the rocks at the shore, Miramar Castle in the distance, whence Maximilian sailed to Mexico and his empire, to be shot by dark midgets, as he called them, why don't they love me, and they love me so much they want to see my blood, to see me dead so I can become perfect in their love.

Well, sitting on the rocks: a South African woman, an American on his way to Lebanon to look at the Cedars, and then into the desert, when people did such things, on the rocks and being told what is the difference between the communist countries where you cannot get a passport and America where you can get a passport but if you have no money the passport is only good for collecting postcards inside. A half-remembered conversation from twenty years ago, still with me, with the blue glass water, the boats rusting, blonde girls corroding at the edges.

Just going away.

One way or another.

Am I done with Nanny . . . that was her name to us kids, Annie Marie became Nanny because it was easier to say than Granny, Grandmother.

Nanny prayed her beads and the beads were wrapped around her hands, pulled over her chest. She would kiss the cross and place the beads in the felt-lined packet. The beads had been blessed by the pope and brought back from Rome by my mother's father; back when he was still a Catholic. He later remarried and this woman brought into the house a twenty-volume history of the Masons. My mother and her sister traveled the Island to find a priest who warned them it would be creating a scandal if they attended their father's wedding. You sought, in those days, the sort of advice you required.

Father Feeney was talked of and what a bad deal he had been given, though no one knew for sure, God works in mysterious ways . . . poor Father Feeney, thrown out for saying what everybody was led to believe, there was no way to get into Heaven if you weren't Catholic and what was the point of not eating meat on Friday, of going to Mass every Sunday and Holy Day of Obligation, if it didn't assure you of something special, or at least a place at the head of the line, but they were not priests and didn't

know what the priests knew or had been trained to know so after everything was said and done it is all for the best; none of them had any of Father
Feeney's books in the house.

Never many books in the house; though they bought books from the
Dollar Book Club and a Bible from a salesman sent by the pastor when it
was thought every Catholic family should have a Bible and if you had the
Bible you might as well have the two-volume history of the saints,
complete with color portraits, the portraits were disapproved of because
they made the saints look too Italian . . . that's what they have their own
parishes for—so they can have statues only Italians know anything about.

No, am sitting here with the voice of my grandmother wondering why
in all that is sane and good and proper am I still in the City, after all the
years and times and trouble your father laid out for you to grow up out
there in the Island, away from all of those chains that can only, finally, drag
you into the river, down where Italians store relatives.

Out there, he moved, away from the street where he grew up, away from
all the people who knew him by face, by reputation, all those years with
the American Can Company, those cars, always a new Chrysler every
other year, when they married he bought Dodge, it was still made by the
Chrysler Corporation, but they did have the responsibility of the house
and the living on the lane and keeping up the property—every time you
turn around there is something needing attention, you can't begin to
imagine how much money it takes just to keep the walls, the roof over our
heads, a son of mine repeating what I have said, and this son here now
typing does not echo those words though I do not have a roof over my
head, rather another apartment, the apartments to either side, luckily
filled with older people who do not make noise, but above the tides of
water and crashing of furniture, and this is what he gave up his life for

a son and daughter to move back into the City, into the slums even your grandparents avoided . . . even grandparents didn't live in such places, and on your
mother's side of the family they didn't approve of the City as a place of habitation
in over a hundred years and before that only with reluctance

Just what happens, I might say in my defense. I have to live somewhere and here is where I hang my hat, lay my head and sit, on my way to
Patchogue, points east . . .

Sitting with many a tune in my head.

The tunes have always been of drawing boxes and triangles. Just about covers the acceptable shapes. It could have been wiggly lines or splotches of crayon, no hidden meaning. Please. Anticipation is so much better.

To go out of the room is to fail.

I sit and dream of going out. I am not storing up time to be subtracted from my debt to the coming fire.

I could go down to the avenue and walk to St. Marks. I could pass through the milling street sellers. I could pass the men with their cupped hands. I can be startled by sudden noises and expect to fling myself pitching over, hit from behind by a stray bullet. There are enough of those to go around for all who wish for such a sudden exit.

I will not carve estuaries on my wrists. I will not go to sleep. I will not splatter my blood across the wall. I will not ease myself from a window. Four flights up might not do the job. There would be lingering months in the hospital. The visit from the sister, from the relatives, who would scent their cue to go on stage at my funeral. A funeral always brings out the best. Will not frustrate the stage critics with a closed casket. No longer are the viewing hours stretched out for most of the day. Eventually, even the strongest break under the strain. Now they slide the corpse past with a tape of folk music in the background.

I am not ready, please, just yet, I have places to go. I must be getting myself to Patchogue.

The train is on hold. The people are waiting. I will be catching many a person unawares. How they will react to my interest in them, they who haven't given me a thought in twenty years.

To appear and avoid the rope of Judge Lynch. Accused of reminding people of what the years have done to them, the lines, the aches that appear, the loss of taste, the loss of . . . he's not a kid anymore, a healthy young man who was up at the drop of day. Where is that tune?

I yawn and rub my eyes. I walk about the rooms. I drink Pepsi Cola. I listen to the radio . . . no, I do not listen to the radio. I do not like the idea of not being in control of what is coming through the air. What mood may strike, launching me back to the town without pity where Liberty Valence waits for the rope or Troy Donahue. He is, and was, a real jerk, is said if asked but do not believe it.

I am at a loss. Something should have happened. Something must happen to get this show on the road. The stage is leaving and you must be on the next one out.

To be going away.

Do hurry back. You'll be missed. What assurance have I of this idea. Imagine: to be missed.

Of the grandfather not a word is to be heard. He was long gone before I was even a suggestion. Dad never talked about his father. There was one story. And time enough for it. Have to delay telling that story. Have to overcome: I am feeding on myself.

About the old man's old man all you can say is you have to assume there was this man. That he did live, spent a lot of time talking about being left alone, of wanting to be left alone. Dad did not want to be left alone but he was left alone. It was an easy way of getting through the years of being on the train, every day of the week—four hours on the train, every day, and then eight hours on the job. Twelve-hour days for the kids to grow up in the country.

Did you miss your father when he was in the City?

No matter how the question is answered . . . hesitation tells us the story or all that has to be known.

Still getting ready to go away. Have to be sure I am ready. Sacks for the vomit and tears. Sacks for the kisses and the kicks in the arse. Sacks for the dollars, ounces of gold, silver, platinum. Sacks for memories, the photographs, sonnets occasioned by this journey.

This going alone is still a bother. Trying to hold conversations with myself. How much more enjoyable it would be to have a fat ear listening at my side, to drag up from the depth of a puddle such wisdom as his class possesses. Of course the certain wit, the things I do not understand, do not get, am not exposed to, me with my book-learning and him with his experience of life, life, LIFE, LIFE.

That's what I got the vomit sacks along for; to fill up with all the puke I will encounter. Take it back to the City for further analysis in the precincts of the 55 bar.

OR, I should be setting forth with the blonde woman of dreams and be led into fantastic adventures coming about with her disappearance within the first steps of the journey. Have to get her back, to find out what happened to her, if she meant it to happen, if I was but the agent for her setting forth on her own adventure without her telling me she was so doing and already had an iron contract from a major New York publisher complete with movie option, paperback rights sold in England, translation rights in Finland, Holland, Italy, Germany, and Spain in the wings.

Or, I could fall among interesting men and women and become part of a crusade or an expedition that lost its way . . . most unlikely given the destination of Patchogue . . . though do remember I am also setting forth to Europe and all that that implies.

I am setting forth to set forth.

Or, with my soul weary, spirit broken, heart in pieces in a sack at my side I will be found standing by the side of the road, the adventures about to begin.

Or, a letter will arrive in the mail saying the village sank beneath the waves.

Or, a letter would arrive from Melinda or Barbara or . . . their lives were so full, no time left, not even a minute of time . . . the kiss of doom is for your statues in the city. Here in the country we have only time for the moment at hand. The crops have to be planted. The dead turned over in preparation for the stacking of the bones this coming September. If you care to join us then you would be most welcome . . . it is a pretty sight enjoyed by many, the stacking of the village bones, strands of tiny roses are woven through the eyesockets of skulls to join others woven through the rib cage, creating tapestries remembering in the richness of the colors and the intricacy of detail a time long lost, gone before we made our appearance in this pesthole called Patchogue.

Got to get those bones stacked: legs in one pile, arms in another, rib-cages like chicken cages in the shop on Thompson Street but less smell and to be sure not all those bones are Italian while the shop is Italian. Those people like fresh-killed pigeon, chicken, rabbit, blonde pussy while their Chinese cousins like a spot of duck and dog.

Out there, yes I know, out there is drawing me, like a drawing salve. So going out there and the immediate sadness of before leaving. Why did I ever get it into my head to go forth onto the wilderness of the Island. And without a car, without a guide or protecting animal. Without letters of introduction, the assurance of friends waiting at the station, just to go out there. COLD. I should stay where I am. Bury my head under a pillow, place arm on pillow and wait until hell freezes over before I am to move my ass out of this house, can't call it that, this apartment in this building.

No one asked me to go forth, to leave this room. No one is asking me to come back. All of these voices have little rooms within my brainbox. They are constantly undertaking suburban sprawl, turning rich potato fields into housing tracts, a swimming pool for the kids to hang out near: all these self-created and managed voices are getting their wires crossed and the sudden fuckup has the little men running around looking to plug the leak or stop the short circuit.

Still here going on like a kid though I will have passed forty before too long. Where was the station that should have yanked me off the train. Where was the car waiting with wife and children. Where was the house on the lane, the porch to sit on, the backyard to keep clean and the front to get into shape, again, this year, maybe we should pave it over and paint roses upon the asphalt or invite some Italian kids down. They are good at painting roses. I would trust a mick to paint us some shamrocks. Roses painted onto the asphalt and out back we . . . Out back? Who is this *we?*
     Just to begin.
     Now would be the moment for the phone call. The phone rings. I go into the other room and am invited by a long lost friend who tracked me down, after all these years . . . come over and visit when, any time you want. We will make you welcome, lists of parties to go to, places to see which will not disappoint you, adventures you have only read about, and only read about twenty-five years ago, not that made-up adventure of today all filled with self-conscious young men or women who go forth dulled with inner suffering.
     Yes, inner suffering.
     Surely you jest or are being foolish in suggesting these people are capable of inner suffering. I cannot believe it from what I have seen.
     Don't worry I am still here in this room. On this avenue. In this city. I am getting ready to go. No baggage as far as I can tell. Possibly as the moment for departure springs upon me I will have to break down and not travel as light as I hoped to . . . how did those guys get everything into those tiny saddle bags, or am I just confused by the saddle bags that were made up to be used by kid cowboys growing up in Patchogue in 1951. No lurch, just yet, into childhood memory.
     I am marking out the territory to be explored, continents to be by-passed, cities to be overlooked, dreams that will not be dreamt because I cannot fit them into the words already within my mouth. Some dreams

have no words attached to them, or at least words I can readily believe as coming from my mouth. It is a clear night. You can hear a pin fall out of window over on Fourth Street. The moon is full; the cats are crazed.

The rain was heavy and now it has let up for a couple of hours. The newspapers covering the man down on the avenue are soaked through. They are coughing and sneezing to keep up their spirits. They should have made their way to the shelter. Not armed they have had little chance of surviving with parcels intact through the long night. How long those nights are with the man in the bed next to me saying his rosary, another one coughing and moaning out his last night on this planet. The man at the head of the bed is talking to his girl from a little town in Indiana. There was no reason to pour gasoline all over yourself, set match, then run into the setting Indiana sun. No reason at all. I was only kidding, but you didn't believe me. Can I hold the match next time? Another man at the foot of the bed is silently sharpening his teeth getting ready for a midevening spring for my throat, the clamp of jaws, blood sprung from the flesh-case called me.

Never a clean handkerchief, ever again. I am too severe with myself. This is no journey into darkest Africa as if Africa is anything but dark. All that sun. If you listen to the guys in the Eagle or the Oasis, Patchogue is approached by way of Africa and some would add by way of Little Puerto Rico, or Spictown if they are of the literary mind.

Should I polish my shoes? Should I brush my teeth? Should I comb my hair? Wash behind my ears? Clean out the water ducts at the corners of my eyes? Extract the stuff from belly button, gunk from under the big toenail, pieces of dried shit attached to the hairs in the crack of me arse—the crack of me arse, has a certain lilt to the words. Could turn it into a Newfie traveling song, in the crack of me arse she rode for home, bent for leather or something like that, in the crack of me arse.

Just polish up the car and make sure I have some of the lines down ready for the tip of the tongue. Make sure I know my name, address, telephone number, social security number, number of my dependents; am I married.

These walls have seen the last of me. I am leaving.

Packing up my old kitbag and smiling, smiling all away, as much of a smile as can be managed in this day of the age.

Pulled down by hesitation. How to get the motor turned and have head yanked back to make sure they are not gaining on us . . . who is this they—

suddenly dragged on to the scene.

Another time. I am almost one foot in front of the other and on my way. Almost.

Just a moment. There is always time for the final reconsideration of all plans, the final moment before the trigger must be pulled, the step off the chair, out of the window, in front of the train, off the bridge.

No regret and no song to hymn the fact of no regret. Still just sitting here, with the sudden heat, while all the previous moments of this waiting to get up the gumption, the energy, the balls out of the pocket-pool game. The chill temperatures have lightened my mood, eased the sense of desperation. With the heat: have to get away. Seek out the chilled thoughts of the mountains, though who can trust a thought growing on a mountainside, a thought broiled on the beach.

I am going away. I am leaving behind the short fat ear, the blonde woman of dream. I am going forth: the final gasp of breath, sip of water, the dregs from the dusty bottle. Of course I have left nothing behind of any value. I carry myself upon my own back, carry everything of importance within the brainbox between my ears.

At least sit down, get my head on straight, screw down the loose connections, know I will find nothing, that nothing will be lost and every-thing I seek can be found within three feet of where I sit.

No person is ever where they are supposed to be. I have grown up in rooms without windows, without a breath of air, as is said, rooms while furnished in the latest page from *Casa Vogue*.

I am sitting in New York City, waiting for the moment when I shall leave and go forth to Patchogue, to Europe and points in between and far away. No attempt will be made at local color or foreign color. Everything will be in black/white given the poverty of the publishers and my own imagina-tion. I am incapable of dreaming in color. I learned to dream in the age of black/white television. Isn't that the old . . . we always dream in black/white. I am leaving the city. I wish a voice would appear out of the proverbial blue, from under a rock, from behind a cloud and let me in on the secret of my setting forth. I am cured of traveling before I set out. I do not have a single smell in my nose to jog me into longing as would happen when living in northern Wisconsin: the sudden smell of bus exhaust or the hot smell of iron, perspiration, hot dogs, the breath of a man in love with Thunderbird . . . and knowing I would be back in Patchogue with the hope of seeing Melinda. Other names could be mentioned but I am in mourning. I am not wearing black and grey. No time to fasten a black band around my arm. The tears do not come. No swooning. All gone. All gone and now I am a son without a family. Musical accompaniment of slow violins, muffled drums, and of currency being counted, slurp of thumb and finger and the ruffling through the wad of bills. No reason to leave. I have left nothing behind. The past is my only ghost. Nothing will stand in my way. I have drained myself of surplus fluids; must wait the passage of time before the reservoir is filled to the bursting, awaiting the state, the famous state of blue balls.

Yes, slipped out of the city. Went to the station, bought a ticket, hopped on the train and in less than two hours I was getting off the train in Patchogue and after a length of time I was hopping back on the train, into the city, off the train at Penn Station a quick drink in the Boxcar, dining and drinking at its best or we'll ship you out, the jukebox always runs the songs, a bit slow so no one gets the feeling they are becoming run down with the eating up of the time before the last train is called and the anxiety of what is waiting for them at home.

Back in the City before I was missed. The leave-taking did not make the papers. The return is unannounced.

I have to store up some images, rituals, arguments, strategies to deal with what lurks out there in Patchogue, what is hidden out there in the hovels by the side of the road. There are castles but they are mainly of the mind and not easily approached. The roads are not clearly marked and often landslides and other natural disasters occur. There is no way of knowing ahead of time; just a prayer and wallet full of money are all you can count on when confronted by the road system of Patchogue, a place some claim is a parking lot with a village attached. This is both to be over-looked and taken into account when dealing with the natives. Life in New York City will little prepare a person for what he will encounter in Patchogue. It might be good to be clear about what one is leaving behind so what and who one sees in the course of this journey into Patchogue and again away from Patchogue can be placed into a comfortable and easily accessible context; rewarding too!

If I leave these rooms and then this floor and then this building I will find myself down on a street around the corner from an avenue. A tree is now green in front of this building. Not as many men are sleeping against the building as before. The Greeks in the restaurant have taken to shooting those who linger longer than an hour. They fill up two and sometimes three dumpsters a week with the remains. No one has objected to this policy. Some have stopped for a coffee and expressed their thanks to the owner for ridding the neighborhood of what it had a surplus of to begin with: a bunch of mouths that shit and piss all over everything. Not leaving even a scrap of poetry behind. So, I am on the avenue. My head turns at the white-bloused tits and the blonde hair. Long blonde hair has been under assault for quite some time and is in danger of dying out. Blue eyes are the next to go. No specific face turns my head. It is more and more just another sad day. I see my aging face and balding head being worn by many on the streets of this area. We have or I have like many another been left behind. They have a rubber bag and chrome tray prepared for me in the hospital. I have not chosen the music but I hope the attendant doesn't do the Y-cut to the pop tune of WKTU.

Once I sat in close-up in that building across the street and had a tit pushed into my mouth. A wrinkled tit. The upper lip was hairy and wrinkled. Her eyes did not even know I was in front of her. The only blind go-go dancer for five hundred miles in any direction. They came from all over and wondered at her technique.

Never to see the results of her work in the spreading stains on the front of tight teen jeans. The club only tolerated the very young and the very old. The ones in the middle, those caught between the past and the dim possibility of the future, were not allowed. The young were drained and the old had been drained.

The building is closed up into itself. Like the people who walk by it. No, that is not exactly right. Too many of them are all out there, all over the place, parts of them being led on a leash—pulled by a rope—all over the sidewalk, they walk with dreams and complaints equally mixed. Not a care over who hears them. Not afraid their jokes will be stolen if spoken aloud. Other things go on in that building. Men gamble away the baby's milk money. That much is certain. They have been known to throw in the wife's pussy in the hopes of making a real killing. Right to the White House, for many a man who has entered that building. To the White House to discuss philosophy and the mechanics of the spirit and the moving business with Ian. The hotels on the Bowery are segregated. Across the street is the roach motel. Spanish not spoken.

So, I am standing on the step in front of the building in which is the apartment where I sit and write about going out to Patchogue. I will turn to my
left after hesitating about going to the right to see what the teenage
hookers are doing at the corner. So young et cetera and not even a hotel,
finally, or a café to eventually become the proprietor of. No role, no
future, no sense of a real calling. Just two orifices promised and trying to
get away without having to use either of them. Never giving a fair day's
hump. As Mr. Brady once said, They sit on their asses counting my money.

So, around the corner past the Greeks supervising the feeding habits of
people who have tried to get their thoughts together to face the rest of the
night. Then past the Oriental guy who got this liquor store. Just pints and
miniatures. Sees no reason to stock the larger sizes. He keeps his customers'
needs in front of his mind.

I am not interested in reality. I am not taking dictation from reality. I
could go on and get lost in describing the whole fucking block and planet
and then the other blocks up to St. Marks and then along St. Marks in
either direction but why stop there. All those other streets and then the
roads, the gutters, the sky overhead. All just so much of OUT THERE.
Sounding like I am throwing myself back into the late-night college conversation of windows painted black, black curtains, men and women
dressed in black: purple lipstick and eyeshadow, and it's all changed
anyway.

A guy was sitting on the trash barrels, pointing to his head: this head has
been hit with a hatchet, this head has been hit with a hatchet. The words
are noted down, the comment recorded ready to bring up at the next
dinner table. Don't have to go to darkest AFRICA to find items of conversation. Or even a street in northern Sweden or Ireland . . . the guy was
white and his ear was black. The ear wasn't saying anything just yet. There
was still a couple of inches in his bottle. He would be getting back to
words. In just a moment when he would need to put together another
bottle to get the poetry out of your man, the poetry is the thing. Every
body needs some poetry in their lives and while the hatchet hit this guy in
the head it didn't knock the poetry out of his head.

Not a single clarifying picture to lodge in my mind, to carry as my
talisman into the wildest parts of Long Island. I wish I was using heavy,
how many pounds, of what, irony, when I talk about the wild parts of Long
Island: the jungle, the desert, the wastelands, the hills of skulls are where
you find them these days. They are no longer safely stuck down on the

page, something like colored stamps you get ten to the dollar and paste them in their books while the milkman is taking around the week of June 6th. You too can get involved in the modern search for the appropriate waste place to send the children and their descendants, there to find love, poetry, and fine dining.

On the next block over from the street on which I live is the police station. Buckets of blood are carried out every morning and spread on the roots of the trees, growing in a row in front of the chain link fence. The blood keeps these trees in manageable form. You have to be careful when carrying a bucket of blood. Bloodstains are notoriously difficult to get out, in particular out of the blue cloth they use in the police uniform. Much thought has gone into the origins of this blood. All these thoughts are frozen in the windpipe. A little boat could be sailed across the blood puddle created after the watering of the trees.

As I was saying: to walk out of my front door, this front door with its three working locks, its two inoperative locks, to walk out of this door, to hear the door close behind me, to turn and turn the keys in two of those locks, to walk out of this door to walk from this door, one foot in front of the other is to travel to Patchogue, to Europe, to the moon, to the far deserts of China, and low mountains of Ireland and Bulgaria. Too far away and yet it's to just go over to First Avenue and sit in the McDonalds and have hamburger and a cheeseburger, just a napkin, don't need any more salt and catsup, plenty on the burgers, to sit midst the old people and the young people. I am going on my way. I have sailed my shoe across the puddles of blood in front of the police station. I should have known better. Blood attracts cockroaches. They thrive on it like they do on the bindings of books. They dance. I am not creating a cast of characters. Patchogue would be more than a match for any character I might run into or create at such a last minute.

So, went a ways down Second Avenue to the tombstone shops. And next door to them are the flesh and bone shops. Where people are made ready for their final performance, a difficult role but performed lying down, most people are able to give it a good turn, a good run for the money being spent. Requires little practice and only one condition. The flesh is stripped from the bones. The blood collected in large glass containers, then deposited in the special compartment of the hearse and when the hearse stops at the check-in point at the cemetery and driver can be seen rushing into the office with a large parcel, this is the glass jar filled with the blood, no longer of use to the occupant of the wooden structure being carried in the hearse. I am not trying to be cute.

Don't get cute with me or be cute with me trying to show off your learning. Anybody can get some learning if they open a book. But who would want such a bit of learning? They give it away for free and you know what they say about boys and girls who give it away for free and if you don't then kiss my cookies, as the sign in the gas station says.

On a sunny afternoon I go along to the flesh and bone shops to see what is being offered. It is not a rewarding experience. Something is missing. They do not give souvenirs of the visit. They do not charge admission. There is no postcard counter and while the toilet facilities are adequate there could be some little touch to remind one . . .

I do not like to look at aged flesh. What can any living person say about this heap, the chunk of remains. Now give me a young, a youthful exhibit and I will sing you the songs of promises that won't have to be kept. I will sing you of loves that will not begin only to end, of hatred that has not been allowed to bloom into fantastic flowers for sale in the shops of Madison Avenue. To think, to think, as the chorus of the song goes that is always played at these occasions and is always on the lips of those attending. What to think, what to think, what can be said that the song hasn't already thought of. It is the wide swath of possibility occasioned by these young people. Not today, sadly, and not for some time. This has been a time of nature settling accounts with those who have been around too long. You got to clean out the stable so there will be room all summer long for the youth of the neighborhood. The old people sit in the shade and make bets on which of the young will get the call. They sit in McDonalds collecting and averaging the received wagers. There has been comment on the changed character of the neighborhood. The lack of young people. All these awful people in the middle, not young enough to die and not old enough to appreciate the spectacle of young death. All these people filled to the gills with life's juices, secreting them, they are, all over the place, into every unattended crevice and orifice.

Ah, the pleasures I am leaving behind to set forth on my expedition to Patchogue. To be there at last. A dream fulfilled. A dream left behind fit only for reruns. To go to Patchogue is to go to Dublin, to go to Sofia, to Vienna, to Paris, to Venice, to Milan. It is to go and to come back filled with interesting tales to be told and retold until the moment of invention takes over. To go down to the avenue: a broken thought fit only for these

68

final moments before leaving. Toothbrush packed, as it must be, cats sent to the hotel, the electricity turned off, the telephone disconnected. To be back before I know it, before any of you know it. Isn't that always the case.

Finally.   Away.

Getting into Patchogue late one night in an oysterboat, there was a drunken Dutchman aboard whose wit reminded me of Shakespeare. When we came to leave the beach, our boat was aground, and we were detained three hours waiting for the tide. In the meanwhile, two of the fishermen took an extra dram at the beach house. Then they stretched themselves on the seaweed by the shore in the sun to sleep off the effects of their debauch. One was an inconceivably broad-faced young Dutchman —but oh! of such a peculiar breadth and heavy look, I should not know whether to call it more ridiculous or sublime. You would say that he had humbled himself so much that he was beginning to be exalted. An indescribable mynheerish stupidity. I was less disgusted by their filthiness and vulgarity, because I was compelled to look on them as animals, as swine in their sty. For the whole voyage they lay flat on their backs on the bottom of the boat, in the bilge-water and wet with each bailing, half insensible and wallowing in their vomit. But ever and anon, when aroused by the rude kicks or curses of the skipper, the Dutchman, who never lost his wit or equanimity, though snoring and rolling in the vomit produced by his debauch, blurted forth some happy repartee like an illuminated swine. It was the earthiest, slimiest wit I ever heard.

—Henry D. Thoreau

IN PATCHOGUE

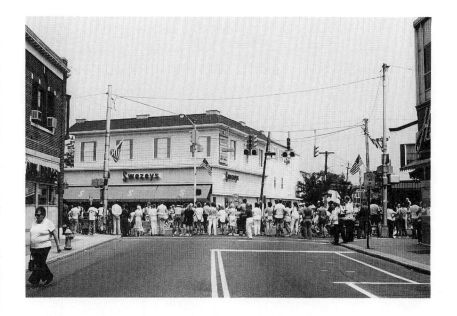

The spirit of modern literature is essentially a traveling one.
—Maxime du Camp, *Le Nil*

Patchogue, that's where Frontier Town was, and back then, in the early '60s, it was the frontier. —Flip

There is also the matter of so-called emotional life which can even at times degenerate into love. —Hemito von Doderer

I came to find myself on the train to Patchogue. The journey does not take as long as it once did. I did not find the train uncomfortable. The seats did what they were supposed to do. Bottom and back were supported in a certain fashion. At the hour of my travels there was little noise of a human or other kind. There were no incidents with conductors, traveling sales-people, religious types of a Protestant persuasion. Jewish faces did not fill my field of vision. Catholic children were seen, occasionally, but not heard except for one moment when passing a building that was at the very moment collapsing into rubble. A child's voice piped up with the O, O, O, and the words, Is that what they're going to do with Grandma's house? No adult reply was heard and the train continued to stop as it was scheduled to stop. No accidents or near accidents. The emergency cord was not pulled. The conductors did not have to unsheathe the nightsticks they were still carrying during the day. This might be an indication that something was expected, but nothing occurred to justify the apprehension of these civil servants, who move from car to car with punches punching out braille holes in the tickets offered up in exchange for allowing the seat to do its job. Of course back a ways money was exchanged for the tickets. I am unwilling to go further back into what was exchanged for the money out of fear of ending up as a money crank, leaning from a high leather chair after the cognac. I did not expect anything out of the ordinary to happen on this journey. The expectation was fulfilled, in spades, to introduce a certain ambiguous way of putting it. In the seat behind me was a colored couple. I have left New York City and on Long Island, people refer to these brown people as the colored people. O, the elected officials, people at the public trough, will make mention of the word *black,* but these two colored guys in grey suits were talking about property values in Sayville and how they just missed getting in on the ground floor, just before prices shot through the roof and now all we gots is buckets o' shit falling about us and no oar to row our boat out from under the excrement deluge.

Now, ain't that right, silly, this brown couple, a man and man, an

educated couple, not traveling with their Siamese cats which they had left
with their white houseboy.

I came to be on this train and I came to get off at Patchogue station
much changed since previous gettings-off at this station. The old station
had been torn down. The brass counter sold to an antique dealer who sold
it to this lady from Little Neck who wanted to use it in her basement fifty-
dollar-a-throw brothel. Enough of this material from an old movie seen in
Brussels, in French with Dutch subtitles, when I was on my way from Sofia
to Dublin, via Istanbul . . . those cheap Turkish flights from Brussels,
bused in the middle of the night from place A to place B, hustled onto the
plane, cash in hand, all another story of buckets: used rubbers being
collected for aging beatnik writers who like to sit around . . . this is getting
eccentric and my interest has drifted from the subject at hand . . . arrival in
Patchogue and now standing in the parking lot of the station. Seems to get
bigger with each year. Always can count on Patchogue to be adding to its
supply of parking spaces. A parking lot is the lifeblood of the community:
always tear down a house, uproot a tree so everybody knows: we believe
in parking lots.

> I wait for the train
> The train was called
> I boarded the train
> I sat on the train
> I arrived in Patchogue
> I took a room in a boarding house on South Ocean Avenue
> I didn't know how long I was planning to stay
> It didn't matter
> As long as you pay
> in advance
> you can stay as long
> otherwise
> N O   C R E D I T

If only the air were filled with perfume, the odors of freshly cut flowers or
even some good old-fashioned industrial pollution . . . nothing for the
nose to do. Keep it in shape for parties later when the insurance agents run
amok.

Off-the-wall might be a way of describing what is happening. On out of
the city with the prospect of actually walking across grassy fields, to cut the

sandy beach to the shore and there skip a rock along the flat waters.
Ah, ain't nature something, a real kick in the head.
I am in Patchogue.
As if you couldn't tell. The grammar is falling apart. I would like to
create a tunnel under the covers, pulled tightly over head, with blinds shut,
keyhole stuffed with sodden cardboard, now properly dried, ready to
catch fire if that kid I saw a couple of hours ago had his way: likes to see
people jump for the meager remains of their lives, even the ones who talk
about their lives in terms of time that has to be gotten through . . . would
squawk if suddenly told: this is it, buddy, no time to pack those packs, the
journey is over and you have banged your head against the wall for the
final time.

A little city poem, left over and now found as he stands in the parking
lot out there in Patchogue, at the station:

> beauty persecutes
> me
> narrow face
> blonde
> ponytail

Have never dragged my ass out of the junior year of high school. I am still
standing, the shine off my nose, against the glass of the shop window. All
that sweet stuff. All it gives are cavities and years of going to the dentist
and then the gum specialist, just when you think you have finished with
the dentist.

Walking across the parking lot. At least I am not struck with the idea in
riding the bus in from the airport in Dublin: why in all that . . . am I back
here, AGAIN? Can I refine this being hit in back of the neck. The size of
the oak trees in front of the church, St. Francis de Sales . . . a certain comfort, plant life continues on indifferent to whatever. They haven't chopped
the trees down, yet. I can think of reasons to get rid of the trees: insurance,
possible hurricane damage, you can never be too careful—the trees just
have to come down . . . the money saved will feed x-number of deserving
children in whatever slum you care to mention, and do you think anyone
misses a tree; there are lots of trees still in Patchogue. These people, the
last time they thought about a tree was when it got pounded into their
heads in the form of a poem by *the Catholic poet,* Joyce Kilmer, and you see
what happened to him: ends up a rest stop on the Jersey Turnpike, more

respect has never been shown a poet in this day . . . look at Walt Whitman, old greybeard himself, turned into a parking lot, a savings bank and a drug treatment center in Coram for preteens who have caught the habit from older brothers and sisters. One could see Old Walt down there grabbing a young leg when he could.

A narrow escape from a terrible death occurred yesterday when the 7:20 A.M. train came into Patchogue on its way to New York. Orrin Gerard and Arthur Searles, who drive an ice wagon for George Saxton, were driving up Grove Avenue on their way to the village and were just about to cross the track when they heard a rumbling sound. They turned quickly only to see the swiftly approaching train not more than 200 feet from them. Both men instantly sprang from the wagon leaving the horse as they supposed to be ground into pieces. At this moment, a sudden and shrill whistle from the train so frightened the horse that he gave a leap and just cleared the track as the train went rushing by. The horse plunged wildly on until he reached the Old Oak Inn where he was caught and kept until his half-scared-to-death drivers could get him.

Where is the welcoming committee? Didn't they know I was on my way out here? Didn't they pick up the scent, hear the vibes, as the street puts it?

No flowers in the fist of a first-grade blonde-haired tyke. No scroll of welcome, no prepared speech and poem by the resident poet of the *Long Island Advance.* (I was raised with the idea that the *Advance* was the *Patchogue Advance.* I know. I know. They changed the name of paper to reflect the real audience . . . et cetera . . . how dreary . . . dreary as all get out.) The *Advance* ain't here to cover the arrival. It has become the hometown newspaper now that there is no hometown hereabouts. They do a good job at listing all the ones on the way out in the obituary columns, less of a good job with the weddings.

And here I am. No bells, to be sure, on my shoes, no pocket sound system, soapbox or message to be delivered from a soapbox, but surely a little testimonial at Felice's is in order. Don't understand what is the matter. I am on time. The weather is fine. There have been no natural disasters, no tragic car crashes devastating two or more families giving the kids a day off to attend the funeral.

Weather should be discussed along with the noon whistle, the Angelus bells and the nothing else marking the day, village-wide.

Where to go?

The first question upon arriving after having traveled some distance. One does have to go somewhere, otherwise one wouldn't have left.

But I have my head under the covers. I do not want to surface. I have seen it all before. I have seen the veins traced on her legs. I have seen the bloody rags collected in the enameled basin. My eyes have watched very carefully making sure their chests are going up/down.

Going on I am and almost quoting myself doing that. I am here in Patchogue. I am imagined as being in the parking lot of the railroad station of Patchogue. I have not been met. Standing alone and wondering in what direction does the story move.

Standing. Though I have now walked over to Ocean Avenue. The town hall is across the street. On the other corner is the American Legion Hall and behind that the village hall. Down the block on Ocean Avenue is the junior high school, next to that what was once St. Francis de Sales School; the Board of Education has it for some sort of office. It still remains the school I first went to after kindergarten over on Bay Avenue . . . as if the whole world should know where these streets are and what they mean. To trace the pattern of the meanings. To pull the tears out of the trees, to carpet the pavement with the smiles once seen.

Last Friday a noisy tramp was found on Main Street in Patchogue. With the combined efforts of Officers Davis, Chapman and Rope, he was gotten to the lockup where he remained overnight. In the morning Justice Conklin sent him to Riverhead jail for 30 days.

I do not have that much time. None of us has that much time.

These are clichés that must be said. To lay the foundation for all that will come in the wake of the boat sailing out of the Patchogue River to Leja Beach. To the island, then the ocean, and then Europe or some approxima-tion. . . . I am away, am I not: Patchogue a mere stepping-stone to Istanbul, Main Street flows into Istiklal Caddesi and on into Cumhuriyet Caddesi: I am walking into the Hilton for a hamburger, and if I am quick enough, up into a room for a shower and view of the city before the maid sends me in disgrace to the native entrance. This is called fancy and not imagination— is that Coleridge barking out by the white birch, a delicate tree that does not survive many hurricanes.

Certain decisions have to be made. We are at a standstill. The wheels are spinning smoke and no fire. Luckily, the weather is warm. No need for heat in this May of my travels to Patchogue. A high blue sky with few clouds and most of them blown out to sea. The sun is bright but only warm. The grass is green, undamaged as yet by the sun. The trees have their leaves . . . that's all the nature stuff I know. I have run up against my ignorance. Once it wasn't always so. I have become a City Person. All this green stuff makes me nervous. The only green stuff I understand is the folding kind. To give these pages the American idiom, though what else can I be using since I am moving through this landscape which could be none other than, into the grave, into the grave it urges. A landscape has no use for people because people have made of it a nightmare. All so easy to report but how to get it into the flesh and not allow the flesh to go tumbling out the window.

In the shade next to the control tower where the crossing gates go down with the passing of the trains, at the tracks, is seen, is reported to have been seen:

I couldn't tell whether it was a girl or a boy. It was lying on its stomach on top of a green and chrome medical movable table. It was dressed in a flannel pants suit, playing an electric piano with its tongue. The arms are stretched out along the creature's side, paralyzed, as are the legs splayed out behind. The arms look like webbed flippers, but are too skinny for such a large lump of flesh. Every once in a while it looks up and gives the long pink tongue a rest. Its hair is done in cornrow style so I assume it is a girl, a Negro girl. The use of the impersonal pronoun does not reflect any prejudice, just the poverty of the English language; maybe there is an American Indian language which can supply the word . . . the poverty in that here was a creature, human to be sure, but of such an indeterminate nature, its human quality was the only visible distinction though the human quality only really came upon observation of the creature's keeper who was standing by the curb, smoking a cigarette, keeping an eye on the tin can into which people dropped coins and dollar bills. Here was a man who was fully conscious of the human nature of his creature and he might as well make a living off of it and the strangers who pass thanking their God that . . . not even a grunt from the creature between the stroking of the keys of this mechanical piano . . . a glistening pink tongue trying to create a tune for the early morning passersby.

On previous visits I had not seen such exhibits. They had been hidden away and were thought to be bad for business. Time passes and new fashions come to be. It had been noticed in the papers: once upon a time young mothers had photos made up of their babies and had these photos blown up and transferred to T-shirts; now they had pictures made of the aborted fetuses of children not wanted. And wore these as a token of how much they had become in Patchogue: in days gone by a child was like an extra set of hands around the house . . . now it was just a mouth and asshole requiring shoes every six months.

The structure for this visit. I am here and what am I to do? I have done this before. A quick run round the place, then the long drawn out, waiting for the train back to the City to talk about waiting for the train back to the City.

Suddenly, almost shy of my past in this village, as if I had grown up to a moment when I was so tired of what had happened to me: who could be interested in the life I had lived in this village, when with the years I had lost my own interest in shaping, reshaping, honing the experience that flung me from this town in August of 1965, only to return in later years as a visitor and never overnight because I was not on such terms with anyone in the village.

To have lived in a place for twenty-one years, all the years of one's youth . . . and to have no one who was, as the saying goes, one's best friend, a person I could look up and unwind the conversation and still to be in touch with to await with actual sadness his death . . . instead this certain morbid fascination of when will he/she bite the dust, for the last time—a lot of false starts on the part of people these days . . . but finally they all do go under ground, no matter how hard they hold on.

Would you rather jump into the tale of

P A T C H O G U E: THE MUSICAL

Or the story of a brother who was writing on commission the story of his older brother, to be used as an inspirational text by the American Management Association. Or my own story. Or there is the movie set in Patchogue:

WHAT ARE YOU DOING HERE?

At this stage in the development of the last project there is still some question as to whether there should be a question mark or exclamation point after HERE.

I should get this old sack of bones to the Oasis, before it closes for good, to have one last memorial beer to my own life. Have to decide, now that I am IN PATCHOGUE, if I will be staying overnight and will require a

room in a boarding house on South Ocean Avenue. It is still early and they
have yet to clear the rooms of last night's victims. If I told you what was
going on in the village last night you would not believe me. I stand on the
corner of Division Street. To go south, to go north? To go south is to go
toward the bay, to eventually stand on the Mascot Dock, to look to Fire
Island, to look to the ocean beyond, to look towards Europe.

To go north is to go toward Main Street, toward the Sunrise Highway,
towards the north, and I could imagine it would be thought I was going to
the north, to Newfoundland, to Finland, to the Shetland Islands, to the
blonde lands.

But I already know what waits for me in the north: disappointment. My
odor repels the blonde creatures. They can smell me a mile away. Can
smell my hunger for the touch of their hair, for the taste of the hair, for the
hope I perceive. The fool's gold, of course, what else—the fountain not so
much of youth but as a spurt of grease to slide the body into the earth
without regret. To lie in the deathbed and know: life continues and I am
not part of it. Dusty hands move across blonde flesh, all the time.

Going out to Patchogue.

The first thought is when will I do it again even though other thoughts
did get themselves stuck down on paper as coming before this thought
which is actually the first thought, even though . . . can't you keep your
voice down? You have to remember this is real and it ain't a movie. The
Rialto Theatre has been torn down to become an empty lot. An empty lot
is much cheaper, tax-wise, than a building on the lot that ain't paying its
way. People don't got the time, as they say, for the movies in Patchogue.
They like life to be real bloody, a piece of steak being squeezed before it's
set down on the grill; the blood running across the tops of the fingers,
filling up the wrinkled skin.

Only the Patchogue Theatre, for now, is still open and I could not go in
there, down front, because I might turn and see Melinda sitting in the
center of a middle row . . . and he is still sitting next to her. He has his arm
around her shoulder; blood drips from the fingers of that hand hanging
over her shoulder. The whole front of her dress is bloody. She is smiling
and cannot see what is happening. She is entranced by what is going on in
the movie, *Johnny Guitar,* for the third time, the hanging, the burning
house, and Nicholas Ray will die in a loft above New Morning Books on
Spring Street. All those words of hope cannot add flesh to the body being
shrunk by cancer. She cannot see what is happening. I will not be able to

tell her. It is not my place. I'm always too far away. I do not speak the same language. It's never the right time: either too early or too late. Once upon a time, or never upon a time, just waiting to meet up at the brink of being shoveled into the hole.

When Ferzler first started as a movie doorman he worked at both the Patchogue and Rialto theaters. In the late 1940s he worked exclusively at the Patchogue Theatre. Ferzler is tall, quite spare; and admits to being near retirement age. He has remained single. "I'm married to the movies," he said. He lives in town and walks to work; he neither owns nor drives a car. He is a shy but friendly man who is proud of his collection of a few hundred postcards—only of Patchogue, he says—and likes to recount the history behind each one. He trades the cards by mail and attends a collectors' show once a year. "There's a fellow who drives me there every year," he said. Ferzler usually carries a few of his prized postcards in his jacket pocket, ready to show an interested visitor. Charlie's hobby would interest many whose roots grow deep in Patchogue. Collecting postcards (he has about 500 of them), exclusively of Patchogue during the early 1900s, is what he enjoys when he is not working. United Artists may have closed the Patchogue Theatre for the last time on Sunday evening but it's not "Goodbye, Charlie." The Patchogue native who chose to work in and make Patchogue his home says he'll stay and just take it easy for now.

So. After all these years I am back here, again. Nothing has changed. The same bad guys are in charge. The same good guys are seen in the shadows.

Lack of drama, my good man. Who will believe your assertion? They have seen no drama. They haven't even seen a village board meeting written up in the paper by the local poet to make ends meet. Always on top of things because she puts their thoughts into complete sentences, when she can, when she herself can understand their attempt at the English language.

And the fear: death will grab me before I make it back to my hovel, there to die alone. But at least it is within walls I have some familiarity with. To close my eyes on cracks, falling plaster, dust accumulating . . . to be undone and no one to know my name, to know I went to St. Francis de Sales School, to one year of Seton Hall High School, to three years of Patchogue High School and there in the final year to see for the first time: Melinda.

Self-centered lout. Ignorant shit. Who gives a flying fuck that you lived, that you will die!

Will you believe me if I make an effort to take into account the whole village of Patchogue, even those areas just beyond the incorporated boundaries, once dark territories explored on bicycle but now over-populated by City People growing used to mosquitoes, high oil prices during the winter, the lawn, the lawn.

For a number of years around the turn of the century, Patchogue was one of the leading bicycling centers in Long Island. Patchogue served as the terminus for Brooklyn's "Century Runs"—the 100-mile round-trip from Bedford Ave., Brooklyn and Roe's Hotel on Main St. Patchogue and return. It was a colorful era in Patchogue history in which some prominent Patchogues Nat and Henry Roe, Arthur Terry and Clarence "Mose" Ruland enthusiastically participated.

Little moments, distant relatives to the *petite mortes* of the French, if you can imagine one without sex . . . in America, quite easily, don't you know, easier done than said, it seems, given your flounderings around in this village. Have yourself on Division Street, symbolic and all that, in the village of your first love, first deaths, first goings away and no one writing letters wanting you to come home. Ain't it a shame.

A good time is being had by all. Even if I have to say so myself for everybody involved. The party favors were much appreciated. Nothing was stolen or broken. No fights broke out back under the maple trees. As if nothing had happened.

I have the feeling that just around the corner is the house on a shady lane between two large streets that ran from town to bay. In the summer, children walked by the house in bathing suits, hopping from hot paved bits of lane to cool patches of grass. In the winter there were always hours and sometimes half a day before the lane was passable after a snowfall. A good place, as is said, to grow up in. No one was murdered on Furman Lane. There was never a break-in. No one even died on the lane while I was growing up. People seemed to live forever and to have been living there forever. More people lived on the lane in the summer than during the winter but even these City People seemed a different sort of chopped liver than those who can out for just a quick weekend over on the Island. In the winter the lane was quiet and the dog had the run of Furman Lane and the street into which it ran, Maiden Lane. There were a number of maidens in the vicinity, but they were of the old-maid variety, a type of woman who has disappeared in recent years. The house next to 41 Furman Lane was always used by transient people, by people who rented or who tried to buy the place, but something always happened. Across the lane was a little bungalow inhabited by an old man who died . . . well, he did live but then he was dead and Mr. Nellis was remembered for his kindness, one of the fifty-six billion people who have died since the earth got its . . . one of the dead and down the lane, Miss Fisher is also now one of the dead people. As is the father of Mr. Nellis's landlord who was described by the Queen of Roumania as a "man with the heart of a Viking and the simple faith of a child." As are the people who claimed to be my parents and who I claimed as my parents: dead, they are . . . moved away from the lane after August saying good-bye to Melinda. Sentenced to exile in northern Wisconsin. . . but not being poets or politically involved and this not being the Soviet Union, what can one say. That's how the cookie crumbles. Them's the breaks. That's just the way it is. What can you do about it. At least the company paid for everything: kept your father on his job, we were able to make sure you and your sister could finish college, what was the point, if after all these years, you had to interrupt, as you get older you simply decide to forego certain pleasures; you begin to see there are other things and your father wouldn't hear of it; was his idea to move away from Brooklyn. I couldn't have cared less. I was happy anywhere. Here my mother's voice breaks off.

You never get out of the village you were stuck into by fate, by birth. It's the old story you got and it's too bad no one got murdered halfway through the tale: the remaining pages would be filled up with detection and guilt. Some stories are supposed to appear out of the woodwork. People sit around the table, sing happy birthday and do not wonder who will not be at the table next year. Though I always wondered who would not be there. What would I do and it comes to be a time when I have to think twice, whatever that means, as to when she and he actually did die and there was no word, no waiting by the door, in the white-walled black-vinyl chaired rooms and told: "Sorry your mother passed away . . . or your father . . . he wasn't in pain, I can assure you of that."

Dead, they are.

I am back here in this village that did not see them off, did not wish them a bon voyage. Where were they going anyway? They were not going south to Florida to send back announcements of gold prizes won, daughters or sons married, that final anniversary and into the earth with . . . *a former resident of Patchogue . . .*

A reunion of Patchogue people was held in Boca Raton, Florida, at the Boca Pointe Country Club February 24. The guest list of 95 was comprised of former Patchogue residents now living in Florida, those who just spend the winter months there, and those who commute for short vacations. David Gottfried, the Master of Ceremonies, set the tone with fond and amusing remarks about Patchogue in the "Good Old Days." Dr. Maurice Fletcher, who left Patchogue 40 years ago, spoke about his special memories. Sanford Davidow spoke of how he came to be in Patchogue and all the good years that followed. Marjorie Schwartz told of the great things she found in Patchogue. Al Chuichiolo gave a humorous report on "Patchogue Today." There was dancing throughout the afternoon and it seemed unanimous that Patchogue is special with special people who have made it so. Reportedly, a second annual Patchogue "South" Reunion is in the planning stages for next winter.

I would walk down Ocean Avenue and check into the Smithport Hotel. It is not there. I would have to make allowances for certain geographical difficulties on the copyright page. Check into the Smithport Hotel and then into the bar with the bottle of Miller and watch the little boy pissing and the slogans: why I order beer—what goes in must come out.

There was the story of the gold buried in Dead Man's Hill. Gold as much as any person could ever want. Turned out to be a dead body and it turned out to be just . . . Someone stuck two split-level houses on the lot where Dead Man's Hill was located and I am sure there are strange goings-on in the broom closet. I am not going to invent vomiting washing machines, streams of blood flowing down the cellar steps, a pile of fleshy matter in the corner of the garage. Can only report the stubborn silence of the village.

If I had not gone away, I would not want to go away. I would not want to go into the City. What's in the City anyway? Look at all the people who're always coming out here from the City. Why aren't more people rushing back to the City? No, every Friday they come out on the train, grab a cab, dash for the ferry to make the cocktail hour on Leja Beach and then the dinner hour and then the after-dinner hour and then the hop into bed for the morning wake me up and let's do it again *real soon.*

I have stayed on in the village. I have grown old and subdivided the stomach. I cannot see my cock when I stand to take a piss. I stand, reach, and on faith am met by flesh. Life is always over before you think it has begun. Down at the corner taking a swig from a paper-wrapped quart of ale is the strong narrative of expectation and loss. Walking along South

Ocean Avenue. Already passed the schools, St. Francis de Sales Church, passed all of these and of course will have to get back to them, to make visible the stigmata between my legs, on my back, in the center of my skull. Came, they did, that afternoon; I am sure it was an afternoon.

A most depressing story or *WHAT ARE YOU DOING HERE*
CAROL   TUESDAY   SANDRA   KIM   YVETTE
People go to Florida to play golf.
They come back to die in Patchogue.
Others go to Florida;
they come back as obituaries:
candy stores
bar
launderette
clothing stores
library
the dock
the station.
  On the 15th of June he came back to Patchogue. He had been away for more than ten years. He was thirty-six years old. He had the look of a married man, a man who was no longer married or he was living in complicated circumstances. His eyes undressed women. They did not enjoy his attention. Call this guy LAR.
  It was a hot day in June in Patchogue. One can feel how uncomfortable it must have been to be a kid still sitting in a classroom. And sit they do.
  The train arrives. Middle of the day. LAR is standing on the platform. Near the broken newspaper racks. One taxi is parked. The driver is chewing gum, a cigar. The twelve noon whistle goes off. Some sort of symbol . . . if you want. No one knows for sure.
  LAR walks down South Ocean Avenue. Past the school, the church. To the grocery store near Pearl Street. He's hot. He goes in and gets himself a sixteen-ounce can of Miller's from the beercase. He goes to pay. Squats to look at the *Long Island Advance*. He stands taking the money out of his pocket. He notices the woman.
  This is CAROL. She's a couple of years older than LAR. Say about forty. She has blonde hair. They knew each other in high school.
  Don't I know you?
  LAR and CAROL are sitting on kitchen chairs in the area behind the meat counter. A baby is in the playpen. The baby shits in its pants. He does it again. LAR and CAROL talk. He is sad. She is trapped. He remembers. She remembers. LAR says he has to go.
  You'll come back for a bite?

Yes.

Jack will be back from work by then.

You're married?

For seven years, two and a half kids. She pats her stomach. LAR says he'll see. LAR will show up. This is a depressing story.

LAR continues down Ocean Avenue. The trees move in the breeze. Young people pass. Old people stand in front of STOP signs waiting for them to change.

LAR sits on the dock. He watches the waves. The scum against the dock

But come to think of it, around ten in the morning, only a young person would have something of significance happen to him at ten in the morning. When you get older, ten in the morning is just about the time you are reconciled to being alive, once again, after passing away the hours of the night. However it is the approximate time when I saw Melinda for the first time in the upstairs hall of Patchogue High School while the burden of carrying along a review once read of a novel by Jack Kerouac— some guy in *Newsweek* or a place like that where they have these contests to see how fast you can write a review, how slow, how many different difficult words, be arbitrary, contrary, sour grapes and apricots also, this guy was typing, when a writer runs out of his primary material he starts to write about his childhood and somewhere else there was an article about how Americans never grow up; they are always harking back to the magical period called childhood.

Should be meeting someone. Need a little flesh in this book. A number of possibilities. Get myself hit by a car. Find myself in the middle of a holdup or an attempted holdup. Witness a murder. A guy or girl has trouble with the car and they're walking home and would you know it, just this one time and who did I run into but you, you wouldn't believe it . . . of all the people, of all the millions of people in the world, not yet dead, who do I run into, and in Patchogue, on Ocean Avenue, who do I run into, what's his name.

Too ironic. The extra step of thought cannot be taken in Patchogue. I would have been grabbed at face value, taken home for supper, talk, and then, do you know what's on the tube tonight, I have been waiting all week for tonight, it's so rare there's something really good on TV, not that I watch it all the time, what with the church, the kids' school, and the softball down at the Shorefront and the firehouse.

I have not run into anybody. I am with myself and am not unhappy with the company. I could be doing worse.

You have figured out where I am, all through this. I am in Patchogue
though I am actually in New York City. I have blood on my hands. It was a
bad bit of business. I should have known. Everybody told me it was going
to happen. If only I had listened. I didn't or I couldn't. It doesn't really
matter what I did or did not do. This blood on my hands, in my nostrils. I
shouldn't have been picking my nose. I can hear her voice start up like a
lawnmower in need of an overhaul: You should have listened to me and
you wouldn't be in the mess you're in and you can wipe that expression off
your face. It isn't funny and when your father finds out about it: right
through the roof and into orbit, just like on television. Ain't true. Dad
never hit the roof because he's spent too many hours hitting the bottle.
You should not talk like that about your father. If it wasn't for him you'd
be living in the City with all those other people. With the smell of other
people's cooking reeking in your clothing, never able to get away from all
of them and all of them becoming more and more, I can't, like your Uncle
William, put it into a fine sweep of language, a sweep of language knocked
him into the grave; so it did, and what, he still knew what he was talking
about and it killed him, pure and simple as if one of them people walked
up to him and pumped six slugs into his chest cavity, but what are you
getting at, what am I getting myself into? You wouldn't know the end up if
you were knocked over the head by it and you ain't about to get knocked
over the head. I was always afraid your cousin would drop you when she
was watching after you when I had to go down to see your father's mother
to pay her the rent every Monday morning. That woman sitting in that
kitchen of hers, with everybody creeping in to see her as if they were some
sort of Mexican peasant crawling on knees to see the Virgin's statue down
there outside Mexico City, where you and your sister will take him after
I'm dead and gone. He would never have gone to a place like that if he
knew, but sitting in that kitchen of hers with her hand out to grab the
money from my pocket and into that dress of hers faster than a mouse
across the floor and the cat right after it and I had to get back upstairs
because I was afraid Pat would drop you on your head because she was so
jealous of first your brother who didn't live and then when you were born
she cried, that is all she could do, was cry, because now she knew Hughie
was no longer gonna be only thinking about her, she who had been the
apple or the potato of his eye. Those micks of his family, they would twist
any decent saying to their own ends, not like my people, sorry, my family:
they were not people, only common people referred to their family as

people, my mother who was now dead and my father who was in Atlantic Highlands, the end of a telescope was as close as he would get to the City, close enough to know shit don't change its color—he was then saying, pardon the language—a certain authorial flaw, the mother would never use such a word as *shit*—as near the truth as any man can get to it who has never given birth, which sounds so old-fashioned to a person like yourself now living in that ghost city, for how else to describe the City, except as a ghost city, even you know that: who has ever composed anything of merit in that place . . . there is the curse of Adam, Cain, Abel, and John Smith and Frank Brown and anyone else you care to mention: that city is a blight, a curse, a cold sore to grow prosaic and pathetic as I am sure you are thinking.

I have never thought anything, where my mother is concerned. I have never felt anything towards her or towards him or towards the idea of being their son. They are givens like the sun coming up and going down.

No way to escape their voices which sometimes can be seen as a crude convention: people in books and on stage are always hearing voices or like the famous stage directions TO HIMSELF . . . loud enough so the deaf guy up there in the gods can make out every syllable, though not child enough in me to understand the attraction of the theater because no wit is showing its true face at forty-five dollars a seat: just a place to be seen and to remind this or that person; then to the theater and now they had better deliver.

Cousin Pat appears for a time, then is whisked off the stage. She had been sent to France to work on her music. Time passes and there are changes in the convent: she finds herself in Hartford working with teenage pregnant girls and drug-addict boys who would be better off dead . . . it is so satisfying, she is saying, to work with live children rather than the dead notes of music on the page. A piece of paper breathes only metaphorically. Pat would fit into Patchogue. She could parade her charges down Main Street, be introduced to the mayor and the Village Board, be saluted for the fine work she is doing, be told she had better get Jack's cousin over to rewire the place 'cause it will never pass inspection. But it was just wired and approved last month. That was last month and this month you have to. But the children. Those children are not from Patchogue. Who ever heard of such children in Patchogue?

To be eaten by the Village of Patchogue. The main order of business and then we can all sit around and have a good time. Serve up the kid and let's get down to brass tacks.

I should be back in the City. Back in the dark sweaty dream where the heat muffles the sounds of the passing cars. Snow does the same job. Nothing to it. Every once in a while you got to have some nature. There ain't even a tree in Mr. James Joyce. Too many trees in that famous Patchogue visitor, Henry David Thoreau. Always trying to slide his uncut dick into an oak in the fall, into a maple in the spring.

Thoreau being the only famous person to ever make it to Patchogue, well, that is, except for myself and Philip Evergood, but who are we and who is Henry David, when you come to think about it. Of course Elizabeth Oakes-Smith is in the cemetery: lecturer, reformer, and poet; she became our Liz! I can imagine Whitman, though there is no mention of his getting himself through this place and there is the possibility of James Thomson being here. In fact I know he was here in Patchogue. He left his odor behind and I smelt it again in Highgate Cemetery, two rows over from where we used to keep Karl Marx before they moved him next to those Polish airmen dead in exile, two rows over and in a grave not his own. James Thomson. The author.

pause

The City of Dreadful Night. Now you see why I have smelt his presence here in Patchogue. Discovered Thomson in the pages of John Rechy's *City of Night,* bought in the Patchogue Stationery Store. They must not have known what they were selling. Into Bryant Park for a little love and discovering where he got the title from. *Naked Lunch* was also a book of Patchogue but every Tom, Dick, Jack, and Jim on the road has heard of that book and, what more can we say, until Burroughs goes to count the final celestial congregation of worms. A lot of people pass through Patchogue on their way to the Hamptons, on their way to Fire Island. They are always on the way somewhere. In Patchogue the life is so interesting, so all involved, there is no, well, to be honest, there is only a little reason to travel.

Ocean Avenue has been paved over. The brick gutters no longer are visible. No slush at this time of year. In the spring I am hammered by: he is living in the City. To think he had so much, look how much his parents did for him and still look: he is living in the City. In what can only be described as slums, the sort of place where people live who have no other choice. It is where you end up at the end, or maybe in some cases, at the beginning of, and then you go elsewhere; it does matter where you go, it is either the

Bowery, one block away, or it is
                    the world
and still a kid at heart. Nothing has penetrated that thick and large head of
his. Always the largest baseball cap for him. Doesn't seem to have led to
anything, if you ask me. How can he live in there? Not like here, where
you can take a breath of fresh air and not smell your neighbor: what she or
he had to eat last night and for all eternity, it seems.

Where are all the fucking people? Didn't they know I was coming, surely,
they are not all deaf. How loud my words seemed to me sitting in New
York on Second Avenue: surely the whole world has heard of my pil-
grimage to Patchogue.

    No miracle to be performed, no earthquakes, rivers dammed up,
bays gone dry. Just a steady stately procession sitting on my seat in a car
of the Long Island Railroad. Off the train, at the station, walking down
South Ocean Avenue, not a soul to be seen, heard, or an arm waving in
greeting.

    Maybe I am too eager for rejection. Have I called anybody? Did I write
ahead of my arrival? You have no one to blame but yourself. I know this
cliché.

    I should cut over to Cedar Avenue. At least I could walk past the Lang
house: two blonde daughters. What didn't they do, or who. The stories or
legends resulting in chipped nail polish and divorce with the complaint: no
one understood me, let alone myself. Why can't it be as simple as when
every man born then lusted after me, promising?

    I walked past the Lang house. The lawn is kept neat. The drapes are
across the picture window. Could a great poem be written today using the
phrase *picture window?* As if anyone had that ambition: to write a great
poem. How to avoid the discussion as to what:

                            great
                            poem
                            phrase
                            means(t)
    Thirst provoking workings of the mind. Here I am on the one street in
the village without a place to whet the whistle. So, back to Ocean Avenue,
down to Felice's, into the joint and sitting at the bar, adding to the gross
totals of how many shots consumed, having a beer to back it up, turn to
look out to the bay and see nothing happening on the water. Thought I

would see what was to happen, what had happened, what is happening. Instead dull waters. Doing what it always did. Separating Patchogue from Fire Island, the ocean beyond, Europe beyond that. Bartenders, like cops and firemen, are getting younger every day. The street is full of everything I never had. To begin is to cheat my own story. Blood should be on my hands. I should be here doing a new version of *Macbeth.* Who would believe it? That shouldn't stop me. I was planning to do a new version of *Romeo and Juliet,* down on the Patchogue River, that wide passage of water flowing from or to bay from or to the Patchogue Lake, down under the railroad tracks, down under the bluff on which Reedy built his house. That guy owned an Irish bar on East Main Street. Moved to Florida with all the other Irish in Patchogue. Went to Ireland once but couldn't understand the natives . . . not much in common with my life, I can tell you, Reedy says, yeah, I heard a lot of names like those I grew up with in Brooklyn, but over there, all the faces seemed beaten out of the earth or beaten down into the earth. There was no spirit, that's the word, what happens when a people have been leaving a place for two hundred years or maybe more years before that, but who's counting, just what you have left behind: them's that got no get-up-and-go or there's them that had it so good there is no need for them to go, they got this army of people who walk along the street with their noses on the pavement, sharpening it up so they can stick it into any business that suits them. With noses so sharp you could be stuck, gutted, and left for dead before you knew someone didn't like the cut of your eyeball, but a nice country in spite of all that.

Sure, it's not a place to live in but you can visit it; they got a couple of colored people on display in the center of Dublin, but they feed them real good and when I was at Blarney Castle, I know it's a dumb thing to do, but this guy leaned me over the wall and I kissed the stone, had a piece of tissue in my mouth so I could wipe the stone before I got my lips to touch the stone, and this man was telling me if the guard had seen the tissue drop out of your mouth there would have been the usual hell to pay and you would have been sentenced to twenty years of supervising coachloads of visiting Americans and then Germans and then French people all coming to get their lips on to the stone, but that was the only touristy thing we did in Ireland and it was about enough for me and the wife.

We went up to the North to see some of the war which we had seen on the TV but it wasn't much of anything or maybe we just picked an off week and everybody was nursing hangovers, but it was a strange sort of war because everybody spoke a variety of the English language. You get so used to wars where one of the sides doesn't speak English and you never know what is going through their heads, but somewhere I read or it was one of the guys coming into the bar saying, whenever a soldier died the last word on his lips was always *mother,* unless he was a real pervert or something, but we haven't met or heard of any of them in Patchogue or at least those kinds of people don't come into my bar.

There's bars for people like that but I wouldn't know where to send you; they bend you over a rail and stick it up your. You know what I mean or if you don't, then, who said you could come in here, but in Ireland— Ireland is one of those places you just have to visit and get it out of your system because you'll never know for sure but after visiting Ireland you'll know for sure, there ain't no reason to ever leave Patchogue. I know it's hard to believe and I've been all over the world. And now it's to Florida here I come.

And Florida here I went. Like a lot of them, just like Frank, Reedy went down to Florida and found out the place was crawling with people. People he didn't like: niggers, as many as maggots on a dead cat . . . spics, spics who ain't even spics. Why'd we ever piss off Castro, Frank said, all he did was send us all these people with fat daughters, wearing ankle bracelets, and Jews, it was like over in the bungalow colony except all of these were working on heart attacks and hating anybody who wasn't just like them and native people, we met a couple of them but all they did was work on the roofs hammering nails all day long and have brains like people who have been hammering nails all day long; a sad bunch of people who seem like they just got run over by a car, who was it said, the state animal of any one of the Southern states is a dead dog by the side of the road.

Florida's got one season: hot.

Patchogue is best after all is said and done. At least you got four seasons and though they get mixed up sometimes, you still got four seasons and not even a youth center named after the seasons.

And who knew me down there, Reedy asks. Not a soul extended himself one quarter of an inch, Frank said. All that famous Southern hospitality; if they could they'd still be lynching and they don't much care if the body they be lynching is white or nigger. Maybe now the sport would be to lynch white people just to show they ain't prejudiced like them northern Jews are always saying.

Them northern Jewish girls, just a lot of Jewish broads hot to trot to fuck nigger dick, that's why they're so for the integration thing: not that I'm prejudiced, mark my words, Reedy says. I just have to say things the way they are and come hell or low tide I'm stuck with what I know and people have to accept it or they might as well move to Bellport where you got the types from the Lab and the City who'll listen to anything and probably give you some money if you touch the right spot in the middle of what they call their brains and hearts . . . they're very modern in Bellport and in Brookhaven, they are after modern, going beyond hearts and brains and are thinking with other organs, if I follow what I heard when I visited my friend Malcolm over in Bellport. He's always liked the colored people, but still keeps a shotgun under the bed just in case and he was telling me the other day he's thinking of running electricity through his back fence. You can't be too careful and the electricity might cook up a set of low-swinging nigger balls going over the fence; you can't be too careful even though I like them as a people, they really got the short end of the stick and have always gotten the short end but then we have always gotten the long end and more shit collects on the long end than on the short, so you can say we ain't had it all that good; lots of trying to figure out how to get the smell of shit off your hands and all that poetry and movie-going and music don't help. It's in there right into the protoplasm.

Reedy doesn't want to go into all the things that happened to him in the bar on East Main Street. Who wants to know about the past? It was a dry or wet fuck depending on how you remember such things. Personally, it was like sandpaper: wore my dick, wore this mick down so he was so smooth you couldn't tell where the bar left off and the flesh began. It didn't bother me for years. I knew how to smile and get that extra drink into the patron, the extra drink that was the profit, the bucks towards Bob's college tuition, but finally one night I am standing behind the bar, watching the Yankees win, for a change, and I look up and realize the whole bar is full of coons. Now I ain't got anything against them, no, I don't, their money is as good as the next, but here I am, find myself the keeper of a nigger bar in a village I always thought of as a white man's paradise. Where did all the white people go? Not far, far away. They just don't go out anymore. Leave the streets and the places of entertainment to them's that got the color of skin liking the night. You can ask Spitale why he split for the Island, and he ain't even queer like a three-dollar bill like some people over there. I know he adds like he's always adding three-dollar bills, even he's got out of the bar business and here I am pumping the stuff down shit-brown throats.

Next month I sold the place to these two Cubans and haven't been back since. I drive by and they got the windows cemented up into two tiny nigger bar windows out of which you could barely point a .22. Maybe they are on to something and the race riot is gonna come down Main Street and a lot of white people are gonna be found hanging from a lamppost by their balls.

And still here standing, not knowing which way to go and still going, I guess, and have the title:

Patchogue and Sofia

a love story

Either it says everything or nothing at all including it at this point in the book. Of course, maybe it has been on the title page and is on the cover or at least the spine, in gold foil. The polar cities of my heart or whatever it is I have stuck my life upon and allow it to turn, in the wind, as a former president had it or one of his advisors. Run it up and see if there is a breeze of interest.

Still waiting to be run into, have my hand shook, my shoulder tapped, my ears caressed with my name called out and the sound of running feet, so glad to see you, after all these years, what have you been doing with yourself, who has been doing things to you, have you been having as much fun as I've been having or has it all been a drag like it's for everyone else you meet these days; the painful waking up, the final exhausted falling into the bed at night with only dreams, dreams forgotten even when we have said, I will remember, though what is the point of remembering dreams unless it is to carry around with you a permanent record of what you could have been *if* only things had gotten worse or better.

But it's a hard life with fear grabbing you by the nuts twenty-four hours a day. Life in this village: fear of—and people don't even have to particularize it, or have the time or even know what the word means. They are just afraid and it shows in their faces, in the way they walk, in the way they don't walk. A person in Patchogue will not stop and say hello unless they have arranged to, ahead of time. What is the point and you never know what you are getting into. And nothing was ever gained by these casual runnings into down in the parking lot behind the old Grant's store. Even knowing there was a Grant's store, where the library is now, is to get yourself locked away for more years than you can shake a stick at, if they catch you laughing to yourself: HOW THINGS CHANGE.

The melody was the same as last summer but the tempo was louder and more strident as residents of Rose Avenue joined by the owners of Carvel and 7-Eleven came to the Patchogue Village Board meeting Tuesday night to complain about the hundreds of youths who hang out in the Rose Avenue parking lot. "I've made numerous calls to 911, all the operators know me by name," said Joseph Libatore. "The problem has affected the entire community." Mayor Whitey Leavandosky noted he has visited the parking lot these last three Saturdays. "I was there Saturday night and it was horrendous."

Off the wall, that's what it is in this place. Gets so being off the wall is the only way you can keep a level head on your shoulders. Out here in Patchogue and I might as well be walking across the Galata Bridge in Istanbul for the level of comfort I am walking through. So young, man, so young and so full of complaint. Younger than the old geezers going on about me? What does he know about anything? We who have been to Montauk Point when the boys came back from the Spanish-American War. They didn't call it that, then. Called it the Cuban thing as later they will talk about the Vietnam thing, and that Korean thing and that Bulgarian thing and the Afghanistani thing or that Togo thing: boys are always going out and getting messed about, coming back with a taste for new foods to get packaged up and you'll hear the young men sitting in Felice's talking about being glad to be back in the land of the smooth armpit and good old-fashioned American pussy. You can imagine what it's like to undress one of them and find this crop of hair under the armpits. You would think hair was like gold or something and then there are those who have it growing down their legs like it was some kind of moss and some of them taste, smell, feel like beds of moss. Or, the girls are back from some place near the sun: you should have seen these guys: walked around like all they were: peckers with teeth and you were supposed to walk around on your knees while they strutted about, and boy, after that, now I know what they mean by strut, you feel like if you don't get out of their way they would walk right over you—ain't they heard the Nancy Sinatra about who is supposed to do the walking these girls can't be that young or the old geezer who was doing the listening is so old he can't tell the difference between a collie dog and the woman who comes to clean out his slop pan once a day. You do it more than once a day and all they do is fill it up quicker. A little discipline is always appreciated, mark my words, a little discipline, that's what's needed in this here village.

To sink into Patchogue, away from all the rubbish of the world, to allow my heart, my soul, the very center of my being, as the poets say, to allow the tops of my fingers, the corners of my eyes, the callouses on the bottoms of my feet to enjoy the pleasure of once again walking, creating character and conflict, the resolution of conflict, the settling of the story into some sort of drumming into the sunset or sunrise depending on where, when and how I am able to get myself off this island and back into the City. Many miles to go. Even though Patchogue is but a tiny village on the south shore of Long Island, no longer a tiny village. They kept moving people out to work at the IRS over in Holbrook.

Jim Farley was telling me: sometimes, once a week I find myself driving down Main Street just to feel like I'm some place. When you live in a place like Holbrook, there ain't any place, in that place. There is no place in the place sounds like some sort of poem by e. e. cummings; but who quotes him anymore? How quickly they go out of style. Can't keep up with the turning pages. Well, anyway, history is my field, not literature, and history never goes out of date, just more of that stuff piling up all the time. Well, I go over to Patchogue, drive down Main Street, then down Ocean Avenue to the dock, stop for a minute or so, catch the sun going down, down over the Sandspit. It's something like the way it must be to stand in Venice and watch the sun go down behind the horizon of church steeples. On a teacher's salary there is just no way to travel. If we get away upstate once every two years we're lucky. Just everything is getting more and more expensive and the salaries are about as high as they can get and Flo ain't working yet. And she has nothing to go back to work at, so we are stuck.

No rugs on the floor. They do not answer their mail. They must be saving money on postage. They will not let me know I am still alive in Patchogue. To be alive in New York City, who cares, who even knows, but to be alive in Patchogue and to look forward to an obituary that will be read, while in New York City, just another chunk of meat with a disposal problem.

To be alive in Patchogue and they deny me that privilege. Me: : : : : : : : : A Patchoguer of those streets with the paved-over trolley tracks. Should I then drag in the kids' sport of wallball behind the junior high, now called something like the South Ocean Avenue Middle School, or pick up ball down at the Shorefront Park:

and you have to take him
and you have to take him
and you have to take him

Doesn't the passage of twenty-eight years cancel out that voice? Never to forget the slightest hurt, to treasure and store it against the moment when they dare to come looking for me and, there, dump from a high spot the bucket of shit moldering away in the corner of my room . . . only four flights up . . . probably wouldn't hurt their heads, hard as stone they be, the finest cement and not even an air pocket in the middle where the particle of humor might find itself lodged to be used upon the spur of the moment. I am not going to tramp down to the Shorefront Park and stand in the outfield waiting for the fly ball that will never be hit my way, because they know, just stand there out in right field underneath the tall night lightpole and wait, wait, wait, and just over there in the front of ceremonial boulder I took Melinda's photograph and that photograph is wrapped in some sort of plastic covering. I watch it yellow and orange to disappear, destroying the image, eating it up as if it were in a burst of orange and yellow, a mockery of my heart's ache which must now travel to new places and never, never will it beat faster, never will it leap to the idea of possibility. Now, just the slow descent into fatherhood and waiting for the child to turn and spit, spit for all it's worth at the bent shoulders of its balding father who has now acquired the same toilet habits as his father: liking to sit on the toilet for a time, with door closed reading, I am, while Dad liked to just sit and smoke a cigarette, alone with himself, no one to come and ask questions without answers, the idea of fatherhood and the slow death we see each day as the child grows and acquires what it needs to get on in the world, as my powers fade, as I fade and prepare to be eaten by the earth, to have a child would be to say, all my life has been a lie, all of my despair for naught, all canceled by this creature.

Here I am in Patchogue, where the hard lessons are learned. Where nothing is forgiven, learned, or remembered; constant repetition and always the same people on the top and the same people on the bottom and into the set sun while supposedly it sets equally on all which might be just a slight exaggeration probably worth the effort to sort it out . . . but nothing is ever sorted out in Patchogue—just stew, stew, stew.

I heard the rumor they are preparing a little surprise for me at Felice's. Can I will it into being? Saint Thomas talks about faith as being mainly a case of willing to believe. I will, so therefore, a dinner for me at Felice's on the bay, with the waves crashing beyond the bulkhead and memories of the Mascot Bar. Ah, the Mascot, and the busted-up saltwater pool, the ruins of which you can still stub your foot against, if you know what you are doing. Who will come to this gala affair?

All of them. But all this silence and I hope it ain't even a metaphor or a posturing looking for a sacrificial fuck on the part of the moist girl in the class. Just the other afternoon this guy, Madison, was telling me (this wasn't happening in Patchogue) about his new book, not the one he had just handed in to the publisher but the one he was working on at the moment, and probably at this moment, he is so doing, working on a novel about a guy who goes to Rome to help cut a film and runs into, ends up sleeping with the wife of the guy he's helping on the film and runs into Bulgarians, among others, as plot complications and I am here in Patchogue waiting for one of those plot complications. I will not allow it to happen to me. These things just don't walk up and bop you on the head as you stand at Carman Street. I could drag in a French movie on that note, but anyway there is a Carman Street in Patchogue, named after another river on Long Island, all these mighty rivers of Long Island, haven't you heard of them, where have you been all your life, guy walks up to me, as I stand waiting for the stop sign to change colors, an allusion to an earlier joke, okay, waiting, and this guy taps me on the shoulder. I know who you are.

You do?

Yes, you were two or three classes ahead of me at Patchogue High. You went away. I stayed in Patchogue and now you're back here. I have a proposition for you.

Any money in it?

There could be a lot.

I didn't remember this guy. You can't go through life remembering everything.

You had a crush on.

I did.

You didn't marry her.

That's right. How did you know?

I told you, I was two or three years after you at Patchogue High. Everybody knew about your saga. Most people have forgotten it but I still have the copies of *The Red and the Black* where you used Melinda's name but not her real last name. You got your hero killed on her birthday but you didn't know at the time of the writing it was actually her birthday. You found out later, years later. When it didn't do you any good. Only made you more miserable and sent you all the way to that communist country and now you're back here and I'm tapping you on the shoulder with a proposition.

I don't know whether to believe you or not.

Does it matter? I know what you are up to.

He seemed to know. That was for sure. He offered to walk me to Holzer's to get us a couple Pepsis.

I can't go in the Oasis. Something happened in there.

Don't tell us.

I won't.

Enjoying yourself back in the old village?

I am trying to. No one met me at the train.

The telegrams didn't arrive in time.

What telegrams?

The ones your secretary sent.

I don't have a secretary.

You're just being modest. The secretary of your fan club.

The story turns interesting.

She's a good girl.

I hope you are a decent . . .

The man pauses. This is going in directions I have not wished to explore in Patchogue. This idle conversation could go on for hours. It usually does: the filling up of time before time runs out.

Walk away from this voice that has a name like Bernie attached to it, or Jay or Nat or Mark or Bob . . . names of people who follow, who ask questions for which there's always an answer. Here in Patchogue. A complication almost arose and the story wanders down the aisle of Troy Donahue. He's this guy who lives over in Blue Point. Had to sleep on the beach when he had an argument with Mom and Dad. A lot of people claim to know Troy. I don't trust a single one of them. When a person gets to Hollywood; but he ain't there anymore. Lost in the world of just another pretty face from a town near Patchogue. You would never catch a face like that being born and raised in Patchogue.

I don't remember the telegrams. He might be right. I will have to check up on it when I get back to the City. Any number of reasons for this slipup. Just part of the game, part of the role I have to walk through. Nothing to worry about. I have to go and create myself a little mountain.

But they didn't act on the telegrams. Says something or it don't. Maybe they will still act on those telegrams. Now that I have put a bug, as they say, up into the man's bonnet. Get him buzzing around the streets and avenues of the village, see what pops out of the woodwork. What can pop out of the woodwork in a village like Patchogue!

Momentary hesitation because I am afraid of what can pop up. I am not talking of flesh and the desire of flesh for a hole of any sort. I should get my speech in order. Names like Bernie call up short, fat, plump-faced, narrow-lipped, dark-eyed, stubby-fingered boys who never become men though they are now in their late thirties. The pants are too tight; never did fit properly. The belt is narrow and rolled at the edges by sweat. The white shirt is stained on the front pocket by a leaking ballpoint pen. A shaving scar on chin because this Bernie is heavy-bearded: granted he could have been one of those guys who has three chin hairs and grew them like whooping cranes.

The guy who tapped me on the shoulder was called Nat. He was just like this Bernie fellow only a little more striking in physical appearance. Not that much more striking, just striking because he wore an eyepatch and spoke with an Austrian accent, it could have been a Danish accent, it could have been, but wasn't. More like a passed-over section of Brooklyn, moved to Patchogue with a father going into the City to drop dead of a heart attack at Hunter's Point Avenue, an awful night for Nat and his mother. Didn't know what had happened to her husband, your husband, in Nat's phrase, your father in his Mom's tone of voice, Dad, when Nat wanted to get at his father, down there in the little marsh of father's thwarted ambition to be a man-about-town. Only rich people can be both a father and a man-about-town, otherwise it takes too much of a toll on the flesh, Nat would later argue, not in Patchogue but at the state teachers's college, upstate, where he was for two years before dropping out because he wasn't learning anything, and why throw good money down a rathole like when I could be out here on the Island striking myself into ratholes . . . get me another drink.

No, Nat did not say the last sentence. It would have been unlike him. It would have been out of character, it would have been a literary device. Nat liked women and was always on the lookout, but no one was on the lookout for him, for his type of man.

Something's bound to happen, right, was the way Nat put it.

Sure.

Of course, I'm sure. I stayed here and you left. You don't know how decent people behave, living all those years away from this country and then living in the City. How do you expect to know how decent people live if all you do is associate with foreigners and City People?

Your father was a City Person, I said.

And so was yours . . . but they got themselves out of the City. What can you find in the City . . . just disease, I'll tell you, disease and preparation for disease.

I should walk down Furman Lane. See the old house. The lawn, the two maple trees, the shade of a late afternoon, September, driving out from Patchogue, the last time, when I had a home, left behind and saying good-bye to Melinda, to drive across this country to Wisconsin . . . to come back in May . . . to go to Ireland in October after a summer in Los Angeles, to Turkey, to Bulgaria and back again through all of those countries, always looking for that moment to appear and at THAT MOMENT have a sword in hand, slay it, transform it, and drag in some complicated medieval legend in explanation: a dragon does not have venom in its bite.

Forget it.

Well, Nat, how's things doing?

Okay.

Only okay?

More or less. Could be better, were better, as you know, maybe things will get better. They should. I hope so.

Nat or, as he would like to call him, Bernie, and I slide carefully over this little complication, eventually it will get cleared up, just like those telegrams. Well, Nat had a paper route back when I had a paper route. He was the City kid whose parents moved out from the City. He got himself a paper route and they had a contest on the paper to see how many new subscriptions each carrier could get and then all the names got thrown into a tub and his name got picked and he got to go to Spain for ten days. He also got to go to Steeplechase with all of us on the bus. We each got a round admission ticket for twenty or so rides. You had to be careful not to use up all the rides on riding the horses around the edge of the park . . . that feeling of being on the horse holding with the knees against the wooden sides of the animal . . . the slow coming up the track and the sudden stop at the top . . . pause . . . looking out at the black ocean, then a hard left and along the side, the ocean to your right and not looking because you knew that faster then . . . the hard left and the race down to the end of the ride . . . it was the only ride worth . . . well, there was the one with long climb up wooden stairs and the sliding down the polished wood onto revolving disks.

But I am out here in Patchogue and I have all of these thoughts of going to an amusement park in Coney Island in the 1950s, late '50s, please, just before (name that group) made the whole place unsafe for the likes of us coming in from Patchogue. Afterwards they gave away tickets to the base-ball games at Shea Stadium, so I was told, eventually the *Long Island Press* went out of business.

We delivered the *Long Island Press* because *Newsday* was seen as being pro-communist and anti-Catholic. I have never investigated exactly why this was and is so.

Nat got to go to Spain and I got to hear the explanation: it is better to be glad for someone's happiness than to be a bunch of sour grapes.

Nat slaps me on the back and says can I buy you a drink?

Sure, when is this gonna be, the year after hell freezes over, or as Flo wrote in the eighth grade autograph book: when the ocean wears under-pants for its wet bottom: can't you hear the argument walking along Ocean Avenue towards home—is the bottom of the ocean wet or is that just an idea we have here walking along Ocean Avenue, past Dead Man's Hill and the bay in this distance . . . does it, well does it?

Nat turns away. He is grown up and is not prepared to throw his mind back to when.

I said I would buy you a drink, not a trip back down memory lane. Memory lane is where the niggers wait or as we said back then: the boogeyman lies waiting to suck your balls off, courting a mouthful of soap from the priest who got sent away.

Father McHugh?

That's him, a real son of a bitch, if you ask me.

Said I had the map of Ireland on my face.

He didn't know his geography very good, Nat says, looks more like Uganda.

Them's fighting words in another village.

You're right but this is Patchogue and we just don't.

Better get me that drink.

There was drinking.

And good-bye and promises to stay in touch until hell froze over. Better get organizing that welcome-back-to-Patchogue dinner down at Felice's for me, Nat, I'm counting on you, as an old buddy from back before we knew what girls were for.

The conversation disappeared and I should have gone over to Rider Avenue to check out the house where I wanted to install one of the clam-digger families who will Romeo and Juliet in this day and the age: : : : : : : : though the reader will not be burdened with reading any half-assed poetry.

Who do you think I am: ain't one of them City People who come out to Patchogue with Goethe's *Italian Journey* under arm and a paperback of *Girls I Have Fucked,* the latest Belgian surrealist novel to be translated, with nose craned to the sky and wearing white gloves to touch for dust the bartops, drawing conclusions about the sanitary habits of the village inhabitants.

However, just spat upon, because I forgot to wear my gold jewelry about neck and wrist. Lost in the journey was the hairpiece for my chest. Patchogue has to maintain standards in an age when everything is going to shit and this shit ain't golden and no one is deluded anymore into thinking his or her shit is golden. Well, some claim their farts are gold but they get carted off to Pilgrim State and there tell the other jokers who claim their farts are silver and the one lonely lad with the platinum farts sits in the corner making fans from Popsicle sticks.

Three men are sitting in a pickup truck drinking beer. They are just off work. Any sort of job will do.

LAR nods to them.

They nod back.

A sense of menace never realized.

That is another movie.

LAR goes to Felice's. The Rotary Club meets here on the second Thursday. Lions Club on Wednesday. Plaque for selling 1,000,001 shots of B&L Scotch. Lunch has just ended.

TUESDAY is sitting at the bar. She got left behind. Another blonde.

Or got pissed off.

Or is just waiting.

The problem of real life in movies: in real life this would not happen.

I know you, TUESDAY says.

You sure?

You went to Patchogue High.

I did. Class of '62.

I was '63 . . . it was '64.

Conversation.

Can I buy you a drink?

No, let me.

HUSBAND IS IN MEAT. Wholesale. Hamburger for the county that sort of thing.

TUESDAY didn't want to just settle. Her parents couldn't do anything for her. Dad worked at Republic . . . boom or bust. A new car or a rustbucket.

She wanted to go to Florida in the winter.

She married the guy so she could send a crate of oranges to her friends from Florida in the winter.

From that place where she was getting her suntan. She wanted to go to Rome . . . Rome, Italy, not Rome, New York, dummy.

VINCE LIKED HER.

LAR and TUESDAY talk.

The husband is a busy man.

He'd break my legs.

The kids are in school.

Break my legs if I open them for another guy.

Why don't you come to the house.

I'm busy.

Why not. LAR agrees. I have to get going. Find some people. A place to stay.

LAR leaves.

I don't believe this scene. TUESDAY's husband comes in. VIOLENCE.

Why you talking to . . . VINCE is the man who's forgotten his pinky ring. An ass toucher. He likes suede-covered steak.

A friend.

I'll break his head.

A friend from high school.

From twenty years ago.

A piece of shit with a mouth. I should have flushed him down the bowl when I had the chance. Back then.

I'll see YOU at home. VINCE says.

Yes sir!

Two cars leave the parking lot. White Lincolns. His sparkles; hers is dirty. The cars go past LAR who is walking along Maiden Lane.

Things are getting complicated. Expect this visiting stranger to get lynched, everything should suggest this will happen.

Ordinary fear.

LAR walks to the Sandspit. Watches the ferry load up with a couple of City People for Fire Island.

Don't get sand in the crankcase, a kid yells on the sound track.

LAR is standing between cars taking a leak.

BOY, what are you doing? A girl, a woman in tough-guy manner. SANDRA after all these years.

Taking a leak.

Wish I could do the same.

Why boys and girls are different.

There's not that much.

SANDRA did go away somewhere and has come back home too.

Her big tits didn't last long. Always a new girl in town, after, now, she is at home.

You hungry, she asks.

Yeah.

They go to the hamburger stand.

Must avoid getting involved in these characters. What they did or didn't do.

Could have happened.

The possibility is the horror.

The torture.

Sends people to the bars.

LAR asks SANDRA if she lives in Patchogue.

She does.

Do you want to see where I live?

Sure.

SANDRA lives on Brentwood Street.

A small frame house. Busted-up car out back.

My older sister isn't in.

They sit on an aluminum camp bed.

Do you want something to drink?

Sure.

SANDRA gets him a beer from fridge.

There are Canada and Mexico posters on the wall. The two alternatives. You could say: one of them days . . . better than Europe.

SANDRA is listening to Chad Mitchell Trio music, Kingston Trio music, maybe even Cisco Houston music . . . Pie in the sky.

One thing leads to another.

LAR and SANDRA fuck.

Taste lives between the toes.

And you taste good too, SANDRA says.

LAR and SANDRA are again sitting on the bed.

Well, SANDRA is lying on her side of the bed and LAR is sitting on the floor. They did what they could.

A quart of beer is between LAR's legs. He is wearing a Mello Jello T-shirt. They talk about did you know.

Did you know when.

A lot of talk.

LAR gets dressed.

SANDRA is wearing a black bra and panties.

She is old-fashioned, I guess.

LAR sees a photo of her sister.

Who's this?

My sister.

Your sister.

My sister. KIM is SANDRA's sister.

Remember: TUESDAY's husband is getting drunk in the finished basement. He is sitting at his small bar playing with a toy cannon. He is drinking from a black glass, an eight ball.

He goes upstairs, abuses TUESDAY.

She kicks him in the balls.

He is on the floor gagging, pukes.

She runs out of the house, gets into her car. Is away.

VINCE staggers to his feet, about and about. Goes into the garage and sits in his car.

The audience is waiting.

KIM will be back home later. Do you want to stay for supper?

Miles to go.

You ain't a postman on vacation?

No, the milkman.

He pinches her tit.

This is out of character. I guess. However LAR is a little . . .

LAR has to find a place to stay.

I'll see you later.

You sure?

Yeah.

We'll go out.

Sure.

But if you keep doing that they're gonna cart you off to C.I. Can't remember what it is I am supposed to stop doing; it wasn't jerking off: sex, thank God, was never talked about in the house on Furman Lane. Sex was left for the street, the lane, the beach, among the ruins of the old saltwater swimming pool . . . except for:

why doesn't she comb her hair; it's all over her face; how can she see?

My mother did not approve of Melinda but she did cook Sunday dinner for her and we used the special china, and the special silver though when I was younger I objected to the silver forks and knives as being too heavy and continued to use the steel knife and fork even when we had company for dinner.

Nat's gone off to chat with Bernie and get things organized. He didn't have a hat to tip saying good-bye. Remembered an appointment that couldn't be missed. My ass'll be in a sling ten different ways unless I get myself over, and then the head got turned and he was saying: I would like to stick my tongue between her toes. Janey Banker walked by. Old Sally Ann Banker, to be exact, or as she was really known (and no one is better known than at the ages of sixteen or seventeen): Sally Ann Bang 'er for all she's worth and never a bad time was had by those who did so engage her in night combat. The delights, the awful descent into the grave after knowing and then never again to know the dream thrill of hand under the waist of panties, the first touch of concealed hair . . . and he is wandering down the pages of Forty-second Street.

Certain upset to his system. Running into people not planned for and the not knowing what to finally say to them. Too bad we couldn't find a bar and get ourselves into those fine memories back when I was watching Flo and there would be Melinda. All gone. All gone into the just get married and not a thought to leave, not a thought: now just the waiting for the trip to the cemetery.

No great ruins to tour, no gardens to wander midst, no great villas to walk by and wonder who was visiting this week and what was being discussed. No cathedral to enter and adjust one's eyes to the comforting darkness, allowing the eyes to travel upwards to burst of colored light, stained light and the possible vision. Also no dim streets of broken hovels where the peasants lived in mild distress; no interesting music filtering out of drink shops and the wail of children left to the street and the ghosts appearing in the dust; not even a roadside shrine to provoke a second of prayer. All fine thought has been left behind or never got itself this far. Who's to say these people are worse off because of this: not much to celebrate but at least we don't have to walk knees caressed by the heaped-up corpses.

Ah, to be in Patchogue.

I am on South Ocean Avenue in Patchogue on Long Island, in Dublin, in Ireland, in Europe . . . and Barbara will not walk by and I will not stand and watch her walk away, not able to say a word. The minutes pass on the watch I got for delivering newspapers with a good·attitude for three years . . . they would have given me the company if I had a better dream. I walked in the opposite direction and within a certain period of time: reconsidered and she was not on Grafton Street . . . a mistake, a mistake, and now I am walking down South Ocean Avenue in Patchogue, while Nat is off talking with Bernie.

Bernie, sorry, Nat, didn't have anything to say about Gail. What had happened to her. I was told she had been lost to the streets of New York and was seen once, just once, for a couple seconds being taken out of an apartment building on the Upper East Side, on a stretcher, the sheet pulled over her petite nose, covering her large and now sloppy breasts. Gail would have made a good mother, a good wife, a good girlfriend, a good friend, a good Joe, an all-around decent egg, except . . . and this is where the story got lost and no one was saying anything about anybody's business and no one knows anything except her priest, her tax accountant, her morgue attendant . . . is how Marty Talbot put it just the other day when he was hoisting a couple down at the Rendezvous.

Marty got himself around, if said so himself, and Chip his best friend was one to agree, if he did say so himself. Marty's people had come over a boat or two after my own grandparents. They didn't know each other, didn't come from the same county and did not attend church in the same parish in the City; they just were friends in an ethnic sense. Green ties, corned beef and tongue with cabbage, turnips and boiled potatoes, Coleman's mustard on the side . . . his friend Chip, whose real name was Jack or Sid depending on the mood, was from London but had lost his accent and taste for rubber underpants in the years he had been in this country. No singing take me back to the old country where Sid or Jack or Chip wanted to sound Italian and get the goat of one of the parishioners from Our Lady of Mount Carmel, not a single one of which came from Pavia. That's what you get when you get wops mixed up: they all come out of the same ministron . . . Sid left off the *e* to let people know he didn't eat that kind of soup. You got to have some standards and Rick's hamburgers are okay by me.

You know that place up on the Sunrise, don't you, Sid asked me when I last saw him. If I had the car out of the shop I'd drive you up there and get you a taste of what a real hamburger really is; damn shop got the wheels and they ain't about no house trailer, get it?

I didn't but it was okay.

There was a certain Mediterranean air about the conversation, as well as Irish. If you don't get something the first time around: always a second chance though don't think of it as a second chance because then you will always be coming up with less change than you're due.

And to be away is to be arriving back where you started. Something like that, as always. And it would be nice to run into Maria as I turn and walk into Lee Avenue. Don't know how I got here as I don't know how I began to talk to Maria in a cafeteria in Helsinki. She was sitting at the next table. Each table had a bright red plastic-shaded lamp hanging above it. She was looking at drawings completed at a class she had just come from. Her mother had brought her back from Canada, and herself, the mother, was never satisfied. Neither here in Finland nor in Canada. Always in the next place and this is as good as any other, just like me sitting in the City and knowing I would run into this feeling out here in Patchogue: why come all this way to find out I didn't want to leave the City? I had filled my mind with every possible reason—nah, you don't know what is waiting around the next corner. It could be the smile with the retractable teeth.

Maria had worked her way through the Scandinavian capitals, liking each a little less than the one before. The pits had been in Oslo, is that how do you say it, the pits, she asked.

It is, I replied. Something like going to Bellport and finding everything closed, the expectation acting as a sort of club.

I didn't have that many words for how I felt. I just knew that Oslo was not a place for a person like myself.

Just like Patchogue, I wanted to say, if only I could avoid having to echo every kid who finds the village where he grew up is just too small for the imagination which comes packaged up with an ambition that would send me to walk the squatter hills of Ankara, or take myself to the baths and have the dead skin rubbed off my back, upper arms, and the man hands me the cloth to rub cock, asshole, and balls . . . the dust of the streets, even in

Patchogue, the dust catches up with the eyes. I could burst into tears. Or is it laughter I am to burst into as I go about these streets, trying, hoping to force, through language, that moment, just as when in Menasha I had stood on the shore of Little Lake Butte des Mortes, how's that for symbolism, and knew: you don't know a fucking thing and your mother had her elbow up your asshole and your father was sniffing the crud between your toes and your sister had a toothbrush stuck up her pussy, cleaning the teeth that bit off her boyfriend's dick when he was trying to prove to the world and anyone who'd listen through the cracks in the walls, he's a man and not just some sort of flower nailed to the shithouse wall.

You should watch that mouth of yours, Joe is saying. Could get you in a pile of trouble and no one around here got any spare pitchforks to help you out from under the heaps of dung thrown your way, if you only so much as open that mouth of yours . . . everybody remembers your mouth . . . or so they say or so you say, they say; ain't that more like the real story: you, your own storyteller because no one got the time anymore to wonder: what happened to.

Ah, Joey . . . I remember when we were standing for some reason in the playground of St. Francis and you've just said something about your older brother—his coming back from Los Angeles and how much he liked the place: the place was real neat, I think you said, he said, not like Long Island. In Los Angeles everything smelled like today and not like a pile of clothes in John's Bargain Stores . . . is that what he said, you said, but what I do really remember and too bad Joey ain't around much these days, out on the end of the Island a lot, with those people he now calls friends, well, anyway, someone said Joe had the touch: he just had to walk by and girls walked after him or they turned their heads and felt good he had walked by them. Irish charm, you said it was, Joey, but I remember wondering how Italian gangsters had the same last name as you did: remember Frank Costello, but you were Irish, as Irish as my own father, one was as Irish as anyone can be who is born in Brooklyn: crash course in forgetting everything about Ireland, which wasn't a lot because his own parents had come to America as young people, away to that place which Julie Smyth's mother said in Portadown: a Catholic, an American Catholic, you're almost a Protestant.

I should be ordering up these scars. Make them intelligible in themselves and not hope, *people will get it.*

Just armies of them from Muncie, Indiana, to Patchogue, Long Island, New York; armies of them and not a clue as to why and then what ever did happen. I would kneel down, I thought, embrace a shrub. Know I was back in *the* village. Always a lot of usage of *the* as in *the* town, *the* village, *the* City . . . particularly, distancing ourselves with the walls of those words.

Here in the middle of May I find myself celebrating Christmas Eve in Flenburg. Only the machines are working. A dog is barking. I am reading F. Scott Fitzgerald and am staying at a youth hostel, alone, in a place built for five hundred, alone and reading, the dog, the oranges and Coke, not to be touched except the next morning going to church and yes, getting the Latin Mass, but missing the sermon and after, walking with the families along paths tramped over fresh-fallen snow, the bright sun, as bright as this May day in Patchogue and not a smile, a tip of the hat, a hand extended, making my own way and hoping, one day, it will mean something; wasn't that always the hope: it will mean something, or it won't, comes another voice. I guess but I do not have a room into which to place these voices. There is only the avenue and maybe a park bench down at the Shorefront or at the Sandspit. And I would be sitting in a room looking out through a lace curtain, to the park sitting in a drink shop in Utrecht, down the block from the house where I was staying in the corner of a student's room, in a student's house. You can tell students live in the street, Oda says, because of the plants in the window. Old people think windows are for looking out of at the world and down their short stubby noses, plants are a way of saying no to this idea.

But one doesn't look to the street in Patchogue. One does not look out or look in. There is no value to either way of looking a person might say and tell you his daughter just finished the second year of college upstate and was thinking of maybe dropping out for a course in secretarial science, something, you know, that puts gas in the tank, a new dress on the back, and a new pocketbook to carry the loot home in.

Not trusting to the details, man, have you noticed. Too many lies are packed behind a description of South Ocean Avenue. Green paint peeling, three FOR SALE signs on the rundown house, but what does the rundown house look like?

What do you care . . . just shoo the flies off the face of the dying kid being held by its mother in a little street of San Juan Latrane in Mexico City. Did my father look into the sugar skulls and see his own empty mouth, teeth long gone, and kept in a glass; did they sew those teeth into his mouth when they buried him?

He makes me want to puke, Nat is telling Joey. I was meant to hear their conversation. They couldn't hide it from me. Next he'll pull out his story about Mr. Mahon going on about being the undertaker in Gleneely and the problems of the hunchback and getting him into the coffin, nearly broke my heart, Mr. Mahon said of the fat woman on the hottest day in the month of July in Donegal, almost though I would need a tire iron to pry her into the box or the man who was too long for the box we had made up for him, something defective in the tape measure. Yeah, something like that, Joey is saying or he'll hiss out, you should go suck your mother's balls.

If he says that to me I'll stuff him into a meat grinder and let Ligouri sell him to the county home for Sunday lunch or maybe the colored guy, Turner, out in Bellport, could use his carcass for his followers in North Bellport.

You got something there.

I know I do.

We all do. Don't worry.

This book will not become a long conversation. Just want to get to the action, as soon as, should have known Gail would get disgusted and take her cookies home with herself.

What am I going on about?

This is Patchogue and I am walking myself about the town, sorry, the village. Maybe we'll see a good lynching, a cross-burning, a Star of David desecration, a pissing on the crescent.

About time you flew right.

Don't I know it. This flying right, as far as I can tell, not a single person in this village even knows what flying is about, let alone how to fly right, you get what I am saying, fly right and you fly right into the sun and are dead as the doornail some kid is always tripping over.

Knew what Gail was saying. Sure, I did, as I stood by the side of the road in Hanover waiting for the ride which will never come so having to trudge back to where I came from. Like swimming all the way across the ocean only to wake up on shore across there at Leja Beach with a smile on my face like I just ate out the whore of Brighton or had my ashes hauled from there to London and then on to Patchogue . . . the toothless wonder . . . came she did from a family who had the teeth pulled out of the heads of all the girl children just after the permanent teeth arrived. No sense waiting around until they got rotted or knocked out of your head, now at an earlier age you'd be able to give suck to organs willing to pay for the pleasure if you can call it that: standing in the rainy shadows of a London slum.

In Patchogue, Gail is saying, you have to go to a motel and share your dreams with a welfare family. We have everything the modern city has right down to the idea of a welfare motel. You know what checks in but don't check out.

Board member Anthony Aliperti had little regard for Econolodge, saying he had seen some run-down Econolodges in Florida. Weber said there may be some facilities that were older, but that he had the highest regard for the youthful leadership of Econolodge. Aliperti said later that he thought "youthful" may mean out to make a quick buck.

Gail you're always good for a laugh.

I wish it was still the case. As you get older all you hear is laughter from behind hedges and there is nothing there when you go to look, nothing except the memory of when you were there and nothing was there, then.

In St. Charles over in Port Jefferson they had this kid from Argentina who was born with no arms and no legs. Mom said not to repeat this to anybody because all you would do would be giving people something to laugh at; you can't expect people to do anything more than laugh when they are told about a kid like this poor kid from Argentina, there but for the grace of God, you should be praying, and don't let yourself ever forget it. Years later in Tijuana an armless legless woman is suspended in a harness over this guy who has the biggest cock which he was supporting, erect, lying on his back, his hand seemed tiny when compared to the cock which he was supporting in a vertical position from his recumbent pose and at the sound of the music from somewhere the woman was lowered from the ceiling, an American flag in her mouth, her teeth grabbing the little gold-plated staff, a breeze rippling Old Glory and down she came to be impaled by this guy's cock. A human top you might say, but she didn't revolve as quickly, no hardly, they pulled her up and then lowered her again onto his glistening cock. This went on for some time. The viewers got bored and wanted to see—what else could they want to see: how should I know. I could imagine someone chopping the woman's head off and the guy slipping his cock into the bloody stump of her neck.

I had been seeing things like this for twenty years or more. It's always the same. The rooms change. The languages change. Even the reasons change. History is stuck into our heads. Well, some of us have it and are the worse for it. The majority, this'll put them to sleep, could care less, can't blame them, a vast Chicago, if you ask me. A woman sitting in Cicero is telling me of fifty men in five weeks. Sometimes two a day and every one of them said he thought he was in love with me. I just can't fuck them and leave. Or they can't, have to run the mouth down into some dark lane and smother what they want to do with a lot of words. When they leave, I read Rilke.

What are you doing here in Cicero?

I don't fuck men, women, or dogs anymore.

In Patchogue with more reason than any place I have ever been. I tried to create a reason for being in Amsterdam, and met this guy, he was from one of the former Dutch colonies and he was saying, she left so fast in the morning she left her pants behind. He pulled out a pair of red panties and waved them about. I thought she must have been uncomfortable. He was sorry to see her leave so quickly. She hadn't fallen asleep and he didn't have time to go through her pocketbook. He hadn't gotten paid for the fuck and all he had to show for it was this pair of red panties; if people don't believe me when I tell them what a time I have every summer when all the girls come to Amsterdam asking for me. I am famous.

Someone is saying if you have to travel more than half a mile, the love won't last. And some say if you stuff your fingers up the nostrils of the skull of Oliver Plunkett in Drogheda Church it will bring you good luck. And some say you read too many novels and mistake what you read for being the truth. And I say if you tripped over the truth you wouldn't recognize it. And you say it looks like you tripped through the truth and have ended up with not even a post to piss on. When you had that job in Blue Point sorting gun parts you had more of a future than you do now living in the City, in the slums, with the sounds all night of police cars, fire engines, ambulances, breaking bottles. You had a drink instead of a vision.

Ask me, the voice of Kevin says, if you dare, if you have the courage, and I'll tell you something went awfully wrong for you to end up where you have with barely enough to come out to this hole in the ground and not even a car to get around with, having to walk up and down Ocean Avenue like a nigger or a vet. Don't get me wrong, I have nothing against them. They're all God's children but some of them are—

But what matters: what happened to you, that it brings you back to this place. You ain't dead. You sent the notice of your mother's death back to the village and it was noted. Your father died, this we found out later and now you bring yourself back. Are we to give you some certificate of seaworthiness? Should we pat you on the back, send you on your way?

How to answer. No angel to carry my heart into the hole in the wall as with Canova's figures allowing an art history lesson to arrive from Vienna: city of the dying.

O, glorious city, so in love with the dying: you have a museum for the dying, for the dead and a man to guide the viewer about the room: well, here in Patchogue they have, it is true, added on to Robertaccio's Funeral Home: the little funeral director who passed on the chance to do his own mother.

Active in many local organizations, he was a life member and past Grand Knight of Patchogue Council, Knights of Columbus, a Fourth Degree Member of the John J. Shea Assembly, Knights of Columbus, a former trustee of St. Francis de Sales RC Church for 35 years, and past president of the church's Holy Name Society. He was also a 40-year member of the St. Vincent de Paul Society, a 30-year member of Catholic Charities, a life member of Patchogue Lodge of Elks, a life and exempt member of the Van Guard Hose Company of the Patchogue Fire Department, a member of Patchogue Lodge of Moose, charter member of the Patchogue Fishing Club, a charter, life privilege and past president of Patchogue Lions, a past deputy district governor of Lions Club, a 40-year member of the Patchogue Chamber of Commerce, a member of the Domino Yacht Club, past president of the Suffolk County Funeral Directors Association, former director of both the Metropolitan Funeral Directors Association and the State Funeral Directors Association, a 30-year member of the Small and Independent Business Bureau and a member of the Long Island Better Business Bureau.

What had all the years of experience been worth only to miss the chance to do your own mother, fix her face in an expression: GET ON WITH IT, in the shabby way you have always had, as was the painted-on expression on Mom's face up there in Saugerties because, mark my words, they have a room reserved for you in Islip, no doubt in my mind or in your own father's, they have that room and you will be first in either of the families to get themselves carted away to the hatch and there you'll be able to do all the dreaming you want; carry on with all those delusions about being a writer: who ever heard of the likes of yourself being a writer and look at the material you have given yourself:

PATCHOGUE

Yeah, Kevin says, Patchogue when you could have easily given yourself Vienna.

How can a person be in love with a city where he does not speak the language? That is part of my problem in the City. I do not speak the language. I am not invited out of my room. My conversations all take place in bookstores where the words are limited by the impatience of the clerks to be getting on with and there is always another conversation waiting to walk in off the streets. Not like in this place, a place where I have never said more than hello, do you have, you should, who do you, and what do you mean, sorry, sorry, sorry for even suggesting you might be alive. I should have known better. I have found on the dirt floors of Milwaukee that—pause while I try to imagine what I could find on such floors . . . something like what I have found in the Oasis. No one is ever there when you really need them. Always after or before the fact and there when you finally get to tell your tale you might as well have the Glasgow gas pipe down your throat for having a quiet sleep before passing on to the marble slab where the guy makes sure there is no foul play, other than life itself, your man adds from the proverbial dark corner of the bar, even in the Oasis they have this guy sitting, just off his clamboat with the new story about what the daughter of the captain tried to bring home to meet the parents. Her old man almost blew his gut all over the guy's shoes. He was so angry, he says, playing poetically to the chorus of chrome-headed bottles.

You got the head so far up the shithole, Kevin says, you would need a search warrant from the Supreme Court to make contact with the famous ounce of reason all of us have been stuck with. Why in all that is . . . come back to this place?

For the same reason you did. I read that you were working with property in Florida.

The Patchogue Dream. Florida. Working with property, you say. You must have heard my mother talking. Worked as a doorman in a building with rich Jews, Cubans, and then niggers. The place was going to shit without even going through a constipated stage. Right into the cream of diarrhea. No one was throwing out any life preservers. I stayed at it for a couple years. Something like five, three more than Frank, he could only hack it for two, don't blame him. No one to listen to his tales of woe. And they were tales of woe and him with nothing but a tale of woe. I can't even remember what he was going on about. Just a tale of woe. Like Venice always sinking.

You've been to Venice?

My brother was there. You remember Hughie, don't you? The size of him, lost a bit in Vietnam. Scared shitless, he said he was, for the year he was there. All that weight right down into the shithole.

Never does one hear the name of a foreign city mentioned in Patchogue.

Yes, there is a travel agency but they package up Catholics for the Franciscan tour of Niagara Falls and the Dominican tour of Washington, D.C., and the Jesuit tour of Puerto Rico.

I just wanted, quickly, to go to Mattituck and be walking among the trees surrounding the construction site of Melinda's mother's house. No way to arrest time and who would want to. Just add that little tag to show I am not about to fall into a violin for the old days, always good.

Kevin is still going on and changes the subject, a little, I hear your parents moved to Wisconsin, got themselves into Oshkosh overalls and began to pitch the cowshit.

As good as any story you're about to hear. They did move, much against the will but once decided they did not ever again permit the word *Patchogue* to be mentioned. The word called up the humiliation of the move. They had to leave Patchogue and go into exile in Wisconsin. Same climate as Siberia, Dad said, and the people less friendly to boot.

That's what I hear, Kevin says, but can't be worse than Florida where people buy paperback novels to keep in the bathroom and use for toilet paper. They think they are making a cultural statement and have received some notice in a City paper for the daring of their concept: the killing of how many stones with what sort of bird, is how they put it, and I didn't see any niggers get lynched or crosses being burnt. They have more interesting ways of getting back. But only if you have been there a long time will you be able to ever find the words to describe them and always you will come back to the impossibility of what is undergone in Florida.

I tried to stop my ears with words, Veliko Turnovo, but Frank *the Protestant* wormed his way in: you litter the page with all these names of cities, but who cares, since 1964, anyone can travel and has done so; who do you think you are, who cares; where is the conflict, the resolution, the interest, the development? Yes, Frank, and Veliko Turnovo are still pretty words and a city as unique as Venice, built on the sides of cliffs and it is up

and down, much like Venice, with the up and down and over the various
canals, fuck Frank, what did he ever do for me, that is Protestant Frank,
what does any of this do for me: Patchogue has never been driven past by
myself. I do not know what it would feel like to get off the highway at the
Patchogue exit and see-what-happens as I thought to do in Lille and in
Yugoslavia. Just get off the train, find it is days until the next train out; find
I cannot and do not want to leave. Everything has been ordered to suit my
imagination. I am happy and trimming the grass on what will be my plot in
the local cemetery: death arrives: I am into the ground. It is always possible. Something would happen and I would end up in Brussels and be
caught in a city with two languages and not knowing either one of them,
find myself living in a district where a third is spoken and still not speaking
that one, all this very far away from Patchogue where they are getting
ready for high-school graduation, where the campaign is underway to
remind the kids it's their duty to go out and get drunk, get drunk, get very
drunk and see who can come closest to wrapping the car around a fine oak
tree on South Country Road . . . everyone is woozy in the car from the
groping sex down by the bay; sad the church won't be as full as it would be
if they had been done to death during the school year but even then, there
would have been the risk of doing it after the deadline for the memorial
page of the yearbook—gets filled that year with only a sixth grade teacher
who has known a bunch of the kids since those years   those years
those years.

  I don't know where the fuck Bernie has taken himself. Nat, I hope, is
getting the dinner arranged. It doesn't have to be formal. Not as elaborate
as *Christ's Entry into Ostend.* Ensor didn't get around to finishing the painting; the drawings have been lost. But much interest was created in the
possibility, after viewing his *Christ's Entry into Brussels* while many a
painter has attempted an *Entry of Christ into Patchogue.* A lot of trouble as to
whether it should be along West Main Street or East Main or just come
down from North Ocean Avenue. No one can agree and the rabbi will not
intervene: one monthly Wednesday luncheon for the Christians and Jews
is enough for the rabbi. Let them kill each other: they will enjoy it. As is
the thought, like Derry, a lot of Patchogue ain't there anymore. It must
live on in an imagination such as my own.

                    ALAS poor PATCHOGUE.

Many a good time, though if I get too close to the good time with the words the time evaporates and I am left with the puddle of who paid and did I pay my share or was it really worth it when all is said and done, done with it.

Kevin says he'll probably see me at the dinner, at Felice's, right, yeah, I'll see if I can drag Larry along.

I must resist this cliché. This dinner business. No one would ever do such a thing for me.

Don't worry, they will. I have my doubts about it, writes Hemito von Doderer. Even though they have a museum for me in Vienna it's only open on Saturday; they know what they really think of me.

At least Patchogue is a real village, not like Levittown, though that sneer is no longer accurate. What was her name? I don't know. Someone said she moved to Texas, that other destination of people fleeing the Island. Probably in Houston where they give you a pair of hip boots when it rains. We necked at Jones Beach. Her uncle is a priest; she has a half-brother who is to be a priest. She didn't think she'd like all the floor-washing that goes with being a nun. To go the extra hour and a half beyond Levittown, to Patchogue, to risk a reason or an attempt at why.

Muddle, boy, you can't have this muddle if we are gonna give you a dinner. Remember, you got to say something at the dinner. Get up before the tired jaws, tired from all the steak which has to get eaten, so we know it's an occasion. At least you ain't one of those vegeterians. We had one of them as a speaker. Someone asked him if human flesh could be eaten. That was an easy question: man is an animal. Right you are, someone shouted from the back of the room. It was Buddy, who else . . .

Harold (Bud) Rooney, triple-threat athlete of Frank Merriwell stature during his years at Patchogue High School died at the age of 28 in St. Vincent's Hospital, New York City, during an epileptic seizure last Thursday. A free-lance photographer "Buddy" was living in an apartment on Greenwich Avenue, New York City, when he was stricken by the seizure. There is no known record of his ever having been subjected to a seizure prior to the day of his death. A wake service was held Monday evening at the Ruland Funeral Home, Patchogue, and among Bud's many friends in attendance was Joe Namath of the New York Jets. Bud had worked with Namath at his football camp. Bud played two years with the Jets farm team, and then went into modeling and photography in New York City. He also did bit parts in such movies as "Love Story" and "Owl and Pussycat." He played varsity football at Patchogue High School under Coach Joe Agostinello for three years and was called "a real triple-threat man. He could run, pass and kick as a quarterback." Coach Agostinello said he started his coaching career with Buddy. "He was in the eighth grade, and we were together until he graduated from high school. He was the best athlete I have ever coached and without doubt he was a boy who never gave up. He never knew the word quit. There wasn't a boy or girl among his classmates who did not admire him. To me Patchogue and Buddy Rooney have always been one. It is a loss and yet it will always be something Patchogue will remember in that Buddy represented Patchogue wherever he went—in high school, in college and throughout his adult life. I consider him as close as my son. I knew him as a boy. To me it was a personal pride to see the young man succeed in the tough business of modeling and show business." Don Campbell, now varsity basketball coach at South Ocean Avenue Junior High School, Patchogue, and teaching science and health also coached Bud and was a personal friend. "A kid like that comes along once in a lifetime. He could have been either a pro football or baseball player. Even when Bud was in eighth grade he could pick up a new sport fast. He'd learned to play badminton one afternoon and two physical education teachers came along and challenged us. We beat them—Bud in a new sport he'd learned that afternoon was good enough to hold his own, and better. Buddy came from an athletic family—his father, uncles, brother Don, played minor league baseball; Uncle Bill was an outstanding hitter. Bud had consistently batted up to .370."

Blonde smiles, did you say, back there? Didn't you go to Copenhagen in the middle of winter looking for a blonde smile? What would you have done if you had been found out? I was and fled back to Ireland. No blonde smiles in Ireland. And in Athens the blonde smiles were only for the dark Greeks who borrow dildos from visiting German men so they could give the women a working over. Those women come all this way just to fuck us: we can't disappoint them. What will they say when they get back home, "I met the only Greek who couldn't fuck." Has that ever happened since the dawn of creation? Lilia didn't go to Greece. She went to Morocco and came back with, "Men fuck like my grandfather and he's been dead for twenty years." She must have been in Athens and didn't know it. I will have to check her passport. She was trying to show, even though she is Bulgarian, that she didn't have it in for the Greeks, as well she should. What did they ever do for the Bulgarians . . . right into an awful history lecture. The old man falls into the soup in Short Hills. You can feel the razor working over his wrists. The rope about the neck, the brains running down the walls.

There is a certain lack of imagination in Patchogue. Suicide is not very popular. Oh, the kids kill themselves ramming their cars into a bridge abutment on Southern State after being told they have bad breath. Can't take a joke and I never did like the pimples on the side of your nose; even the drugs at the Cro-Magnon Club can't help everybody.

Where have I gotten myself? If I knew and if you knew you would have the train back to the City, laden with gifts: baskets of cheer, a scarf for your neck, a license-plate holder saying COME HOME TO PATCHOGUE but no car in the City to use the damn thing on; never have I seen a T-shirt with Patchogue written on it. There must be some sort of taboo against the name of the village. Never when I lived here was there any mention of this. . . . Bay Shore was different; that was definitely not a place to have a T-shirt from. If you were white it was like advertising you had a nigger for a grandmother and wanted your sister to marry a high yeller and peddle her pussy to Spanish trash, while Spanish, you proudly tell people, is your first language and you're going to knock every jerk in the county on the ear with your command of the English language.

What are you going on about, Larry is saying. Always going on about something that's what's wrong with people who stay too long in the City. I lived there, put in my time, and realized my place was back out here, not that I even thought about back out here, it was just I did know here my home was and it wasn't walking on Ninth Street wondering if a jungle bunny was gonna score a couple of points for hacking off my white face. Larry has gone to fat and has a fat wife. He was engaged to Melinda and works for the county jail. Melinda's father got him the job. Don't ask me what she saw in him. I know what he saw in her: blonde hair, big tits, and she was hot to trot, as long as you kept it in the family it ain't a sin and no one is wiser—I wasn't family and struck dumb. Much too close. Might as well shout out the Hermosa Beach magazine and city slogan

HORSESHIT

Larry has two kids and another in the oven. As long as it don't come out too well-done is all I ask. Melinda was a good kid but that's all she was, a good kid, and nothing against her for it, that's what I was and you were off in Wisconsin or in Ireland or in God knows where. You said those things to her and she never got over them.

Larry, it's never so simple, come to the dinner Nat and Bernie are putting on for me at Felice's. It'll get a little clearer if I do say so, or so say

or never, not for a moment have I forgotten that moment when first
Melinda and I kissed.

Who can say that, never, whether in Madison, Wisconsin, or York in the
north of England, my heart dangling on a rope suspended between those
cities, if you can believe it, always at the worst moment, the rope snaps and
dumps me back in Patchogue, standing under the shattered tree in the St.
Francis playground. We are beating up Eddie Kiernan because he is ugly,
because he smells, because he won't fight back, because we hate his guts
and no one likes him, that's why we didn't care; who cares about people
like that, and not even Ray Ditmars, goody-two-shoes himself, came to
Kiernan's rescue. Not even Kiernan's older brother could stop his brother
getting beaten up. That's what younger brothers deserved, as long as it
didn't rub off on Pat Kiernan, no skin off my knees, I'd give him a boot,
just for the hell of it, but he'd tell our mother and my father would beat the
shit out of my hide.

Larry has a smirk on his face: you've ended up with the fear some spic's
gonna shit all over your face and get a medal from the community for
doing it.

Might be right and yeah, he got his paw around Melinda's tit but what
does he got to show for it, what does any of them got to show for it? Sour
grapes. What else can you pick from the hills of Patchogue? No hills unless
you mean the garbage over in Africa on Rider Avenue.

On every corner of Main Street sits a man in a wheelchair, an eagle
attached to a line and the line attached to the arm of the chair. He is with a
group of touring war vets from West Berlin. They are trying to raise funds
for a memorial to the GIs that gave them chocolate bars when they got
captured at the end of the war. It is all a little sad.

You ought to get your head examined, Nat is saying. How can you
come up with ideas like that? Who ever heard of German war vets standing on Patchogue street corners. Now, if you had said they were vets from
the German American Bund summer camp over in Yaphank, that
would've been a different story.

"They're fine American people, fond of their German background, a spirit
which built the Settlement League," said Bob Wheeler, recently-elected
president of the German-American Settlement League of the residents of Siegfried Park, Yaphank, a private community of about fifty homes which is also
infamous for being a Nazi meeting camp (Camp Siegfried) fifty years ago. Every

summer from the mid-1930s through World War II, hundreds of German-Americans flocked to Camp Siegfried and praised the uprising of the Nazi state and of Hitler. According to Wheeler, their intentions were honorable.

That's a secret and not for the pages of this report.

I follow you but I thought you were gonna, as the saying goes, tell it like it is.

I am, with the same boring intensity Lucja describes the Warsaw of her memory: all fur coats, horseback riding, high intellectual discussions over the pigs feet on Sunday afternoons, communist existentialism and Catholic cynicism with the attempts at a synthesis, once or twice a year, leading to either birth or abortion then confession—abortion is easier to confess, none of that nasty restitution that goes with stealing and self-criticism.

Yeah, to think Lucja is a citizen of Long Island these days, then exiled to the nation's capital, where she is chased and chased by jaded bankers right out of romance comic books, all colliding in BMWs, a citizen of Long Island, and from Huntington of all places, home of that boyfriend Melinda once claimed when I called, finally did call, after the first year of college, that summer, wasted in going down to Sayville looking for a book to describe my condition: Thomas Wolfe, *Look Homeward, Angel,* of course, could there have been another book?

Malcolm Cowley is gonna have a rerun of his comments from years ago in Roanoke: longest cocktease in literature, people want explosions, boy, Malcolm said, and you give them a dry hump. Learn from your betters, don't be afraid to get the wick dipped before three hundred pages meander out of your machine.

I am trying. Miles to go and at least a couple of more hours and then I can sit myself into Felice's, eat my heart out when I turn and see.

Don't worry, my friend, Joe is saying, I know Nat will do a good job and if he doesn't I'll have his heart served up over at the animal shelter and I mean the real animal shelter and not the motel in Coram with welfare mothers in one wing giving blowjobs ten days after and before the checks arrive to put some rice and beans on the table for the little future poets of America . . . and in the other wing, young men who'll whip and piss all over you. Don't say Patchogue ain't as up-to-date as the next little village on this island.

So we got Nat, Bernie, Joey, Larry, Frank, both Franks, Gail if she shows up and I am sure she will and I am sure a couple of Pats . . . where is little Patty Kelly . . . if anyone knows where she is, please let us know. She had the cutest bangs, the cutest nose, the cutest walk, the cutest handwriting, and *what happened to Patty Kelly?* Answer me that one: a dark day in hell would be required and Patty Margonof and Nadine Katz and Rita Crocitto. Is your ass gonna be in gear or will we have to get a stand-up comic over from Stony Brook, one of those tough-talking Jews who fancies himself a stand-in for Lenny Bruce. Or you could get that Jewish guy whose father owned the sweatshops in Ridge, you know the guy I mean, the one who flew the spics up from San Juan, charged them for the flight, put them in chicken coops, and when they demanded electricity, he had his cousin give them a dose of Jewish lightning, saved me giving this year to Planned Parenthood, stopped a little population explosion just waiting to happen, with one match, best condom there is when it comes to the spics, if I say so myself.

Nah, I can't relate to Les Bogen, that was the guy's name. Said he was surprised people like me read James Joyce and there he is getting his fingers into Herman Wouk, some people read with their lips; Les read with his fingers. You could imagine him pulling meaning out of the page with his long fingernails; probably is an orifice for rent over at the river: no, now too old: no one loves you when you are old and gay.

So Nat got the table all arranged. On the tape of the background music he is playing a combination of Polish polka tunes, Nico, a hit of Bach once in a while with a smidgen of von Webern to show he has been to the big city, some time ago. Where do I place the vomit bags, Matt Talbot is asking. I don't know, Marty Talbot replies. I can't figure out what sort of throw-the-sucker-into-a-bucket-of-shit party this is gonna be, still not as clear as it should be.

Bad vibes is the word, my brother, Matt.

Watch out for the vibes or the vibes will ram you up the ass every time.

Find myself losing control. I wish I could get the finger back on the button and be ready to push when the signal is given. Get me out of this place. How to face Nat and Bernie, Larry and Kevin and Joe will bring Karen who will have a pile of crossword puzzle books by the side of the chair where she sits; the nerves have her by the short hairs along the back of the neck. She knows something has to give and she is afraid it will be, so afraid, if she, just like *that,* just like, *that,* and right into might as well drive the car right off the Mascot Dock, about all I'm capable of doing and not enough water, really, to do the job or high enough up so the fall would get me. Probably choke to death in the black ooze on the bay bottom.

Larry slaps me on the back. How's it going old sport? Having a good time in the old village, don't you want to know what Melinda's pussy tastes like? Getting them blonde hairs out from between my teeth it was some chore, if you know what I mean, but then all you got are them colored girls in the City. All of them tight little curls of Brillo and a smell you have to scrape off.

Something like that, Larry, something like that. It's always something like that. So glad you could make it.

Marty Talbot dims the lights of Felice's. He knows people after the age of twenty-five are sensitive to bright lights and need the comfort of dim lights, so dim the grey hairs and the suddenly appearing expanses of flesh uncovered by hair do not matter and some say dim light is complimentary to people who have added to their bulk: all cats are.

Stand around in the bar area having a couple. Need a little pick-me-up before I get myself knocked over by the evening. How to get back to the City? Didn't know this was gonna happen. If I did I would've invited Lilia. But she wouldn't have come out here. See enough pathology walking around on the streets of the City: no need to see the rural variety. Joey is wearing a second gold necklace with tasteful diamonds spelling out JOEY. Drink in hand, he has right hand out shaking. He likes to have the hand ready and waiting. Puts people at their ease. Can't stand to have people walking looking like they have to take a shit and can't seem to find a spot to drop trou. And let go with another contribution to mankind. Sorry, for humanity. Karen will have my skull if she catches me using outdated concepts of, something like that, have you noticed how we all sound alike?

So much I didn't see in Patchogue. So many faces, left to the imagination and the possible grave. A good time will be had by all, even if it kills. And I'll have you know: a good time was had by all and all were had by the good time pouring down upon their heads.

Never to recover their sanity, their will to get up in the morning and go out and wrestle a buck from an unforgiving world, something like that happened after his testimonial held at Felice's on whatever night in hell this was and I'm here with my hand being shook by Joey who asks if I need a gun, he can get me a license and even targets if I want to make a little spare change. You're the perfect sort of craftsman we're always looking for. Never know when we need a little garbage disposal, just got to be careful, but trust you, all the way back to the playground of St. Francis, able to put the boot in with the best of them, a little too much of the sanctimonious guilt moutherings on but that is to be expected and allows for improvement of aim: don't want people to suffer unless it's called for in the contract.

Ah, Bernie did show up. Sure, he would. He was the guy giving the testimonial on behalf of the people of Patchogue *who are in the know* . . . a small subcommittee of the Back the Patchogue Committee that seeks to have the Sandspit declared a national monument in keeping with the forward-looking spirit of the village. You got to fill in the blank spots in the village history with what actually did happen and we are indebted to Tom, here, I can call him that, though he does prefer to be called Thomas, but we are all friends sitting about in this room—see how quickly am able to get from bar to sitting around the table in the dining room, with a sweeping view of the bay—and out there is Fire Island and beyond: Europe; just keep swimming and you'll run your nose into a pile of floating shit and you'll know you've either arrived in Europe or are off San Juan, chuckle, please, chuckle.

Hundreds of citizens of the town of Brookhaven turned out Friday in support of the Stick with Patchogue Committee. The committee formed recently to encourage the town board to keep the town hall in Patchogue where it has stood for most of the twentieth century, erected a large sign in front of the town hall. Citizens were invited to affix their names to the sign forming what the committee calls "the largest most visible petition in Patchogue history."

Well, anyway, Bernie is saying, our friend, our Patchogian, patriotic friend of Furman Lane has documented to the satisfaction of everyone on the committee and to the members of the Patchogue Historical Society, to the members of the Brookhaven Historical Society, to members of the Suffolk County Historical Society that just over there on the Sandspit Dock that great American patriot and all-around general ballbuster himself, Henry David Thoreau, landed in a Dutch-driven boat and proceeded to upchuck a dinner of boiled duck and clams, a happy and disappointed man, having failed in his mission to find the bones of Margaret Fuller. There had been talk back in Boston, and you must remember how far Boston was in those days from Patchogue, to make a fine and wondrous stew from those bones and now, Mr. Thoreau had to face the question of how was he gonna get back to the City. There were no great and efficient taxis running from bay to train. (Let this be a plug for the Say Yeah Taxi Company of Patchogue. Fee paid.)

He was alone and, lo and behold, a valiant Patchogian offered to carry Henry David Thoreau on his back all the way to Blue Point where they refreshed themselves on oysters and then got themselves back to the City, in a mood much to be appreciated by the ladies of the Bowery where they went and spent, spent, and spent all the pent-up energies of the seaborne air.

Hey, Bernie, you didn't let the preacher give his invocation. And who got the flowers to make that part of the presentation?

We are winging it, Nat says. We got the preacher but he was out saving a couple of colored souls in North Bellport and will be here as soon as he's done counting the money from the souls and the house they live in but here is Carol with the flowers and a big kiss. Is it for Tom, a kiss like he never got in his whole life in Patchogue, don't let anyone say we in Patchogue don't know how to kiss. Give it to him, Carol!

And Carol does so.

Who is this Carol? I try to focus mind but she does have brown hair and I have never had my head turned by anything other than blonde . . . Flo will be along later (Nat leans over the table, don't worry, we have not forgotten your past and your hopes for the future . . . but living in there, in the City, how can you have any hope, only thing you can hope for in the City is a spic who knows how to aim and pull the trigger, sending you cleanly to the morgue, not to linger on in dull appreciation of his bad aim and your worse luck).

I am kissed and stunned. Little did I know this would be happening to me. I did not expect to be so royally treated. It was not in my plans. What am I to do with my idea of housekeeping in a furnished room on South Ocean Avenue and watching the world, or that part of the world, go by, that goes by on South Ocean Avenue? It is getting more complex than I imagined.

The flowers make me sad. Flowers are for funerals and maybe they know something I don't know. What is going on? No one is letting me in on the secret. Somebody dropped some acid into a drink, but there was no drinking because I couldn't find a place to drop anchor and hold forth, boat anchored into the oncoming waves, up and down, the waves breaking; always wet. That is what I remember: always wet. Like walking around in Paris, either always wet from the rain or just feeling like it.

Kissed and I would like to be sat into a captain's chair with a little plaque
screwed into the seat, shiny from use:

UPON THIS CHAIR SAT MICKEY FUSCO
HE NO LONGER SITS UPON THIS CHAIR
HE HAS GONE TO MEET HIS MAKER
HE IS SITTING DOWN TO THE FEAST HE DESERVES.

and which he practiced for all these long years of sitting here in meeting
after meeting to hear who dicked who; who was getting a piece of something on the side and could he, maybe, yes, he would like to have just one
little slice . . . say ten minutes' worth; that's all you're good for now; got to
watch the heart and the wallet.

Nothing so tacky as the ghost of Melinda appearing. Or Flo. Or Barbara
or Lilia, just stuck here with the reality of the minister getting up, clearing
his throat, taking a sip of water. Tap of spoon to glass. Attention is directed
to the standing minister.

Let us bow our heads in prayer to ask Him or Her as the case might be,
in the tradition you are following, conscious of your obligation which is
really a gift from Him or Her, as the case might be.

Where did you get this joker from, Bernie is asking Nat. I thought I told
you to get one of those Irish rummies from St. Francis and make sure he
didn't work his way through a bottle of Thunderbird, just make sure he
was here on time. Something about scheduling, Nat replies. The Catholics
had two funerals and a business meeting of the parish bingo committee so
they couldn't make it. The wops up at Mount Carmel were pressing an
early crop of grapes and their feet wouldn't be dry. The Jews had business
to attend to. You get the picture, right, so this guy's from Brookhaven.
He's cheap, though I must tell you he asked that his fee be sent to the
Adopt-a-Whale Committee of the Bellport High School PTA.

We are gathered here to honor a young man which does not imply any
qualification either pro or con, to honor him not in his masculinity but in
his personhood.

A door slams shut in the kitchen. Three undocumented workers are
fighting over who can use the telephone first. They are being driven
insane, man, it is better to go back and eat dead worms out of the graveyard than listen to this shit, the fourth sermon by, how do you say it in the
English, by this joker, is that how you say it in the English, this joker with

the little cock who likes to get it sucked by Juan or Raul who gives him the whole banana up the asshole, is it how you say it . . . and then this guy doesn't even leave a tip, just lifts his hairpiece.

This young man has been a credit to the human race, to the world in all its green and other aspects; has sought and continues to seek in a way consistent with the path he is seeking to search out and find, that which is there to be found.

Get the hook, Marty says. There is a crash of dinner plate hitting floor and the rush of headwaiter and waiter. The minister gets the message after going on for another ten minutes, those minutes lost in watching the headwaiter sweeping up the mess, moved the attention did from floor to table by the falling head of a former gym coach, Joe the Italian. Took to the drink he did, when he found out . . .

That's another story best left to another book. No way you can show in the pages of this book what happened to Joe the Italian without too many people losing lunch, even before they have had lunch.

There is a quiet period of time. As the minister requested, when we can get in touch with the muscles doing their job of work.

The one between your ears, you mean, Nat asks.

I got a little lost. A time to catch up. Out here in Patchogue, found I was the subject of a testimonial dinner, am in the middle of it and am waiting for the roof to fall in as it once did in Milan, Saugerties, Beloit, and places even more obscure. A ceiling falling in is not a pleasant prospect and not even arrived at the main course.

What are you going to be doing after the dinner, Nat asks.

I guess walk around some more.

A dangerous proposition, I can tell you ahead of time. You'll run into nothing that'll make you happy: nothing to produce a line of poetry, just more of your face reflected back in passing, no, past store windows, with your elbow now spread out across the top of your skull, the skin peeling; you had better get yourself a baseball cap if you don't want the sun cooking your brain.

Well, I know what you are talking about, what you mean, though I have to get out of here and get some flora and fauna into these pages.

Other people have done a better job of it than you'll ever be able to manage, Bernie says, why not let them have the territory and you can reserve for yourself the human drama, the flesh and guts, blood, sperm, and saliva.

Can one ask for more, Joe says. A little saliva goes a long way when a man has to knead his dough.

Don't talk dirty dirt in this room, Gail says, or it might have been Paula. I have always wondered what happened to Paula, and my search will go unrewarded, as it should. Whims have a way of getting us distracted from the business at hand.

What was the business in your hand, Joey says.

Business, I was to write the history of these two clam-digging families, of their loves and their struggles with the elements, of the romance and adventure they faced each day when they sailed forth from the Patchogue River and of the star-crossed lovers who came from two families that had gone to war over: and that is where I am at the moment. I have to figure out what they went to war over.

What about the time your old man (Frank is saying) had an argument with the doctor living next door over who was to cut the grass on the property line, it couldn't have been more than an inch of grass but that is what they argued about, almost came to blows if I remember right.

You do, of course. The famous War of the Property Line, which sounds like a page-filler in a local magazine, not the subject matter of an argument to find itself locked into the pages of a serious novel, making its way around the world. How to translate *property line* into Turkish, Bulgarian, Albanian?

Too ethnocentric for my taste, Nat is saying. Anyone with half a brain carried around in the brain box resting upon sloping shoulders would know, one of the constant themes of peasant life is the problem of property rights, of the rights to graze x number of months, of boundary rocks always being moved, of bodies being found at the bottom of wells, convenient wells, a long story, in other words, was and will be had by all.

I did get up and give my piece after the water glass had been tapped by a coffee spoon. I would have requested the blinds to be drawn and we were to look into our dining partner's eyes above the flickering candles on the table but that would be . . . Silly, is the word, my boy. Who ever heard of such goings-on? Once upon a time, you were a man of dignity, wit, charm, intellectual pursuits, a man in the gardens of the great house by the river, in the cottage in the Dublin hills where arguments could still be heard in the Latin tongue about saintly matters.

Dermot has arrived. Not too late. Just back from the sands of Libya and before that the green wastelands of England. I do not know what to make of his appearance. It is as if James Thomson showed up and I had to pull three rabbits out of the hat instead of just the one involving your patient suspension of disbelief.

How's the meat upon your plate, Dermot asks.

Just fine, as always, Bernie replies before I can get a word around my full mouth of masticated steak and potato. Eating too quickly because you never know when they are gonna ring the bell and send this vision on its way.

I have eaten myself into the earth with all this coming and going. I don't know what is gonna happen. Have the feeling since the roof has collapsed, the floor is gonna open and bang: into the maw of who gives a fuck.

LAR walks over to Ocean Avenue.
Sees a **ROOM AVAILABLE** sign.
The porch is broken.
Plastic toys in piles designed to break a leg.
Yellow toys under the broken-down shrubs.
Just the place for him.
A guy who barely speaks English shows him the room.
ROOM: so small you have to go in sideways because the dresser and the bed.
Fifteen a night in advance.
Why not charge a hundred?
Next year when we have the new dock.
Always next year.
Always next year.
LAR tests the bed.
Like they always do.
You realize he's thirsty.
He goes down the hall, finds the bathroom.
Takes a palm of water.
LAR goes out and over to the candy store next to the St. Francis playground.
Buys a couple of tall ales.
Goes back to his room.
Sits.
Drinks.
A certain tedium.
Goes downstairs.
The whole family is sitting on the porch.
Man, mother-in-law, wife, kids wrestling.

A dog is being tortured in the backyard.
Speak, you filthy dog.
Speak, you dumb dog.
Be careful, the wife says.
I know my way around here, LAR says.
Just be careful.
LAR should head himself down to CAROL.
Gets tricky. Here.
LAR should head to the Oasis.
He can do both.
Why not?

1

LAR walks down to CAROL.
He goes to the back door of the shop.
He does not trip on the kids' toys.
CAROL sees him standing on the other side of the screen door.
Come on in, Lar. Jack called. He got to stay a little late.

2

LAR walks uptown.
Past the church
convent
hall
railroad station
sees himself getting off the train
just for a visit
past the boarded-up shops.
The Bastille of Rock.
Goes into the Oasis Bar.
Sits at the bar.
BARTENDER is slow to get his gut over to the end of the bar.
LAR has a five on the bar.
What'll it be?
Beer.
A couple vets are sitting at the bar near the street window.
The TV news is on.

The natives are restless in Africa.
LAR drinks half the glass away.
Calls the bartender.
A shot of gin.
Transaction complete.
LAR drinks off the shot.
Stands and heads for the bathroom.

3

A young man, his hand wrapped in a bloody handkerchief, is talking in the
phone booth.
But Mom it's awful. Everything is over, all the years and she . . . the fat was
dripping off her. She'd. She didn't wait. After all these years. How could she. It's
okay. I'm in Patchogue. (This is LAR years before, as if you didn't guess.)

4

White convertible goes by on Ocean Avenue.

5

LAR is looking at *TV Guide.*
CAROL's told him.
It won't take her long to . . . make something for supper.
Just pop it in the oven.
Just like on TV.
Just like on TV.
Well, I didn't go away like you did, CAROL says.
LAR looks at her.
There is silence.
Broken by a baby crying in the playpen.
Saved by the bell, CAROL says.
Sadly, LAR replies.
What should have happened is . . . on to the couch grabbing at clothing.
Fuck.
So far the audience and never will the audience know why.
Neither do the two: LAR and CAROL.

It would be nice if she pinched the baby's penis. A lot of trouble brewing here, she could say.

The dinner is served.

Do you have some butter, LAR asks.

Salt and pepper. They never put enough seasonings in these dinners.

LAR could do his Madigan routine.

It ain't a routine, CAROL says.

It's life and it ain't even original.

Nothing is.

Night has fallen.

6

VINCE gets out of car and goes into Spitalie's.

He orders a Cutty on the rocks.

7

LAR has his back to the bar top.

He is swinging his legs back/forth.

Three men have come in and are talking about Fire Island.

Fire Island conversation.

Sand in the crankcase.

My dick's been sucked so much it's goin' to fall off.

8

Why did you come back, CAROL asks LAR.

Because I wanted to. I was in the City and I—

Do you still have family here?

They're dead.

Do you want a beer.

Does a . . .

Okay.

CAROL gets into the shop and brings back a six-pack.

A potato and (LAR points) you got a seven-course Irish dinner.

Don't I know it; married to one.

When did you say Jack was coming back?

He's gonna be late.

They've finished dinner. She folds the aluminum containers and stuffs them into a garbage bag next to the kitchen sink.

What do we get for dessert?

We can watch TV.

Maybe another time.

I have to be going.

If you have to.

I have to, maybe I can see you tomorrow.

I'd like that very much. You can meet Jack.

Are you happy? LAR asks, opening a can of beer.

Who gave you the idea I wasn't? Why ask such silly questions?

I was just asking.

I'm so busy. I don't have time for questions like that. The baby, the marriage. When you have kids. Are you married?

I was.

This has gone on too long.

Who wants to know why.

LAR is ready to cry.

CAROL doesn't cry.

A mother does not cry.

A crying mother is a bad example.

Difficult to believe this is going on in America.

Or maybe not.

9

In the Oasis.

If I don't move in time her tit would have crushed my . . .

That's what you get for going out with a one-titted broad.

She's got two tits.

LAR gets the bartender over.

Another.

The kid is crying in the phone booth.

10

I didn't think you'd ever get married, CAROL says.

Me either, LAR replies. I had to . . . not what you think.
Children are just too optimistic.
That's because you've never had any. Children just happen.
That's what I mean. They happen like the sun coming up and going down.
I better be going.
If you have to.
I do.

11

LAR leaves and walks back towards the rooming house. Changes his mind and retraces his steps, past the shop, he sees CAROL in the shop holding the baby in her arms. Her blonde hair glows in the shadows caused by the beer and soda signs. LAR's step hesitates. He goes on. He walks down Ocean Avenue to the Mascot Dock. He watches City People crabbing. Some kids are drinking in a broken-down car. A girl giggles in the middle of three men.

12

VINCE goes into the men's room to take a piss. He locks the door. He takes a Walther automatic out of his coat pocket. He unloads the clip, checks it. He looks at himself in the mirror. VINCE puts the end of the barrel against the side of his head. He aims the gun, arm extended. There should be tension in his face, registered in the mirror. He smiles. He puts the gun back in his pocket. Goes out to the bar and orders.

13

LAR goes into Felice's. The second visit of the day.
He sees the sign: **NO SHOES   FORGET IT**
He sees the captain chairs with the names of famous drunks painted on the back.
You were in before, the bartender says.
Yeah, took a walk around the town. Nice day for it.
Walk 'round, come 'round or something like that as the song by Charlie Manson goes.
He was one weird dude, the bartender says.
Yeah, he was.

LAR drinks and notices the sign

1,000,000 drinks sold in this bar

A lot of drinking.
Always.

14

TUESDAY is driving an MG. She is up on Sunrise Highway. She pulls into Dave's Hamburgers. Sits in the car. Kids look at her. She gets a couple of burgers. She eats the burgers and drinks whiskey from a flask.

15

LAR walks out of Felice's, cuts across the village beach, passes the bathhouse, still closed up, gets dried white paint dust on his rubbing palm. He is going to visit SANDRA.

16

LAR is walking along Maiden Lane. He hears a voice from a car.
Hey boy, what ya doing in my town?
Gene!
Lar!
Should I do a repeat?
Nah, I don't want to kill you this time.
You might be right.
Remember we met when I ran you down with my bike.
I remember, before you moved from the house on Ocean Avenue to the one back of the other house.
Where the needles fell off the Christmas tree because my old man bought a cheap one and didn't put any water in the basin, he was drunk.
All fathers are drunk.
Or something like it.
This is one of those dumb sentimental chance meetings that should be the highlight of any movie about a man coming back to the old home.
GENE and LAR knew each other when and then lost track when GENE went

off to play tennis for some state school in Pennsylvania, marrying a girl from PA. They will talk and promise to see each other. GENE is shaking his head and LAR is ill at ease.

17

LAR knocks and waits. Insect noises, of course. The light comes on. Blinds on door rattle. SANDRA peeks out.
It's you.
Himself and himself. How's yourself.
As well. Fuck it. Why did you leave before?
I had to. You inviting me in?
I shouldn't.
You will.
I've heard that line before and it wasn't in a movie.
It was probably on TV.
LAR goes in. The TV is on.
What are you watching?
Nothing. I just turned it on. Kim is late getting home.
Car break down?
No, she stopped for a drink after work with some of the girls and she'll be in later.
LAR goes to embrace SANDRA.
She pushes him away.
You were awful, just leaving.
I had to get a room.
You got one here. I mean you can stay if you want to. Kim doesn't care. I have to listen to her and her boyfriend Jerry, a real symphony, if you get what I mean.
A fifty-piece orchestra.
Yeah, something like it. But all playing on the same note and on and on again. It drives me up the wall. They don't even stop when I put a talk show on the TV; they just keep at it.
LAR and SANDRA drink beer and then go to bed.
They are watching Johnny Carson.
Isn't he the greatest?
Almost like Shakespeare.
Such a wit.
Such timing.
And so deep.
Please no more. This is not ironic.

KIM comes in.
She is alone and worse for wear.
LAR gets dressed.
He has an excuse.
KIM would be nice to . . . but he is a gentleman.
I have to get back to my room. I'm expecting a call.
Who are you expecting a call from at two in the morning?
A secret.
Secret my ass. You just want to.
It's not true. Can we have breakfast?
You're supposed to say that in the evening, not in the morning.
Bad timing.
Yeah, all around bad timing.

18

LAR is walking back to the boarding house
pause
This could be a moment to pull: when in doubt, kill a baby.
LAR sees a woman with an old-fashioned—how fashions change—baby carriage crossing Cedar Avenue. She is run down by a taxi coming back from leaving off people at the late ferry to Fire Island.
Shouts. Blood. Gore. Laughter.
LAR keeps walking.
What can he do?

We cannot have this. We must not have this. It just won't do. It cannot be allowed to continue. We will not tolerate it. I looked to my right and found Dermot getting ready to fall asleep. Already down the tubes when he realized even before he had begun, it was all a lost cause. But this can't be. Just as Dermot shows no signs of being uncomfortable in the heat, dressed as he is in a grey Donegal tweed, frayed at the collar, long-sleeved white shirt, blue knotted UCD tie: he will have to be revived so conversation can either begin or pick up once again.

The mayor has appeared over in the corner. He is moving his grey-haired smile across the room. He is greeting lost and new friends.

You knew my mother even though you were of different religions. Said you were almost a Catholic and should have been when compared to most of the Catholics my father knew . . . and you're a Democrat . . . got those

Republican rascals out of office, all those years they'd been in the village
hall: built themselves a nice little pleasure palace, but the whistle got
blown and now you get blown, but only by the winds of good fortune, I
am sure, because your wife is ever at your side, being an inspiration and
guiding light: also good for a laugh when the waves start to beat about
your shoreline at budget time and every, what do you call them, not in
mixed company, I don't want to say excuse my French. The mayor is a man
of the old school and knows how to read, write, and do figures without
being told at every step of the way. The mayor is pleased to have among us
here today a credit to his village, to his race (a quick look round the room
and seeing it is okay to make this little joke), you all know what I mean: the
Irish race; gifted with verse, song, and saints, and not in that order, neces-
sarily, just the accident to have him among us, on a day like this: during the
late spring Just Before Summer Shopping Days sponsored by the
Patchogue Chamber of Commerce which leads into the Start of Summer
Sale Days and the Massive Fourth of July Celebrations, every week in
Patchogue a festival of a thousand interesting things to do and learn. To
walk down Main Street, is a learning experience that would take week
upon week of classroom instruction, but the honor of having a distinguished
visitor among us and to think he is not going to ask us for, he is not going to
strap on the poor mouth and pass the hat, well, he should be wearing one
given the intensity of the sun over Patchogue, given the state of his defoli-
ated, please, fellow Americans, fellow veterans, do not think I am making
light of the sacrifices of our sons and daughters who placed their lives and
in some cases gave them to their country on the battlefields of Vietnam and
other farflung battlefields in the war for democracy and against those who
would like to, in mixed company it is not the polite thing to even suggest
what they might do, though I can hint at it. Have you ever noticed the
short little dark gentleman who works every Sunday afternoon at Jack's
Stand up on Sunrise Highway, a perfectly legal establishment, given the
bureaucratic mess the town has made of the regulations allowing such
stands to appear like so many mushrooms after the rain, and every one of
them, licensed by *the town* and now in dire competition with the esteemed
merchants of this great village of ours (snores from the corner of the
room), well, have you ever noticed this young man, whose speciality I am
told is tuna fish salad on a bagel, have you noticed him: finger into ear,
rummaging around, almost the beginning of two fingers into the ear and
the finger is lost beyond the first joint. I do not ask the obvious or make

the obvious point—there is nothing within the head to stop the finger, because it just gòes rummaging about the ear cavity and returns, triumphant with a yellow sheen added to the brown flesh of the finger: this is what the merchants of this village have to contend with.

Applause is heard and dies quickly away because there is going to be a patriotic demonstration to remind me, at one time I was a person of political convictions of course quite confused and yet always worthy of attention: you're gonna like this, Nat says.

Yes, you are, Bernie adds as does Joey, yes siree, Bob, as the saying goes: you are gonna like this.

Tonight, is it ready? How times do fly and even without an ingesting of those substances flowing out to this village on the backs of the SS, Street Survivors, our local youth special-action group much praised by the director of the Four Sisters Community Center. But I/we are here to notice and remember both the happy and the sad times of our village and the members of the community who have given so much to make Patchogue a better place to live. (Nat turns to Bernie, who is this? Sounds like he either got the wrong speech or the wrong night. He's the head of the vets, he wants to speak, I thought it would do us all some good and anyway our guest does have an interest in military matters, ain't that right?)

The mayor has previously introduced Don Kaler who is somewheres in the midst of his talk. I missed some of it, having to make a contribution to democracy in the men's room, while the mayor did go on with something really to be missed. I added nothing to the BEND OVER AND SMILE graffiti on the wall.

My brother Richie who you all knew as the King. Richie the King Kaler did not die in vain. He is remembered in the hearts of his fellow villagers, of his former classmates who gave up a minute of their recent reunion to his memory, and as you know he died in the defense of freedom in Vietnam. That is history. His name is inscribed on the stone wall in Washington and on the fleshy hearts of his friends and those of us in this village who take the time to remember: our village would not be here if, during the years of our country's history, young men and women—yes, women, too—if they failed to answer the call to arms, to shoulder the defense of freedom.

The waiter got a cold ale into my fist when I exhibited the signs of passing out.

It is now over nineteen years, yes, my friends, nineteen years since

Richie made the supreme sacrifice and with his life aided his country in a time of war. With his life lost charging an enemy machine-gun nest, dead, Richie was, when finally hours later his comrades were able to reach him. In a scrawled note he wrote, the pencil writing smeared with his own blood: *do not forget*. Richie was not a man of anniversaries: he couldn't remember his own birthday, there should be a little laughter. Do you get it? How many of us remember the day we were born?

So not on the twentieth, not on the tenth, not even on the twenty-fifth, but on this the nineteenth anniversary of Richie's death in the defense of freedom I have brought with me a little memento, a tiny reminder of that death and of his sacrifice, and I will ask you all now to stand, this is not a moment of silence but rather I will ask you to stand and draw your attention to the kitchen. Two of the little dark guys appeared at the door of the kitchen bearing platters, silver platters, and walked slowly to the center table. I have brought with me and I ask you to share in this eaten memorial to my brother.

The platters are placed on the table and Don walks over to the table, removes the covers and reveals four hands in a light butter sauce.

Yes, my friends, I too served my country in the years after my brother's death and through the miracles of modern science and a little help from a buddy in the food services unit of the U.S. Marine Corps, I was able to pack up these four enemy hands and so today, have them cooked up and yes, they do look a little like the legs of some prehistoric bird. I ask you to have a slice, something, I am told, like parsnip à la dente with a secret little punch.

The waiters have carved up the hands and have served them out to the assembled audience. There is a moment, all eyes to the mayor and then to myself as guest and I plunge fork into my piece of gook hand and flesh to mouth for a quick careful chewing. Yes, a most delightful flavor, a flavor of the Orient in spring, fading into summer with a hint of the chill of the passing of time and how fragile our memory is when it comes to even moments of the recent past.

Don sits and the absence of applause is apt commentary on the seriousness of the gathering.

Joey says to me, and to think one of the things I always envied you, there living in the City, was, you could go any day of the week and catch yourself a derelict and broil a bum for the evening meal.

Glad you think me so prosperous, Joey, that I would have an apartment large enough to house a broiler large enough to do a bum on a spit as you suggest. I must confess, though, I have not had the delicacy you suggest. In the part of the City where I live they're seen as rodents and the little kids wanting to grow up to be accurate policemen use them for target practice, a certain failing, though, is part of this practice, since most of the derelicts are not swift of foot and are usually in a recumbent position—thus stationary targets; thus an unnatural situation is drummed into the heads of the future officers of the law; they are only used to shooting suspects when they are flat on their backs. Haven't you ever wondered how it happens so many cops are shot with their own guns?

You forget I am a policeman, Joey says.

I have never forgotten for a moment. There is no need to. You are a twentieth-century addition to that serial of Baudelaire: the priest, the soldier, the poet, and now you got the cop, who offers up his life and gets damn few takers, all the usual interpretations of futility fall down upon you and those who have given any thought to this matter.

Going on too long.

In danger of getting carted off to C.I. Got to watch out for the guys with the butterfly nets from Pilgrim State and there to stand you, against the sky, your form silhouetted behind bars, in the building rising up from the sandy wastes of the Island.

Don Kaler shakes my hand and offers me good hunting.

I am not a hunter.

All men are hunters.

I'm not.

In your own way you are. Let it go at that, at this solemn moment in the history of the village. You are in danger of becoming a City Person, jaded to all the simple pleasures of life, to the pleasure of sitting on the Mascot Dock, watching the sun disappear, watching the waves dillydally; a cool breeze as in catching a breath of fresh air.

I follow you, Don.

Nothing more will happen at this celebration. Only so much can happen before everything gets lost on the participant. A full day and night has been had by all. No sensory overload, please. Don't jam up the channels with idle chat and verbal nudges into the backseat: man to woman implied in these nudges. The other way 'round has not yet arrived in Patchogue. As to male to male and female to female, all another matter and now with the Oasis torn down: where can this issue be teased out?

A loss to the community was suffered when the Oasis came down to make way for an empty lot. You don't pay a lot of taxes on an empty lot. The wrong crowd was hanging around the Oasis. Kind of guys who swiped change off the bar top.

Not even spice to the community, Dermot is saying. You can say that about some people. They might be snorting midst the rubbish but they do add a certain touch. Makes us all feel human to be tolerant of them, but a human who would swipe change from the top of a bar! Reminds me of a man who was barred from pubs for being a bore. An increasing problem when factored into the equation with your barman's greed: wit is always on the short end of the stick—getting its nose poked with a shit-covered twig from a burnt-over tree.

If it was safe to get out of here I would. It is always safe to get away. You are free, white, and over twenty-one. What's keeping you? The dog is waiting for its vomit so it'll have something to eat.

The mayor is leaving. He is shaking, again, the hands he shook when he entered. They are still friends, always will be and always have been. So good to see you, hope to see you again. Always a pleasure and don't forget the check . . . don't worry, it'll be going to charity, a charity of my choosing.

Yeah, his back pocket, Nat is saying. Largest back pocket on the Island. And he's an honest mayor. The others have shopping carts they bring around with them, drive up to a shop and take a tour of the premises. Always something the little woman can use or resell to get something she really got to have before the sun does shine or fall out of the sky. Our mayor is not like that. As honest as the day is long or short or is it the night and something about as long as the stars don't fall out of the sky or fall down on the job. And his handsome wife.

Bernie slips me a plaque with a woman's head in profile. Underneath my name and the year   1984   (5)   (6)
HOMESICKNESS AWARD
Presented by the Patchogue Chamber of Commerce
I should cry. I cry. The tears are wiped from my eyes by. What's her name? If only I knew.

You don't have to be ashamed of showing a little emotion. You are among friends, people who have known you since the time your pants split and you had to tie a belt around your leg to cover up the split in your trousers because you didn't want anybody to see the white underpants because if they did they would nail your hide to the shithouse wall and you would begin to shrivel like a squirrel skin tacked to a board by Mr. Nellis. Something wrong because the skin never did get soft and he was saying they don't build them squirrels the way they used to.

Am I required to make a speech?

You will be called upon at the next regularly scheduled meeting, but what the hell, we're a small organization and you're among friends, so what the hell, as I have said, why not do your thing as is said or as it was and I don't mean get a hand around your thing and give it a wave at the assembled audience: we are a mixed bag but not that mixed.

Sometimes one just doesn't know where to begin or end and when to cut bait, when to get one's act on the road after spending as I was saying.

Have you sold enough of that potion so we can take the show down the road to Bellport and line up those girls who took Latin in the Patchogue Summer School: year of 1961, wasn't it, when you got the image of wealth and all the beauty which would never fill your plate, sitting right in front of you with Mr. Ryan going through the declensions, the cases, the use of the ablative, not a speck remains of those hot hours of class. Change the subject, boy, because you're dozing them off in the back rows.

I was saying I am glad to be out here in Patchogue, once again. What a pleasure it is to find the village still here, sixty miles from the City, to find you, all of my friends, still alive and kicking against the fate God dished out—am I saying this or did they get another one of those preachers over from Brookhaven? They come as a package: one to open and one to close, and in a more religious vocabulary, one to give out the invocation, another to give the benediction, which shows the lack of planning because there should be a third to take up the collection. An old joke. Always the best. Well, at least we have it down pat and are watching for variations in the telling. Not much variety in this telling; not even a smirk curls out of Nat's mouth or allows Bernie's hand to come down as a pat on the back.

When does the time arrive for the gentlemen to retire to the bar for the after-dinner drinks and a discussion of the *possibilities* of before the night is over or at least for a quick couple of hours, honorable exaggeration not taking into account the toll of years on the physical capacities of the men in this room?

I could do with a drink, Dermot suggests, and I have to go along with them . . . so can I, Nat says and Bernie says, Dick Felice says the drinks are on the house and he ain't referring to the bar but the motel his cousin has up on Sunrise. A lot of ashes get hauled between Speonk and Patchogue.

Moving towards getting what you've always wanted to get.

Everybody is standing. And if I knew why I wouldn't be in this place. I am not used to such cheerful departures. I wait for the knives to be thrown, the words tumbling from the mouth in pursuit of the person being driven from the house. Go with a curse upon the lips. You will receive a warm welcome back, didn't someone once tell me in the City. How I lived in the country. How one lived in the City. Collecting the knives embedded in the back. Nat comes up and asks what am I gonna do with the rest of the evening.

Yeah, what are you gonna do, Bernie asks.

Dermot says he is going out on the town if I can find the town and if it will support my weight.

You should allow others to complete the witticisms. You'll get the reputation about town as a man with an ear for his fellow humans, a man for the Mascot Dock communing with the oily waves and I don't mean the Italians who come out and strip the bay of baby crabs to use in their sauces. You know the kind of people. As close to nature as pounds of melted plastic topped with shredded green pepper.

Is the Cro-Magnon Club still open?

Closed down years now, Joey says. Something about licenses not being in order.

Nothing in the till to make a contribution for the kids. What does a couple of bats and balls cost.

Cheap sons of bitches, not a head screwed on right, didn't know we love our children in this village, in face of all the evil coming down the pike on the L.I.E. Hell-bent to force a nigger cock up the, excuse my French.

You are excused and what an interesting accent you have. Dermot drops his Irish charm all over Joey who can't resist and is over to the bar buying Dermot a drink, or what'll you have?

An Irish and what goes with an Irish whiskey, is it . . .

How should I know? I was just born in the place. I didn't write the joke book.

I know there's a joke attached to that. Have a rotten memory.

An English vice, if you ask me, Dermot says.

How do they memorize all those plays on Channel 13?

What is Channel 13?

It's the educational station. The wife watches it and tells me all about it. Better than watching it.

No, that's how bad it is. The kind of place that would do his version of *Romeo and Juliet*. They'd really like to see Patchogue clam-diggers as the guinea lovers.

The clammers got lost in this shuffle though there is always time. Thought they would pop out of the woodwork once I was back in the old village. Miles to go.

Have heard that one before and the one that comes right after it. Or at least I think I do. Should never have made the jump to the big time. Should have stayed a large fish in East Lake instead of being a small one in the City. Could have gone a lot of different ways. Missed the boat, train, plane, and am now waiting for the stage and there is always another one leaving or it went without anyone telling me.

What a crock of shit, Nat is saying to Bernie who is paying the two preachers. Next time, boys, get the message straight. There is an exchange about the words Bernie has used but I am not of a mind to go into it. Pick up a local newspaper in the City.

I have my hand wrapped around a bottle of ale. Have to get myself or this self through a couple more hours and then back to the City. Never thought I would miss it. Never thought I would be longing. Have to hold my tongue with the tweezers of my attention addressed to a pair of tits that walk in unaccompanied by any male protector. Am not supposed to see such things. And then connect eyes to tongue and saying in such a manner: she had a good mind and was lots of fun to be with. She has a sense of humor linked to a profound understanding of her place in the world. She didn't like tits talking for her. She would have had them cut off when she was a young woman, but, she did not want to give evidence, by mutilating herself, of reacting to all those eyeballs plastered to her nipples.

We had nothing to talk about. The weather did not get mentioned. I could not talk about the City and she was not from Patchogue. She came from Mastic. I would have talked about water problems and underground contamination. She was having none of it. I tried to talk about Europe but she said she was seeing America, my country, first, thank you. I did not ask if I knew her from some other place and she did not ask was I from around here. At the bar she told the bartender, I'll have a vodka, if you got the tonic.

Vodka and tonic, the barman said.

With a slice of lime, she replied, with mouth attached to throat, more or less, can't be more accurate because I didn't bring along my anatomical charts. A throat inside a neck on the back of which rests light blonde hair, tied in a modified ponytail. Could talk about Arabian horse tails but the color scheme would be shot to hell. No sense disturbing me because we won't have anything to talk about.

Do you know her, Nat?

He didn't and I don't think it's worth your effort.

How should you know?

He didn't and we drifted about the room. No one wanted to leave. Where was there to leave to?

Ain't it always the problem? I could throw a fire into the restaurant and have all the patrons rush for the doors and everyone will find themselves on the sidewalk, comparing notes on how each had survived: God, luck, the other guy, toughness, you call this surviving.

Here we are stuck in the village, once again, like in olden days, though the highways are all open, the trains run when they can, the water supply is endangered, the news from the City is all bad. The dregs of society have risen up and crowned their own man king. The buildings are swept with fire. The streets are clogged with the dead who go uncollected for weeks.

No, that is an exaggeration.

A couple of days the corpses wait and they are then so chewed over by bands of wild dogs there is little to collect and it is rumored parts find their way into the soup provided by the Protestant and Jewish relief kitchens. The Catholics have other ways of raising food. They have a direct pipeline to the good old days of the multiplication of loaves and fishes. No one would want to touch the seafood. Large cancerous eruptions can be seen on the sides of the fish hauled in from the river. So glad to be out of this village. At least once in a day the air is free of the smell of rotting flesh

no, a nuclear weapon did not fall and this is not some dreadful bit of
propaganda reflecting the moment of composition

but the smell quickly returns and is now woven into the cloth of our shirts torn from so much wear and tear. The shops have been emptied and the salesmen talk all day, each to the other, about what they are not going to do when they get out of the shop at 5:30. So many things not to do. It is a pleasure to enumerate them. What taste and insight they have into what is around them. Among the things they are not going to do: watch television, eat supper, chat with Emily over on Bay Avenue and Jane up on Lee

Boulevard, watch the kid get run down by the twice-daily bus that slowly goes about the village collecting those more alive than the rest. But I can't keep up with all the things that are not going to get done, all those things designed to waste one's life, when one could be down at the bay straining out edible algae, collecting strands of seaweed lying on one's back, collecting concrete poems from the bruises in the sky, as the sun goes down to reappear in a new edition in the morning, again down on the back, this time damp from the dew and with one's hand bitten off during the night from all that passion called up with sounds of the waves, the cities burning: ain't it the truth . . . but free, ain't we all free now, no longer the desire to go forth, to get away, to go away, to seek, to look because now it is all here, right here, in the palm of the hand and while some might complain about the color of the palm and the pockets of flesh looking like busted-out blisters. It is still a palm that looks so comfortable and is the only one any of us has ever really understood and are so happy.

Really, so happy: not to have to get on the train and go back THERE. Of course we must not build this up into some sort of federal case. Just we know what is going on and have less in our brain boxes to get us confused about what supposedly is really going on. Even the overuse of the word *really*, an adverb, is a sign of weakness, some have argued. The nouns and verbs should tell us everything. But it would seem a lot of other things are always on people's minds: the weather, taxes, what the guy next door did just after he killed your dog, bought some sheep to stick on the front lawn to keep the nigger-faced lamp carrier company—chewing away they did, all summer and into the winter when they got moved to the backyard.

So, I am to walk up Ocean Avenue and yes, I will get on the train, after a certain amount of time and the remaining pages will be concerned with getting back to the City, which can take some time, as you can well imagine, given the amount of time it takes to get from the City to Patchogue. I am on the train and am away. I am in the City. So that takes care of that.

Back to walking up Ocean Avenue. For some reason, left to a footnote that will get lost in the shuffle of the pages, Nat, Bernie, Gail, Dermot, Larry, Joey, even Melinda, can be seen walking along the avenue. They are not supposed to be walking. It came as a new and interesting experience. None of them had walked for any length of time since they were sixteen and found themselves behind the wheel of whatever sort of car their parents could afford to buy for them.

I can still remember, ain't I a wonder, the feel of the armrest, when I go
to shift the MGA '58 hardtop, very few of them made. Pure bathos.

  Just letting a certain class of person know exactly where I come from,
either how far I have gone, risen or sunk . . . and of course the very fact
of being conscious of the class-value status of a sportscar . . . can any of
this rival Mr. Yeats and his widening gyres, leaky boats to Byzantium?

So, they string out on the avenue like some crusade across half of Europe.
Being sold into slavery, brothels, murdered, eaten, robbed.

  A poem comes to mind and I was going to wait until the very last minute
to leave you with this poem:

Forget the Future

I left Patchogue nineteen years ago
I have been back
many times

each time,
less

Less of what? Knew someone would ask that. Just less and less. Ain't you
got a little imagination in your head?

  I got it in my prick, Nat says, every time I go for the wife. Have to have
it or I might as well pack the ship up and head for Hades. If my prick knew
where it was going it would come out the top of my head, where your
elbow is sunning itself.

  They all got a call to sort out a family in North Patchogue. Will get Joey
himself killed one of these days, caught in the crossfire between husband
and wife who are just working things out, when this son of a bitch shows
up, butting his nose in where it ain't wanted.

  Bernie has to get over to Blue Point for the dedication of these million-
dollar condos they're putting up. Sure to attract a real upscale crowd,
people who like to mess around with their own shit because the builder
forgot to put in a decent cesspool, but you know these rich people: so
afraid their shit is gonna turn to gold they like to store it up in the closet,
heard there's always the chance shit will turn to gold: look what's happened to the American dollar, turned to shit and who would have believed
it twenty years ago, so if the dollar can turn to shit why can't rich people's
shit turn to gold?

  He's a good Joe, Larry says, but he does go on. You just got to keep plugging away, Larry is saying, as he turns with a blonde smile all over his face. We all know why.

Melinda is not really there walking along on Ocean Avenue. I know this and she knows this. Would not be dignified for a mother of two to be seen now with the man who once upon a time got sent off to college with her love and who somewheres along the road got distracted and now we just say: we all drank a great deal back then.

I should get myself a Coke in Murphy's though it ain't Murphy's anymore; now the Country Kitchen . . . cold cuts to go with homemade salads for the family on the run . . . ain't no country hereabouts when shops are called Country Kitchen.

And then finally, suddenly, alone. With: why are you back here? It's obvious. It ain't, even now.

From Bay to Main Street. All the years since but it still comes back to this avenue. Or something like it. Better get the lines rehearsed. What if I am stopped for an interview by a guy from WALK:

—how did you enjoy your visit to Patchogue

—after the people, I most enjoy the scenery, the sky, the trees, the way the houses were all framed by blue sky and the way the lights blinked from red to yellow to green and back again, over and over again, the way the stop signs do not change color, though somewhere I read Patchogue has the changing colored stop signs.

I was a little disappointed with Dead Man's Hill being bulldozed down and two skinny houses erected complete with kids waiting to broil a cat on the front lawn while Mom was getting hers from the Hispanic Baseball League while Dad is in the City drunk in a Third Avenue Irish bar, waiting to go home.

A fine time was had, again, this year, and everybody went away with a smile on the sole of their shoes from having such a wonderful time didn't you, among the favorite questions when I was out to Patchogue the other day.

KIM and SANDRA are talking about men. What louses they are. But they love them. What louses they are.

TUESDAY is sitting in the MG in the parking lot of the 7-Eleven. We can assume she has been driving, as they say, around.

Spanish kids are messing about in front of the shop.

The shopkeeper comes out. A young man with rolled-up shirtsleeves. Tells them to get the fuck out of here.

Must have been an argument from before.

Fuck you, man, one of the kids says.

Guy goes back into the shop. Comes out with a baseball bat. Get the fuck out of here.

One of the kids throws a bottle at the shopkeeper.

It misses. The shopkeeper goes after the kid.

He swings the bat and misses. A kid jumps the guy and gets a knife into the guy's back. The shopkeeper staggers.

They fall upon him and knife, knife, knife him.

TUESDAY watches.

She doesn't make a sound. The kids run away.

She sits. She sits.

The man is only barely alive. He twitches.

Suddenly everything is very quiet.

TUESDAY sits and starts up the car. She doesn't look back.

These things happen. You get involved, you get burned.

Don't let 'em kid you. TUESDAY turns on the radio.

Classical music.

LAR is lying in bed.

He is listening to a man praying on the other side of the wall. Dawn is breaking. It hurts. Another day to face.

LAR rubs his teeth with his finger. He goes down the hall to take a piss. He should get going. He doesn't.

He lies on the bed. He dreams of a girl walking by a park fence. No fancy cutting: just a redhaired girl walking along St. Stephen's Green in Dublin; she is saying:

> what's the point of anything; everything has been done.
> I'm the one who is doing it
> and you'll be dead in thirty or forty years
> but I am doing it now
> so what, all you are doing is repeating what's been done
>   >CUT<

LAR walks up to Main Street. Everything is quiet.

Early morning. Very early.

TUESDAY is drinking a cup of coffee in the highway diner.

LAR comes in. We can say all this is too much to believe.

Hi, Tuesday.

On what, she replies.

You know.

Yeah, I know. Don't sit next to me. I don't want anybody sitting next to me.

LAR doesn't sit next to her.

What's happening, he asks.

How should I know.

I was just asking.

Don't ask.

LAR gets sunnyside up eggs, home fries, and a Coke with not too much ice.

That's vulgar, TUESDAY says.

I ain't sitting next to you, LAR says.

It's still *très* vulgar.

So this place is *en française*.

You can say that again. Last night or this morning I saw this guy get beaten to death. I guess. I don't know.

LAR is sopping up his eggs with the toast, sipping at the Coke.

TUESDAY is still talking   I think he's dead. He looked dead. Not that I know what dead people look like . . . not that I see dead people every day.

Really goes well with the eggs.

How do you know what I feel?

>CUT<

VINCE is driving. He is wearing dark glasses.

Something is going to happen. We know this. It has to.

>CUT<

Waitress comes over to TUESDAY asks if she wants some more coffee.

Yeah, why not.

Waitress pours coffee.

——CAPTION——

EVERYBODY HAS A STATEMENT TO MAKE

I have to get out of this place, TUESDAY says. It's driving me nuts.

What are you doing here?

Visiting.

Visiting this dump?

I grew up here.

That's a good excuse never to come back. Visiting the dump.

VINCE Pulls into the parking lot.

TUESDAY sees him. She goes out to her car.

LAR watches, back against the counter.

VINCE beats up TUESDAY. Stomps her dead.

LAR drinks his Coke.

Some of the people in the luncheonette see this going on. Someone calls the cops.

VINCE drives away.

LAR leaves the luncheonette. He does not bolt. He has paid his check. He does not look back.

What can you do when you see a corpse being made?

This all sounds heartless.

But to say anything, to do anything is an awful commentary about the usual futility.

LAR goes back to his room and rests or does he.

He can walk down to the Mascot Dock. He can go to the library on Main Street. Look at magazines, a newspaper. He has to do something. He will avoid sentimentality.

——CAPTION——

Here is the desert. In this silence everything speaks to me: and in your noise everything falls silent.   —Joubert

In the library LAR meets YVETTE. They also knew each other.

YVETTE left Patchogue a year or so after LAR.

Now we know LAR grew up here as if we didn't know this.

However, like any visit to an old place in the U.S.A. there are few people who you know, few places that shall be still there. There is no longer much thereness in the old place.

YVETTE was a musician.

She was one of those brilliant people who have to leave.

She went to college upstate for a while.

She was even married for a short period of time.

She painted her windows black and used candles.

Married to a real dipshit.

She traveled and studied in London, Berlin, Istanbul, Venice, but now she is back in Patchogue, driving a 1965 Buick hardtop convertible waiting for something to happen or nothing to happen.

Like LAR she had the "happy childhood."

She was prepared for opportunity.

Opportunity doesn't seem to have been knocking at her door.

YVETTE asks, have you seen your friend Frank?

No, is he still here?

Yeah, he works in Smith's Meat Market. He's a butcher.

I thought he was a schoolteacher?

A half-assed sort of butcher, a cousin got him the job. He's in cold cuts. He's a slicer. An appendage to a slicer.

——CAPTION——

TO COMPENSATE ABSENCE WITH MEMORY

—Joubert

Frank wanted to be a golf pro.

I know. He was in Florida for a couple years.

Why do you know so much about him?

I was engaged to him for a year. If you can call it that. I don't know what Frank calls it.

LAR and YVETTE go to Smith's Meats.

FRANK is sorting the cold cuts cabinet.

Haven't seen you (*looking around*) in an African's age.

Same here, LAR says.

What are you doing?

Visiting. Just out for a visit.

Why are you doing that, your Mom and Dad passed away—

Just visiting.

This ain't a place to visit, this is a place to leave.

Do you get a break?

Yeah, let me see.

YVETTE and LAR walk up Ocean avenue to the Pub.

They sit at the bar. The Pub is an imitation pub, imported from Ohio. LAR and YVETTE talk. FRANK comes in. He is carrying his white apron.

The boss got the rag on.

Too bad.

Yeah.

I thought you had gone to Florida.

I did for a year. Things didn't work out. It's all one season down there and the people are all the same.

They drink.

FRANK after hearing of LAR's being away quickly just shuts up. Grunts, yeah, yeah.

YVETTE says, she has go to the post office to make sure a letter gets mailed. FRANK has to get back to work.

See you around, LAR says to FRANK who heads down Ocean Avenue. LAR and YVETTE walk along to the post office.

Do you still play music?

No.

What happened?

It just stopped. I wanted so much, then it stopped, and I'm back here.

LAR and YVETTE walk back on Main Street. It seems strange to LAR that she never asks him what he does, what he wanted to do. He begins to say something but they pass the Patchogue Stationery Store.

LAR asks her what she wants to do.

I wish I knew. I thought I'd like to meet a nice shallow man, have a nice shallow marriage, have some kids and as long as there is enough money I'd be happy. What more is there, really? You get in deep. You just get cut up and spit out with your wrists shredded and your eyes bashed in from looking so much. That's all I did, looked, looked, and got bashed in for my trouble.

I know what you mean.

Maybe you do and then comes a moment when he says I don't know where this relationship is going and you're standing there all bloody and you always forget to say: where is it supposed to go, because replies are never there when you need them; they always come along too late. Just to have them waiting to use. All they do is rust. They rust in your mouth.

You're not hoeing a row, you're digging a canyon.

More like a grave.

Be honest.

I want to say, you've had enough of these people; your attention span has been stretched and there is no longer any give. You've lost interest. There isn't gonna be some awful burst of violence of humor.

——Things just go on——

There is a sour taste in all the mouths you've kissed.

LAR and YVETTE are walking to the train station.

YVETTE says she is giving him a lift. She has her car parked here behind the library. The parking lot is huge.

Some say Patchogue is a parking lot with a village attached. People get elected around here for building parking lots. He built more parking lots in the history of Patchogue than any previous mayor.

YVETTE is wearing glasses. Getting old, she says. Like the first tooth that has to be pulled.

FRANK cried when he had to get glasses in second grade.

For some it starts early.

You don't have to say any more.

LAR gets out of the car, walks between cars.

Buys his ticket.

Is that the train to the City?

Right.

Gets on train.

YVETTE gets out of the car, stands on the platform.

We will not see LAR again.

YVETTE stands for a minute.

The train begins to move. The train has left the station.

YVETTE walks back to her car.

Gets in.

Drives down Cedar Avenue.

FROM PATCHOGUE

Is not a travel narrative itself the point of departure, and not only the point of arrival, of a new voyage?   —Tzvetan Todorov

For the men who came packed into a ship moving within a resistance could see a branch of fire fall into the sea because they felt the history of many in a single vision.   —José Lezama Lima

I wiped out the village, every living thing except children because a white man had been pegged down and his mouth wedged open and then the whole village, man, woman, and child, urinated into his mouth till he was drowned.
—Richard Meinertzhagen

I have left Patchogue.

I have gone away. I will not return. Even if I go back to Patchogue I will not be returning to Patchogue. I will no longer be part of Patchogue. But then there is: come to think of it, was I ever in Patchogue?

The train takes a body (the mind follows) that is already getting off the train in Penn Station, up from the platform and walking along the passage-way going from where to where, and always a certain confusion about which entrance for the downtown subway and have to take the Broadway local because, no I'll take the express and with only one stop be up out of it at Fourteenth Street, using the Twelfth Street exit, hoping not to see a body being dragged into St. Vincent's, wondering when my turn comes and if there will be time or whether it will be like my father: dead with spectators looking on hoping for a burst of blood issuing from some orifice, rewarded only with purple face and the eventual undertaker's skill in removing this stain of death, echo of poetry there, right: stain of death, across his whole face and those morgue attendants who are either honest or just not on the job because they left the watch on the dead wrist; the undertaker getting credit for honesty by saying he found it when the time came to make the preparations for the body's final performance.

Leaving a place, the place remains like the smoke from all night in the bar, the hours required to fill the cloth with the remains of the evening. And if I said I had been to Patchogue for five hours . . . or eight or twenty years, minus the unthinking first two years of life, though I do remember, in that salty time, the going to look at houses in Newburgh. What fate preserved me from that city or sent them to take me to Patchogue, remembering that house in Newburgh where they grew corpses like Bulgaria grows sunflowers, all over the backyard, puddles of what were once human shapes, and on and on they talk in the front room of those who are now but puddles in the backyard, if what was once and what will never be again and how things change and do not change, though who has ever heard of something that doesn't change in this awful year of Our Lord;

how many years since from the last war and how many before the next; the next and the final one, one hopes, or the visit was for only the moments of this tale telling: of course you, the reader, all along, have known the secrets of this book. Every book has a secret and only one in a hundred who reads the book will get the secret and for them: leaving Patchogue or is it returning to Bulgaria all along, has that been the story to be written, finally, many years later, I left Patchogue so I could return to Bulgaria. Whatever, in all that was once holy, can you mean by such nonsense?

I care little for train schedules, plane schedules, or the reality of maps. They are how the simpleminded keep track of where they have been or as I am tempted to say: where they have not been. To travel is to stuff the eyeballs with sights. With the site of one's death. No way to keep the mind free of what it sees. Or does not see at first glance. To live forever with the second seen objects of one's desire and travel. Sounds like the mind leaked away on the train back from Patchogue. And can *you* talk about the train back from Bulgaria?

Easy. I cannot get caught out so easily. Back to where, is the easy way out. I have never said I will always be returning to exactly where I started and who said just because a book begins with page one that page one is the beginning of the book? German professors have argued that a book begins when it has entered the brain, or the heart or the soul or the large intestine. This book is always beginning because it can have no end, I WILL recognize, as suitable for what has come before and what has to come after. It is late enough. The conductor walks the aisle punching and taking tickets, armed with a nightstick. There have been incidents. And more incidents. Nothing will happen on my journey from Patchogue. It would disturb the gentle flow of the journey. It cannot be so promised of the reading of the journey.

TIME IS MONEY

In the last seat of the no-smoking car the conductor is playing a quick poker game for dinner change with another conductor and a passenger who seems to be friendly with them. It is very late at night on this journey back from Patchogue.

The smell is the toilet leaking, the conductor says. Shit gets on the brakes, the brakes are hot, the shit gets cooked, you get a sample of the Long Island Railroad dining car and never has a person had a better meal in all the days in Patchogue. Just shovel it in and chew, chew for all the worth of your teeth. The faster you get the meal down, the faster more passengers get the chance to sample the cuisine.

With no bar car it is impossible to sleep on this journey. There will be no dreams or nightmares or wandering of thoughts. As ordered as a close-marching army outfit on parade. The idea will hit with thump of massed boots, and yes, they will let up their step as they cross the bridge, doesn't matter which bridge: no lurching into disaster—they will cross that bridge when they come to it.

Bulgaria is sunny in summer. Bulgaria is sunny in winter. Except for those days when it rains or snows. And should we throw in some more weather to let people know we have actually subjected our own flesh, blood, soul, mind, and memory to the climate of that place, that faraway place . . . if one is going to ring in the romantic and send myself traveling through rough places carrying my Lamartine library upon my back, upon the back of an ass; my attire upon another beast of burden and seeing interesting things, have material stored up for years later, when in Paris, in London. To add in New York would be quite problematic since it is probably impossible to think of anything as being stored up to think about in those rooms on Second Avenue, through the window of which comes the sounds of men.

Back from Patchogue and not even a healthy fuck to remember. But was I expecting too much of a place where the men are sent over to Fire Island to fuck a dune, as the saying goes. To fuck all the grains of sand on the beach, to strike a bargain with the passage of time, to write a signature of flesh across the sands and hope no insect is disturbed at a critical moment.

Melinda, Barbara, Lilia . . . just another guy trying to hold on and the what of that holding on is what can lead . . . I missed the train. I had to spend an additional couple of hours trying to figure out what had gotten me back to this place. Had enough of this junk. Where is the hot and heavy fucking and sucking? And if you can't get us that, how about some bodies being dragged out of the Oasis? Now, I am cooking. Bodies. Exploded faces, burst chest cavities, fingers carved to the bone with broken glass. And give us another one, can you buddy? To see us through the night. To ward off the dream wife from last night. Says she is going to Florida to fuck as many niggers as she can in a ten-day period. See if she can cure herself of this longing for dark meat. Ain't it always the case, off to the

north to seek absolution in the blonde faces hurrying to stick candles in
their hair and walk from house to house carrying the corpse of the grandmother which is only taken out twice a year for an airing and a celebration
of just how long these dudes have been hanging around such a godawful
place: if I see another tree I'm gonna vomit and sail someone's face across
the tide of puke.

Broken down. Sitting on this plastic seat. I am being told by the billboards
I should be seeing a Broadway play: this evening, for sure, for sure, for
every year, forever. And my eyes have been played with as has my heart,
if I can drag in some romance from the movies as Carol Lynley walks
towards ME, of course, it has to be me, as it also happens when Yvette
Mimieux walks towards ME and then Monica Vitti is waiting for ME and
I will not leave out Tuesday Weld and maybe even Kim Novak . . . and I
could talk of the girl with the long blonde hair who dances in the crowd in
the wedding scene in *The Deerhunter,* and who will remember to look
because as I travel I have found:

> anything you want to fill in,
> is good, at such moments
>
> ESKIMO SLADOLED

Looking at the theater posters: in the City to see Richard Burton as
Hamlet, up there in the balcony so far away you need binoculars and him
down there strolling about in rehearsal clothes throwing up and catching
the skull of Yorick . . . and Liv is over in a corner of the doll's house
struggling through the English language. Everyone says she is really
striking and she has the smiling child to prove it. But I was alone. How else
could I be sitting in Patchogue. As I also sat in Bulgaria those other times
trying to understand why I had gotten off the train that first time. I could
go down the list of events programming me to getting off the train at five
o'clock or so, on a Thursday afternoon, in Sofia, already dark because the
winter came in quickly, faster than I had expected.

   As I trace back the events of the day, almost night and darkness had
fallen, so you can say it was early night; traced back to the weakness of
Medy's bladder and her need to take a wicked piss and Lilia having to fill
in for her mother in the kiosk while her mother took the piss in the
squatter of the apartment building just across the corner of the park. The
light bulb was burned out, stolen, and never replaced but Medy knew the

way (by heart) to the invisible Turkish throne from years of going from kiosk to piss and back again, though on cold days she took a pan with her and, wide skirts allowing, pissed while sitting in the kiosk: years of such imprisonment, years of working so her daughter would not have to work, those hours so long and so agreeable unlike her colleagues, the business growing only to be taken over by the government in the interests of keeping the streets of Sofia clean. She sold unshelled sunflower seeds and the government didn't want all those shells on the streets and so in the interests of pollution control, so, but for a weak bladder and the weather hadn't really turned and this was a good time for business. If the need to piss had struck an hour before or an hour later there would have been no need to seek out the shithouse in the apartment building; the procedure could have been effected in the kiosk and Lilia had just come from school and was on her way to the tram to head back to Nadeshda to begin on the homework —already wearing a blue pullover because her flesh felt the cold more than most and she had been taught you don't have to put up with the cold, you can do something about the cold. Yes, you can, much in the manner of Dutch people longing for the mountains who fly to Switzerland, fill their eyes in two weeks with enough mountains to last the remaining fifty mountainless weeks of residence in Holland where pimples are much valued as being reminders of the mountains once seen . . .

If Medy hadn't to take a piss I would have walked on into the darkness. I would have walked and walked and have since learned I was walking only into darkness, darkness and more of those tiny shops that sell parts of this, parts of that.

I stopped and asked, as I have written elsewhere, an obvious flaw, one should not mention books another might not have read. (I must be more concerned about the failure of nerve on the part of the reading public.)

I am stopped.

I turn to the mountains and see only sun-bashed clouds obscuring the distance. Ain't no mountains on Long Island unless you've heard: do you know that mountain of shit who calls himself a gentleman or that woman who is a . . . she videotaped abortions in the Sound View Motel over in Ridge. Things being what they are: closest some people will come to having baby. At one time she would have given the remains to the mother in a doggy bag . . . but this is the modern day and age.

Kill another granny and see how she twitches.

If only I had some place else to fasten myself upon. What I am stuck with.

PATCHOGUE   and   BULGARIA

If there is a person in either place who can claim to know both places
intimately, I'd even settle for a person who knows where one or the other
place is.

There should be a definition of KNOW; avoiding the sterility of facts.
To fuck a fact is to have one's cock rubbed to the elastic bone, to have
one's clit scraped off with a razor blade. Facts coat the mouth, stop up the
ears, cover the hands with callouses, and where are we?

Sitting on the bench waiting for the train, just announced as being
twenty-five or thirty-five minutes late and they do hope they have not
inconvenienced anyone and when the train does arrive the passengers will
have a pleasant and relaxing journey into the City, there to find new
worlds to conquer and bring back to your village of Patchogue which
patiently waits for one and all who have been within the village limits—
know that thirty miles an hour is just right . . .

Ain't it twenty-five within the village limits? Another fucking fact; we
might as well talk about speed limits in Nigeria as compared to northern
Finland. The piss is taking a long time.

In the shadows near Hewlett Avenue as I was standing kissing Melinda
my watch pounded out the passing seconds and I knew (how?) one day,
many years later, I would be in Sofia . . . many years later, even after the
first meeting with Lilia: I would never hear the hammering of the watch.

No insects buzz near the light illuminating the platform. If I were a poet
I would be hearing the city groaning in the faraway night. And we fall
down and are dead, dead, dead, and they look on and we see them looking
on and there is nothing to be done, anymore, finally, it is over, we are done
for, gone away, finally, forever, with nothing anymore to worry about . . .
done for, gone, finally. I could go on like this for miles. Miles, do you hear
me, ME, stuck down here in this village waiting for the fucking train back
to the City while I'm already on the train back to the City.

I should have never left. To go away is to take the stink with you, in the
nostrils, on the bottoms of your pants, in the cuffs of your shirt . . . but
something happens and you find the stink transformed into a spot of
perfume. One of those sweet perfumes girls like to wear when they are
sixteen and are leading young men around by the ring stuck through the
tip of the penis, attached to a ring woven of strands of blonde hair. A new
development, as far as I can see. Never having fucked in Patchogue, the

place is filled with an awful yearning, an awful feeling of failure, a sense I have not been made complete by my visiting this place. Just a couple of healthy gropes and spilt seed, down in the swamps worried with the possible appearance of THEM who might come from the swamps and do things to us, so got to hurry and no waiting around to see if, just get it over with and the fast slide to the ends of the summer and final leavetaking.

Going on as is. And am here, once again, in Sofia, with all the same baggage as before, as the mind has come to be called: a vast baggage room but lacking an easy retrieval system, even one like the slow and inefficient one used in downtown Sofia at the central left-luggage office.

Nothing changes. We must be quite clear about this. It would be disappointing if things did change. There must be some constants in this world of shift and change. Sofia is one of them. I do not know how to move through the sunlight of summer. I distrust the shady spots, I have been successful in finding myself always sitting on the sunny side of the tram: obligatory during the winter as a way of keeping warm: but during the summer just a reminder I don't know what the fuck I am doing. Have never known. Just going and have gone and am, now on my way back and where that place is or was, I am, at a loss. Sitting myself on a yellow plastic seated bench . . . not even a speck of graffiti, so no secret message to be conveyed.

Or. It was just another one of those days, even though I had been out to Patchogue and I was in Bulgaria, once again, be away, to be far away, and yet, she would not be waiting in either place. There would have to be a third place, maybe even a fourth place and fifth. I would go to Istanbul, this year and next, plan for Helsinki; it is a habit of mine to turn away from anything close at hand. I do not like to be touched by what I walk through, by what is reaching out to touch me. I would be a knight and am lost in the night. The armor clanking away, rusting; the flesh wilting; the heart carved up by greed and lust.

Got myself onto the train. I am on the train. There can be no doubt about this. On the train. Ticket has been punched. Receipt has been placed in holder on seat back in front of where I sit. A loud argument is underway three seats away. She is saying he is to blame and he is replying she is to blame and if only they hadn't and you wanted to, only because of you, while who do you think you are, trying to get me to, but you wanted to; I did it only for you because you wanted to have something. She looks out into the black window; he looks across the aisle, into the black window.

They are not, now, talking with each other.

Remembering, like a dummy, of course, a dummy, what else could I be, not having thrown away my address book, not having thrown away my friends because they have moved so far away it becomes a once-a-year treat to see them, to catch up, only to go apart and have to catch up, once again, in the next year with the same worry, from when young, of birthday parties and will they all be here next year. Dead in the parking lot with the crowd looking on. Dead in the bedroom while he had gone out to adjust the television: the smell of her warm shit on my arms as I tried to carry her to the toilet. She was so weak from trying to suck on the cubes of ice, her flesh just a heavy embarrassment, not wanting to look at sagging breasts, hair between legs; he combed her hair, she no longer able to do so.

AWAY, here in Bulgaria from all of that. Nothing in this country to remind me of those deaths, unless I pull them from memory and walk them like rats on a leash. Of course, I do carry those memories: I am a human being; I have tried to wash from my wrists the stain of my mother's shit. The smell never leaves, once contact has been made. I wait for my own death. It waits for me. It has plenty of time. It will not get bored and wander off to play, as is said, in traffic. Neither to hurry nor to delay. Ain't got a snowball's chance in hell.

Difficult to snuggle down into this train seat, just the wrong size or the seat is designed to keep the body erect and facing front and center. Take it like a man. Take it like a woman. Tried to close my eyes for a minute and get myself gripped by a dream, even though it has been promised that no dreams will occur. One day, one thing. One day, the other. To hold as many contrary ideas as possible. Never to commit myself or to commit myself to every idea. To be a whore with mattress strapped to back and take on all comers.

So, it can be said I am interested in the people that go away. That have gone away.

Beaten down by these memories and not a place to stick my head against and hope to arrive in the City before too much comes up and I find myself sitting in a puddle of blood. My wrists brilliant alluvial plains of blood. Anyway, on my way and have already arrived, if you have been following the course of this journey and have at the same time, taken flight to Bulgaria.

Bulgaria. Some of the most comfortable park benches in the world but not a single dream to be sought while sitting on these benches. I have posed myself as Artaud at Rodez sitting in the park near the American Embassy or behind the Dimitrov mausoleum or in front of the National Theatre, near the most interesting bar now closed and transformed into a club for junior army officers. No more lurking cocksuckers in the Bambouk, engineers just back from Mongolia, or awaiting the word to go to North Korea, to Syria. Everybody was to do one of those jobs. Like Eugene in London. Paid his dues to the world of work with ten years in the Belfast post office. They took ten years of my life and gave me nothing in return for it. Just a healthy kick in the arse that reverberates up my spine and who the fuck do they think they are demanding I go to work for them, or even use the very word. A polluted word. A brown stain on the wall never covered with the new coat of paint.

I sit in the park and have told Philip of my idea for a novel: two people sit down at a café table and even before the waitress comes to take the order the author has set off to trace how each of these humans arrived at this café table, in this city, in this year. Of course the writer cannot linger too long on this writing. As a critic writes, why spend ten years writing a book that will last six weeks on the bookshop shelf, only to disappear into the furnaces of scrap dealers in New Jersey? Anyway get those two people to the café table and have them sitting and then, back, spiraling back to the moment when Mom and Dad: sperm took to egg, and the adventures on their ways to this table where the usual interruptions for service: the order being taken, the order arriving, the order being eaten, the comments after the order has been eaten, the calling for the check, the counting out of the money for the check, the calling the waitress over, the paying the waitress, the leaving the tip, the leavetaking, or the return of the waitress for another order and the whole cycle begins again because something was missed the first time around. The conversation is repeated with care to get at what was overlooked, what was forgotten the first time around. This could go on, of course, for days.

He ain't got that sort of time. Have to keep the show moving along and damn it, no way to ease the scene to Europe. But where else to have the scene take place? There are no such places in America, yeah, I know, I know that movie about dinner with Andre, but a dinner is not a sitting at a café. God, I have fallen into a cliché as I rummage about in this idea thrown out in a conversation here in Sofia and I, alone, am aware of what a cliché I have given birth to.

On the train, sitting on a bench in front of the train station looking at theater posters, HOWEVER, what was stuck into my head by this place, then, lumps of dog shit against the base of the mortar cemented in place in front of the Veterans of Foreign Wars. The barrel of the mortar has been filled with cement, otherwise can you imagine what would have been stuffed down such a barrel: the cut-off cocks of niggers from North Bellport, collected one night, late in the summer, year before last, when debts had to be settled, lost sheep avenged, one's aesthetic sense having been offended by pairs of large lips walking along Main Street in Patchogue . . . bad enough, fat Greek ladies with photos of their children printed on sweatshirts blocked the sidewalk but those lips attached to chocolate faces: shitsmeared assholes. Cut the dicks off and what a way to celebrate Memorial Day, some might argue, but they have all left the village or never moved to the village. Or the little boy carving his initials into the upper arm of his even younger sister: her own true love and she finding out at an early age: love hurts, really does hurt and later into the City to flog her ass to the $20-a-blowjob crowd in dark corners of the garment district, an acquired taste, Spanish dick smegma, but once mastered.

Getting bogged down in trivia. You want the grand themes, the grand gestures, the flinging of soul and body into the oncoming tide, the stammering out of, never to go away because there is never anyplace to go to while I have tried to go away. Many times I have gone away. Packed the books away, sold the furniture, given away the extra clothing, gone away and the longest time spent in deciding which books to take with me on this going away. What will happen. How I come to loathe those companions of my journey when they fail to provide what I expected. Does this all ring true or are you: suspended between Patchogue and the City, between the City and Bulgaria.

Without Melinda, Patchogue would have been just the place I spent twenty years of my life, most of it unconscious. Without Lilia, Bulgaria would be just a country, vaguely passed through on the way to Turkey. Bulgaria a place to pass through, a place that gets one or two inches in the back pages of the newspapers. But now, but now

BULGARIA

and knowing probably I can find no reason for this getting off the train, for this walking along on Hristo Botev Boulevard, this stopping, this conversation, this failure to walk into the night of that Thursday in Sofia. Further and further into the night though actually, when I look back, violins, please: I had no alternative. There was nothing for me in Istanbul. Anne had been thrown out of Turkey the previous month and was or had passed through Sofia sometime around the time I was arriving. Thrown out of Turkey for doing drugs while at a summer camp for the children of Turkish army officers. But everybody was doing things like that, back then, and for Anne, Turkey had also come to an end. Any of these countries are easily exhausted, some might say. What's the point of imagining a place where you have to give the geographical points of reference? Let them sink in before the words begin to register. Just mention Paris or London, or New York, even Rome can sometimes be held up with this company as can surely Venice and people have an idea in mind, but mention Bulgaria and you get a blank stare or you get the vulgar bulgars or yogurt and more recently pope-killers (aspirant division) while a couple know about the Bogomiles but don't usually attach them to Bulgaria; they know about the Balkan Wars or they know Hemingway on Bulgaria and now, just a blank with me trying to run as fast as I can to fill in the background without turning it into a geography lesson mixed up with history, politics, and sociology—providing some idea as to what I stepped into when I stepped off the train in Sofia, that Thursday in September.

> *Travel Questions/Answers*
>
> Where are you?
> I am sleeping in Ireland.
> With a girl?
> No, just sleeping—
> the dream of Bulgaria
> far away from these rooms in Sofia.

There is a problem of attaching this travel to a quote real unquote place instead of doing the Borges and inventing from the fragments of cloth what the day to day throws up like a dog after eating too fast: came right back up as quickly as it went down. But come on now: you have been disgesting this meal for almost twenty years and the worms have had your father for ten as you write out this prose and you keep talking like these things just happened . . . well, in the quote big unquote picture the events just happened. They are now separated by years which even out every wrinkle and provide the jolt sending the eyes rolling backwards into why in a cold fuck should I give a flying fuck for your personal history . . . how many men have you killed . . . how much money have you made . . . how many people do you command . . . how many books have you published—instead, I offer up the wounds and if the camera was as easily available as the typewriter I would paste picture after picture of the scars on my fingers which I once carved with a small kitchen knife to let my central nervous system know I could feel pain in spite of what people said: you don't feel anything that happens to you; you have a computer instead of emotions . . . I don't know what it means to feel anything but I could feel the knife as it slid back and forth against the side of my finger: first, the second finger and then the index finger, then the fourth finger and, finally, the pinky for the sake of symmetry. Not a ritual of manhood but an admission: manhood had failed to grab me and I was still in that lane in Patchogue from which I should have turned and said: I was a kid, that's all, a kid, and a kid filled with more poetry than sense, filled with clouds, oozing stones, whispering trees, girls with blonde hair and this one blonde girl who was finally by my side and then lips against lips to hear the watch pounding out something.

Boy, who are you kidding, just a scheme to cling to your childhood in the face of the wasted years that are gonna mow you down like the machine gun cleaning from the face of the earth the finest and best of England's young men.

How any life, in particular a life such as your own, can be said to be wasted is beyond comprehension: idiots, idiots, idiots, idiots all of them marching along the avenue and not a glimmer of recognition of their impending fall into the ditch. But nothing happens. Nothing to string into a rosary of repentance and guilt: handmaids to poetry. So! Step out! See what the streets of Sofia have to offer the imagination. Wagging fingers disapproving of what you would like to do. That something is never much of anything. In a country of not much of anything. Just one of those days. The mud is beginning to ooze. The water is turned off in the apartment blocks.

I was walking the other day, as is my wont, in the residential districts just off Botev Boulevard and before so doing I was struck by the composition of a potential photograph. A small old woman dressed in black, sitting on a chair in front of a bathroom scale. She had a small plate in her cupped hands. The building was yellow and was the side of the Elin Pelin Book-shop. This black creature nicely centered against the yellow background. Raised camera to eye. A trolley passes so have to wait and in the waiting I notice a finger coming at me from the right, waving me off from making this picture:

Life in Sofia

I was looking at the composition. He was thinking I would use it to depict the high level of industrial development in modern Bulgaria. Or. The old woman was this man's mother and he had her out there to rustle up a couple leva to pay for her bread and cot in the kitchen where through the winter she is installed next to the stove to stir the pot bubbling away so when the kids come home from school she can say: SOUP'S READY.

> The Soviet Party makes mistakes.
> The Bulgarian Party never does.

Well, anyway, a long roundabout route to understand the presence of rice in the mousaka . . . when potatoes will see a man nicely, thank you, when it comes to that dish, potatoes are your last friend when in doubt, though I might be showing my New World origins and those origins compromised by too much Irish blood in the system, but in Ireland the potato arrives from the New World to provide the last couple of nails in the English policy of eliminating Paddy from the field of vision.

I have not yet talked of the lemon streets of Sofia, the little dark people who wash those streets. Two people working a hose attached to a tank truck driven by another dark person. Or going to the mausoleum of Dimitrov, checking in as it were, after ten years, to see if any flesh had fallen, any changes in the scene to be viewed and to feel the firm poke of the cop when I linger to see if I can see anything up those nostrils and am struck, once again, by the finger on the right hand, pointing, indicating a point, and wondering where the memos are stored giving directions to the team who put together the corpse for display: the arrangement of hands, part one, part two . . . effect to be achieved, desired, possible complica-tions, final last-minute criticism and trying to forecast any possible perverse interpretations on the part of the overscrupulous, though of course when it comes to such things there can never be too much scrupulosity: what if in some future society such a gesture might be viewed as the height of vulgarity, something only rarely encountered on the shithouse wall and even then only in the smallest letters because of the gravity of the offense in uttering these words? That finger can become an object of our study and we would always be on the alert to understand the meaning of such symbols . . . as on Ulitza Andrei Zhadanov, that finger attached, waving me away from taking my photograph and how the traffic cops sitting up in their roosts on busy street corners wave fingers at: those eyes that seem always to look up when jaywalking, just to see if the finger will appear, reminding them of their school-day visit to see the corpse in the mausoleum.

I could have been the little Bulgarian boy sent to the florist to pick up the ordered bunch of roses to leave on the marble bench to the left of the mausoleum entrance, with the other bunches of flowers remaining to wilt a couple of days then collected, always leaving at least one bunch of flowers.

The finger and I do not want any to think I am thinking of the meaning in English, when said the finger. I have other fish to fry.

Back to the City after the day in Patchogue.

Remember we are still on the train.

I am still on the train coming back from Patchogue.

Have to keep certain things straight, otherwise the whole show flies into chaos and we are left to sit by ourselves in the park, head against the back of the bench stunned by where we are.

How did we end up in this place? Bulgaria. How did I end up in this place? Probably in vain, asking this question as once on Mount Desert Island, looking down into the harbor, seeing the yachts and complaining about being born in Brooklyn . . . but at least you are alive, Mom replies, unlike your brother who only saw one day of life. Imagine one day of life after me carrying him nine months. Probably knew what was in store and cashed in his chips early.

Just stick with what actually did happen. How to know, even now, what actually did happen. I am stuck with the sorting out. And the rules are always changing in regard to this sorting out. More material is always showing up. But am on my way. Ain't that a whole pile of news you didn't expect to receive at this late moment in this tale of love lost, love gained, love misplaced? However, he was a man. She was a woman. He walked into the room. She was sitting in the room. There were paintings on the walls. There was a rug on the floor. He said something to her. She said something to him. They did things together. He left the room. She left the room. The rug stayed in the room. The paintings are still on the walls. She was a woman of ideas and he was a man who listened to a woman of ideas. They talked about ideas a lot. They had enough time for ideas and then the usual ritual of life. They were a lucky young man and woman though it was coming to the moment in their lives when they had to begin thinking about what they were to do, now, no longer that young. He didn't know what to do with the things and garb of his youth. She was worried by the wrinkles growing at the corners of her mouth. She didn't want to use makeup. He now read more carefully than before the ads for baldness. Baldness made him feel old, though living in Bulgaria once again reminded him that baldness was just one's fate.

No, he wasn't the American who met his future wife in a restaurant. He met her walking down the street, just like that, back then, and now he was still talked about in certain Sofia circles. Ain't that a kick in the head? To be talked about. While in the City he was alone. His life of no conse-quence. But of course this is true of every life. He didn't want to hear of this. He had his own row to hoe and he would be getting on with it as best as he was able.

The train ride would come to an end. As would the journey to Bulgaria. No doubt about it, any of it. He was of an age when he knew certain things and was not prepared to pretend otherwise. He should be getting his head against the park bench in Sofia. Give it a rest from where he had to live during the visit to Sofia . . . out there, Durvinitza, or out here, if he thought about it while walking between the large apartment blocks. Living out there in Sofia and coming from out there in Patchogue. Always to be deprived. Not to be in the center of things, to avoid getting hit on the head by the whirling of things, but the boredom aches into the roots of his back molars. I flee from places built up by successive waves of eyeballs and cameras. Why add my eyes to the pile the emperor's men are making, yanked from the heads of the captured Bulgarian soldiers: slimy heaps of just rubbish and their former owners are being led back into the moun-tains of Bulgaria.

Muddle, my dear friend, muddle and always the silence and never knowing for sure what one is supposed to be doing and finding out, too late, my dear, too late, and what better time to find out. I have gone off to Bulgaria and I have gone off to Patchogue. I am rooted to a single spot and complain of the roots growing from the bottoms of my feet. I feel their way through the earth, curling about stones, across underground streams. They are never so lucky as to encounter a river and there, drown.

So, alone. In both places. I would drive myself up a wall. But no wall to climb, be driven up, to find my tongue being dragged across. In Sofia, once again, to walk the lemon streets of Sofia, I have recited, to many and all, whenever the moment comes, when to explain what it was like, once upon a time; the experience has been packed up, like Christo packaging Bulgaria to be consumed by passengers on the international trains.

Bulgaria 1967

I left the train at five o'clock in the afternoon
found love
dressed in a *gymnázium* uniform
black with sewn-on white collar.
We talked and she took me to her house;
ate fried cheese and drank red wine
her mother came in later
and since it had grown colder
a fire was lit in the stove.
I told them of coming from Ireland
waited while she translated for her mother
told them of coming from America
waited while she translated for her mother
told I could stay as long
nodded yes which in Bulgaria means no
they nodded no which in Bulgaria means yes.

In the morning
after the night's narrow bed
lying together
we walked the lemon streets of Sofia
viewed the corpse of Dimitrov
went to the zoo
saw the *militizia*-guarded American embassy.

That evening we talked of going to the mountains
and of the coming years

>   not realizing
>   our love would turn in upon itself
>   we would rub together
>   two files
>   going in opposite directions.

gift for languages? The gift of pythons and hotel clerks . . . a language is like a chunk of meat . . . you wag your tail and circle around it, you're intimidated . . . then zoom . . . you dive in! you've got the heart of it! . . . by the rhythm . . . well, anyway

—L. F. Céline

Once the poem is said I am left with the ashes of experience, as I am sure other people have said. Just can't put my fist on it and crush it under the weight of my jealousy for what has come before and what will come after.

Each of these books, each of these pages has to seek the form within the word itself . . . maybe all I have to do is show . . . must flee form, seek a way through this life without form, pure response, pure reaction, one step ahead of the hammer, always awaiting us in the knacker's yard; too many Judas goats walking around, seeking to make a quick buck, turn a trick, turn a screw, light a candle, all the rest of the sentimental rubbish designed to add velvet to the mailed fist. So, I sit in Sofia thinking about my father's death this month, ten years ago, no, eleven years ago, or the years go, and my mother the previous December and toll the years back even further to my being in Bulgaria for the first time, almost proud: my ability with the language has not increased that much; I am still being held to the earth by one language. Imagine those poor people trying to flee one language only to end up with two chains about the corpse, tying it to the earth, mouth stuffed with mud, having to repeat *interesting* facts about all the languages they know: the changeable *l* in the Slavic languages, the use of prepositions in English.

Do I really want to know what you're telling me? Will this rubbish be running around in my brain box at the final moment? Like rats in a maze, or mice, since rats have been overly attended to as the years have gone on.

Two campaigns underway in Sofia at the moment:

9 IX 1944

When I arrived weeks ago they were between campaigns. A certain slackness of the spirit, I thought, but really just a lull to let the sign painters stock up for the next campaign and after

9 IX 1944
comes   the Glorious October Revolution

And the train continues to drag me back to the City. I try to sleep but
my eyes are pinned open looking at myself looking into the night, through
the dirty glass; a smear of light but nothing clearly seen. Wish there was
something to see, to fasten onto, while every second brings another
shadow to cling to and then be repelled because once one gets close to
anything . . . well, you know the story: once fucked an object loses its
interest, once packaging has been removed, once the legs open, once there
has been the explosion of, and all the rest of those dreadful clichés. Who
would want to repeat such an action, except when the fingers have been
broken, the heart turned to mush, the brain evaporated, a cold unfeeling
bastard, that's all you are, a collector of bloody sheets and tears in little
silver thimbles which you mount on a rack in your library next to the
religious books. The only relics you're prepared to admit. No indulgences
granted, save the ones towards your mental capacity.

Ah, if only a dream would occur and relieve me of this dreary reality. A
dream we could come back to again and again, with the hope it would
solve something. Every dream is only of interest to the body that dreamed
it. If the dream reaches towards poetry it might be revealing but how rare
that is, how rare poetry really is, but so many have taken pen to paper and
carved a career of reading themselves before young people. I have heard
of no epidemics of suicides passing in the wake of these poetic travelers. I
have heard pleased noises from the local bankers, innkeepers, sheet
manufacturers . . . but where is the forest of hanging bodies . . . the pools of
wrist blood, the shattered meat on the sidewalk?

To go and come back. Just further away, this time, here in Bulgaria. But
no difference, almost, maybe, I guess, between here and Patchogue. Both
are away.

Comes with looking into the night from a passing train. How long this
journey goes on and NOW: when will it end? How will it end?

And all of them will keep on living, as if nothing had happened. They
will not lower the flag in Patchogue; schoolchildren will not line Main
Street as the hearse bearing my remains passes: when's this gonna get done
so we can go home? The fire department noon whistle will not blare out

its underlining of my passage. There will be no proclamation by the mayor; he will be busy with proclaiming November Aunt and Uncle Month in commemoration of those fine people who stock our childhoods. In the Oasis, the guys won't mark my passing with hoisted glass.

With the Oasis gone as with the passing of the Bambouk both Patchogue and Sofia have lost their focal points. There has to be a bar where the energies of the thoughtful glass can be gathered up and trampled underfoot.
the Oasis   and   the Bambouk
During the winter I would seek out the Bambouk, right there next to the National Theatre, a large room with bar up front to the side, built of bamboo facing and the room continued to the back and around a little corner to where the bathrooms were: a man comes up to me while pissing and points to my cock and makes a sucking sound, *pet leva, iska pet leva* . . . I assume he meant he would for five leva or was I to suck him . . . no, I was younger then and I can only assume youth is the prime meat on the block here, also . . . but don't get the idea this was the only action. There were psychiatrists just back from Mongolia, North Vietnam. They had seen the world and it was enough for them to live on in Sofia.

Sergie was different. He said he was Russian but had lived here as long as he could remember. That he did not remember his birth was and is unusual, given that everybody in America remembers their birth as being the first disappointment in a long series of disappointments. Sergie had been to London and acquired the taste for Smirnoff's vodka; he would not drink the Russian stuff. They piss in it, is that how you say it, they piss into it, before they send the stuff abroad, laughing all the time, at those foreigners, who will be drinking my piss, to think of it, my piss will travel ten thousand kilometers and be drunk after people say *nazdravie*. Smirnoff is the only vodka to drink and so I drink this Bulgarian rum which is not good and is not bad. It does what it does which is more than you can say about most things in this country. Sergie was tall and carried himself like he was about to break into tears, in the grips of the traditional nostalgia.

I have not met Sergie this trip to Sofia. I have met him on previous journeys. But he was getting older, his hands were hungering for young flesh not grown slack from use. That is all an old man can expect, slack flesh, falling away from the bone. The hands rebel against that touch.

To find Sergie is to be a little lost. He is gone. What can I do about it? Nothing, of course. Which is nice to contemplate. To be able to do something about it.

And I have been thinking of Sonya who I met in the Bambouk and with
whom I walked.

Waiting for Sonya in Restaurant Moscow, Sofia

I would say a hundred sentences to you
each would begin with maybe
for I know the sad truth of this city
where the shove is more important than the kiss
where the heart is an inefficient reasoning machine
when compared to the party register
held by crooked fingers
in a building resembling a penis.

Every passing tree draws my eye
I am satisfied only by silence
and then I wish for a vast party
casting me into the morning
when the bottle caps chew my teeth
and I kiss, again, the pillow.

Of course I am passionate
in the manner of grass rippling under the wind
near the great house spilling its wealth into the river
where I have swum with heiresses of boredom.

My watch ticks away the minutes
you will not come
fear is the faithful shadow
our mouths are very poor in language.

Finally the waitress arrives with beer
I shall go to look for you
finding again the empty street
and what to do for a couple hours
until sleep slams dreams into my brain.

Sonya was fourteen minutes late.

And being in the Bambouk with Lilia, getting drunk and not understanding what is going on; Sergie leans over to Lilia saying, what are you
doing with this little American, when you can have someone like me or
like any of the other men in this room: why with this tiny man who is so
young; who is still eating the shit that drops from his mother's asshole?

Lilia stands and says we are going. I haven't finished my drink.

We are going.

We must go and she explains when we are outside why we are going so suddenly. He was smiling at you and insulting you to me in Bulgarian. He was enjoying himself. He is just a drunk. Like all of them.

But still I sought him out because it was interesting that such a thing could happen. Me from that country where people are always speaking, always spoke their mind and took people for how they presented themselves since most of the time there was nothing more to a person than the face so presented, so marketed with a tongue as glib as the Mississippi River.

And Sergie apologized and didn't know what was the problem, didn't that girl know we were only kidding and I told Lilia who says, this kidding, if that's what he calls it because it's a very peculiar sort of kidding that would not take place if you were not there.

How can you think I would insult a man who knows what I am talking of, when I talk about my stay in England and my liking for Smirnoff vodka, of such lamented sense in this country of theirs since I'm not Bulgarian but a Russian and there are such long memories, someday I will tell you about it and how those with long memories go crazy in this country or they grow very rich and powerful if they are able to harness a closed mouth with a long memory and yet know when to open mouth and in what manner, a skill a person does not learn but which comes with the sac of birth, is that how you say it in English, with the sac of birth brings many interesting items along together with the flesh that grows up to sit here in the Bambouk, watching the years fall into the smoke collecting under the ceiling, all so many days and not a day more interesting than the next: some days I have to drink, some days I try to fuck, and some days I have to go to work, it is all like this, weeks after week, years after year. Then there comes a time when there are no more chances and they cart you to the factory next to the meat factory and you are dead, hungry, dead, and once a year if I am lucky someone will print up a *nekalogue* and post it on walls around hereabouts and people will look and say we knew, we know this man, this one, he is dead, unlike us, and we should give him a second of thought because come one day we too will appear on a *nekalogue* while passing along to the hungry field where the meals are laid out only once or twice a year and there comes a time when there are no more friends to bring you a snack of what you have like to eat, drink, smoke.

Back to Sofia. Back from Patchogue. At least I have been to some one place which is more than I can say for most people who live out their lives going from point A to point B and never realizing that is all they are doing.

The secret in Patchogue: what exactly gets people off the scene, as it were. Death is never mentioned. It is only the long lingering lead up and then: what happened. O, he died, did you know? Nothing to disturb the nice flow of little fat people up and down the avenue, with eye peeled for the bargain, to make the day, no matter what to make of the day and be made by the day.

Sergie is one of the missing as is Sonya and Harritena . . . the missing pile up all around me and only I know where their graves are located but I am telling, telling all what I know. The mind is a vast cemetery with all sorts of graves: those that truly deserved the early grave; those who, what a shame, so young, so full of promise: yes, the promise of ruining x number of lives, if given the chance, by meeting them—all of them dead or in some sort of living death, that does not include me as part of their lives, not that I regret it, in all cases, just, so, sitting here in Sofia, so few I have known and most of them lost to the sight of myself and those dead in fact if not in reality, to me.

To walk these uneven streets, these rough roads about the carefully trimmed flower gardens arranged to spell out the name of the Party, to express solidarity, to express the undying friendship between the Russian and Bulgarian peoples, undying, in the face of history: the more a people knows of the other the more they grow to detest the other.

Going to Patchogue did not involve going to Fire Island, while going to Bulgaria, going to Sofia involved going to Albena, on the Black Sea. We all need a break, a pause to scrape the tongue.

The absence of bookstores and churches on the map of Albena provides an accurate reading of the mind of the person for whom the resort was built.

Yeah, I know.

What do you mean? What do you know?

People do not go to a resort to read or worship.

I know it sounds so peculiar, to even say that.

I am shocked in my expectation, truly bowled over by having this expectation and in turn having it insulted by the reality of this place.

All color faded: whyever are we all here? This is really a quick study and I have done a thorough job in three hours, the rest of the time is just a reiteration of what I have observed within these hours: right down to the woman stopping me, leaving a shop, to look into my bag and the man on the beach trying to get away with three *stotinki* on the price of a bottle of Pepsi, it's the little things. Another for instance: there are now three times mentioned for when lunch is: 12:00, 12:30, 13:00.

And as I was saying these resorts are built around: going to lunch, having lunch and coming back from lunch; going to dinner, having dinner and what to do after dinner. To lie down is to dream; these walls being formed up into my casket. And I imagine a man lying on a bed in a room in a resort dreaming of flesh falling a great distance to land smashed on the pavement. He does not know if it is his own flesh or a loved one. He is waiting to hear and is not afraid of what he will be listening to. It is of no difference to him whether it is his own flesh he has seen or the loved one. What can he feel one way or the other? He is in a place where feelings have been left at the gate and the checking room is quite small. Long ago feelings were drained from these people, much as blood is drained from a corpse in preparation for the exhibition just before the grave. But no one comments on any of this. It was different, he is telling himself, once upon a time, but that is the problem, it was once upon a time and not a very good time, as the song takes him along. He is alone on this bed, in this room in this resort. Any person who might be of interest to him is very far away and yet he does not ask what has brought him to this resort because he has no need of knowing the answer to the question. That answer would lead nowhere and he has little interest in being led anywhere at the moment. He is studying the shape of smashed flesh. The face is not visible, the hands are tucked under the bulk of clothed flesh. Only the shoes provide a poignant sort of moment, but then shoes always do, even in the smallest and meanest museum to display a pair of shoes is to truly display a person's once-upon-a-time presence. A cigarette case, a pair of spectacles, the man's revolver, all could belong to another, but a pair of shoes, and while he knew, well knew, never telling, if they decided to substitute another man's shoes for the ones of the man who was being remembered, to do such a thing would be to invite the most awful expectations.

To break the present time of this man: he thought there would be great piles of human flesh on display. So far he has been disappointed. He had looked forward to massive rumps, breasts, legs, chests, heads, necks, feet, arms. He wanted to see flesh rolling on the beach, along the paths of the resort; he wanted to hear the desperate sounds of these hills of flesh

climbing over each other; he wanted to swim across lakes of shit, urine,
cum, and secretions expelled from these bodies, by these bodies and so far
he has only seen the storm clouds, formed up in ranks of grey, coming in
from the sea: from stainless steel, to battleship grey, but no storm would be
great enough to wipe away what he was wishing to.

Again, he was lying on the bed in a room, in a resort in Bulgaria, but he
could have been anyplace in the world, even in Patchogue . . . yes, he had
seen the natives of Patchogue walking on the paths of the resort. He had
seen them slamming their children against the stone walls: why are you
crying, didn't we bring you all this way, just so YOU could have a good
time; what more can a person do except offer all what we have done for
you, you, the ache of our hearts, the hope of our deaths, you, who, just
want to get into the bushes and start fucking the earth.

The bed does not hold him. He wants to go out but, to come this
distance and to find, to go out is to again walk the streets of Patchogue.
With the same set of eyes in the head; age does not add any wisdom, only a
deeper sense of longing. How enthusiastic I was this afternoon when given
the chance to talk joyfully of the thought of war: of how it would cleanse
the earth of so much, and while some good would be lost, how much easier
it would be to breathe.

So to come to this place and now I am confused as to which place I am
in. It is Europe, I am sure of that. Europe, that place of *The Skin*. How few
of these modern Europeans have read *The Skin* and who know what the
flag of the new Europe looks like. Don't I remember when people were
proud to put the collected flags of the Common Market on their cars and
drive south with EU on the back of the car along with the accident of their
birth? O, how much fun a war would be . . . so much more to destroy . . .
but how would the armies of refugees be formed up . . . with so few horse-
drawn wagons and automobiles so numerous and yet so small . . . it will not
come in our day. I can talk about the obituary page as being my favorite
page of the newspaper: to think, to be free of him and him and her and her
and them, a nice batch went this morning, went the other day while no
army has clawed its way through Patchogue—there is a dreary innocence
about the place: a taking of people at face value because that is all they are
worth and all you will get to know: this month's face, and here I see people
without faces, only appetites.

Alone, of course, I am walking in all these places. To be with some
person would be intolerable. It is bad enough I have to think and then

remember and hope and long for, but to be with such a person who evokes all of these feelings, all these capacities of the human mind for suffering . . . NO, that would be . . . I could not get drunk enough to feel the sort of hangover which would best describe the feeling I would have to march through if I was with someone.

To come to the coast of the Black Sea and know that back there, back there: Melinda, Barbara, Lilia.

To come to the coast of the Black Sea, to throw myself into the water, against the waves and then back on the sand surrounded by large naked creatures vaguely described as human, only because for the most part they are hairless, but would be hard put to, no matter, to lie on the beach and remember I must be bragging. That is the only way to account for it. I can remember a feeling—from twenty years ago. Imagine that! What is he doing wrong? No wonder he is in such a place. Alone, notice, ALONE, he is not even singing a joyful song. Filled up he is with dreams of cemeteries and the corpses of young women on display . . . but he cannot tell anyone: the shape of the young woman's lips. He bent to kiss and say good-bye, for the last time, as the song sings it.

To keep going until I reach the City. That is my plan. I have always had this plan. I am keeping to my plan. Even though plans are made to be broken and the City keeps changing its name. Once upon a time it was New York. Now it is Istanbul and later it might even be Venice or Dublin.

If she is old enough to pee she is old enough to . . . a military laugh and an arse is followed out of the room with five sets of eyes glued to the moving hams. To go away . . .

And to find one's self lying on a beach in Bulgaria on the Black Sea and how about that one, gang, boy on the beach in Bulgaria meets and finds his one true love and lives happily ever after. Not likely. Not as likely as getting off the train at five o'clock in the afternoon in Sofia and walking up Hristo Botev Boulevard: she sitting there waiting for all time and I for all time stop having tried to ask in the café just before the park on Botev, and not making myself understood and there were a lot of people because end of day.

Or, as should have happened: I met this girl in high school. It was love at first sight. Later, I could say it was lust at first sight, but before we get any of the complications: love at first sight. She was two years younger than I was. When I graduated from high school she had two more years to go. I went away to college and endured years of separation from her. I did

well in college because I worked hard so I would be able to get into law
school. I finished law school and we got married in the university chapel.
Her father bought us a small house and my parents sent us to Europe for six
months with the idea that two people should see something of the world
before they settle into their lives, I know, I know, ain't this a life, yes, of
course, a life not postponed for two or for ten years. It happens all the
time. It just doesn't begin at a certain day because one gets a piece of
paper, well, anyway, she also had her piece of paper and found a job in
advertising. We lived happily ever after. Have I left out anything?
Damned if I know. A life I have heard about. I am always hearing about it.
I do not know how they live those lives. How do they face the graveyard
or the smokestack; just passing along the ideas and then, POW, the lights
go out.

There is a small mosque in Balcik, twenty or so kilometers from here,
where I sit, a small cemetery surrounds the mosque. The windows of the
building are shuttered, the tombstones lean at angles, the inscriptions are
nearly effaced, time has not had the time to wipe all mention of these lives
from the earth. No one comes to the mosque. The entranceway is over-
grown, the gate rusted shut. I should go through all the: ah, the sweet
passage of time, and I will pass away and this book might never see light of
day and if it does, quickly shuffled to the library shelf, to be, if ever, taken
down and a young person might wonder what a man was doing on a beach
in Bulgaria on 29 August 1984, with this being typed on that day, when this
man had just come back from the beach after lying on the sand for two
hours, carefully noted by watch, down on that part of the beach not
guarded by lifeguards, midst naked, no, nude bodies turning brown all
over, but he was not nude. He saved that for this room in which he types of
this day, 29 August 1984.*

Past. Time already gone and back here in Sofia to copy notes made on
the bus from Albena.

To run into the fields and fall exhausted, looking up at the sky: the sky::
there . . . as the waves are, when dashed into the sea and feeling the water

---

*Revised a year later, 1985, in New York City, typed again on 15 October 1987,
typed again on 9 March 1988, and read again on 12 July 1988 and revised again
this day in Sens, France, 25 May 1989, with corrections again being done on 28
June 1989 in New York City. And a final reading before typesetting on 3 March
1991 in New York City, and a final proofreading of the galleys on 1 June 1991.

against body, and being knocked down and feeling the great green water flow over and the touching bottom, soles of feet, propelling myself back up and looking back at the sharp white cliffs.

Locked within the centrality of the nervous system, all we can ask for is pleasure to be given and to be specific in our requests so in return your request will be specific with no limits, no dashing into the abyss of the avenue that awaits me like the nest of mere worms that is our fate, to see all those broken faces, again, NO, postpone all of that for me.

The City approaches, as it always does. It is not going away, dummy, you are the one who has been away. Indeed, I have and am still away and will be away until the cows trot themselves home to be milked and the long dissection of this experience to be swallowed up by the City and discarded. No, just buried, buried under all which makes a person forget. I am not to talk of the Mascot Dock. The hours to be spent sitting on the bulkhead looking to the bay, across to Fire Island and thus across to the ocean, to EUROPE and here now, in this city bound by mountains and filling up with exhaust, industrial pollution, and the usual pollutions of a human kind.

Where is the cock and pussy? Thought we were going to take an interesting turn and have some real people do real things to real people and then sit around talking or having feelings about those things. Well . . . a letter arrives and I break my rule . . . like signing the pledge to obey the rules; only don't know what the rules are. So many laws in this country everybody has broken several and the authorities are just waiting with their catalogs. Something like a lottery. You have won: fine, reprimand, jail, work.

A letter arrives:

I've looked through thousands of snapshots we have and there is not one of Melinda with the two children. Either she has one or mostly the pictures are of the kids. It struck me how much she plays down herself.

Read this letter in the municipal garden with the ache of watching a person slide into the grave, mourned only by: get out the umbrellas, the rain, the fog, the slippery mud, set the scene, all the usual props, into the earth and nothing left behind but the already fading memories of what her smile was like, the tone of voice, the smell when she was sweating, when the perspiration would skim off her brow. Dead, she will be, as will we all, nothing left behind but flesh to be buried and flesh that will grow weary of the memory, as indeed this flesh is already weary of the memory, though the memory adds a shade to the dread picture in bright sunlight. Me, alone, in the sun, not thinking to raise hand to sun, not thinking to walk into the shade, back from the beach through the mountains, a glimpse of graveyards, towns, dust, little boys playing with a dog in an open square, a donkey-drawn wagon with horse tied to the back, three men dressed in blue sitting in the wagon, weary, I am sure, from the whatever they have been doing.

More local color, any sort will do, doesn't matter which country. Local color is universal and applicable to any situation: drag in the drunk, pretty girl, the shy girl, the old woman with loaf of bread under arm, swarm of all-purpose flies, aching roads through tall mountains, how about a couple of skinny waterfalls, one car/truck accident, though luckily no one had been seriously hurt, the car a total wreck, the gas station that has run out of petrol, a restaurant that has cold Pepsi Cola, for a change, a loo, a john, a *yuz numera,* a toilet out there beyond the tree for the gents, for those able to stand and pee at the same time, the girls line up and squat behind a door, the flies, the sun, the dust, the green fields, the tan fields, the stacked-up tools, the broken-apart tractors rusting behind freshly painted barns, the ducks, the geese, the chickens and two sheep and a goat walking down a country village lane with their owner calling after them: PUP PUP PUP PUP PUP PUP PUP.

LOCAL COLOR

DURING THE PATRIOTIC WAR (1944-1945) THE BULGARIAN NAVY ACTS SUCCESS-FULLY IN CLEARING OUT THE AQUATORIUM OF RIVER DANUBE AND BLACK SEA FROM MINES. SOME OF ITS CREWS DO THE SAME EVEN OUT OF BULGARIA'S TERRITORY.

THE BULGARIAN NAVY TENDS TO A QUALITATIVE CHANGE IN ITS DEVELOPMENT AFTER THE APRIL PLENUM OF THE CENTRAL COMMITTEE OF THE BULGARIAN COMMUNIST PARTY. IT IS EQUIPED WITH NEW, POWERFUL CRUISERS AND ARMS AND ITS UNITS NAVIGATE ALREADY IN THE MEDITERRANEAN.

UNDER THE LEADERSHIP OF THE BULGARIAN COMMUNIST PARTY, WITH THE HELP OF THE SOVIET UNION, THE PEOPLE DEMOCRATIC NAVY IS DEVELOPED AS A DEFENDER OF THE LIBERTY, REVOLUTION AND NATIONAL INDEPENDENCE OF BULGARIA.

THE NEUILLY'S PEACE TREATY 1919 RESTRICTS THE BULGARIAN NAVY, WHICH REGENERATES AGAIN AFTER 1932. THE EFFORTS TO MAKE IT BETTER EQUIPED BEFORE THE II WORLD WAR ARE SUCCESSLESS.

DURING THE PERIOD BETWEEN THE TWO WORLD WARS THE BULGARIAN COMMUNIST PARTY, IN SPITE OF THE REPRESSIONS OF THE BOURGEOISIEFASIST LEADERS IN POWER MAKES A LOT FOR PROPAGANDA AND AGITATION OF THE PROGRESSIVE IDEAS AMIDST THE BULGARIAN NAVY'S MARINERS. ITS POSITION BETWEEN THEM GETS STRONGER AND STRONGER.

OCTOBER REVOLUTION'S AND LENIN'S IDEAS INFLUENCE LIVELY THE BULGARIAN MARINERS. ON 15TH DECEMBER 1918 THE CRUISER NADEJDA'S CREW RISES IN REVOLT.

ALTHOUGH THE BULGARIAN NAVY HAS TO OPPOSE AN UNDOUBTFULY STRONGER ENEMY—THE TURKISH NAVY. IT HAS CERTAIN SUCCESS DURING THE BALKAN WAR (1912-13) ON 8TH/21ST NOVEMBER, 1912 BULGARIAN SHIPS UNDER THE LEADERSHIP OF COMMANDER DIMITER DOBREV ATTACK THE TURKISH CRUISER "HAMIDIE" AND TAKE IT OUT OF ORDER.

THE MAIN EVENTS OF THE HISTORY OF THE BULGARIAN NAVY, ITS MILITARY AND REVOLUTIONARY TRADITIONS, AND ITS LONG-TERM FRIEND RELATIONS WITH THE RUSSIAN AND SOVIET NAVY, ARE EXHIBITED IN THE NAVAL MUSEUM.

YACHT COR CARROLI WITH WHICH THE BRAVE BULGARIAN SEAFARER CAPTAIN LONG VOYAGE GEORGI GERORGIEV CARRIED OUT FROM 20 XII 1976 TILL 20 XII 1977 THE FIRST IN THE HISTORY OF THE BULGARIAN NAVIGATION SOLITARY SAILING ROUND THE EARTH. FOR THIS EXPLOIT HE WAS AWARDED THE HIGHEST DISTINCTION. HERO OF THE PEOPLE'S REPUBLIC OF BULGARIA.

DURING THE BALKAN WAR 1912-1913 21 NOVEMBER AT NIGHT TIME THE SHIP DRUZKI FROM THE DETACHMENT OF THE BULGARIAN MINE LAYERS TORPEDOED SUCCESSFULLY THE TURKISH CRUISER "HAMEDIE." THE FEAT OF THE SAILORS FROM THE DETACHMENT IS A HEROIC PAGE FROM THE MILITARY HISTORY OF THE BULGARIAN NAVY.

The Navy Museum, Varna

Gone. To get the show on the road. To get going. To go. Again and all the rest of that. Leave it all behind even worrying about it and where and when. Tears are made of air. We breathe them. They either taste of roses or burnt hair.

Where is the human life . . . the drama . . . the conflict, the tension, the bloody story . . . right here, before your nose and I know where I would like my nose to be, not heading out into the world, out into the street. To go away when one has only arrived, really only arrived if one is looking at the BIG PICTURE.

No, I have not arrived in the City . . . even if the name of the city keeps changing. I am still on the train somewhere between Patchogue and the City. Penn Station ain't going nowhere. And I will not sit down at the entrance to Penn Station, just behind where they sell *Newsday* to the Long Island-bound commuters wanting to keep up on juvenile rape and crab-grass, get the tirades down right, nothing much playing at the movies, tonight, again, dead, why don't they make movies like *Town without Pity, A Summer Place* and dear, what was that movie with Troy Donahue that all the kids were talking about even though most of us thought Troy was a real scum drinker, a real jerk, not with the kids around, I know dear, but that is how they talk and I am just trying to get eyeball to eyeball with their ears if you follow the first metaphor. Those voices. Am chased about in a small room by those voices. Only on the Island would you have to say: I am sure they are decent people, I just don't want them messing with my crabgrass, though did you see, Dick Felice paved over his front lawn and painted it pink and green, must be the Italian national colors . . . but a good idea if you ask me . . . pave the front lawn and then pave the back lawn and then start paving the living room. I am in Sofia. I will be in Istanbul and I will be in Venice.

Only, *I am in Sofia,* is true—the rest is potentially true as is the going to the City. Am glad for it with the sun rising, Vitosha obscured by cloud and this sexual congress with actual baggage, a lot of sand in the crankcase, can't be fun for either party but gets you over to the other side. When and where. Have my sign downstairs:

DOES ANYBODY
WANT TO go to
TURKEY in September
See Thomas McGonigle
#304

They haven't been lining up at the door. I am to go on alone. Too much sentiment clogging the narrative veins. We want to be swept up by the force of the story and all the local color. Well, you already know the business about the Bulgarians shaking their heads no when they mean yes and the other way around when they mean no: local color, Hapsburg yellow, though the Hapsburgs didn't get their mitts into Bulgaria.

The purest melodrama. It would begin on a Sunday. The last Sunday of my visit, this year, to Sofia. I go to Nevski Cathedral to hear the choir. I stood toward the back so I could see the choir as they leave. The music comes in waves, and is answered or the other way round by the priest. Candles, three lit candles for myself and the other people in my life. I watch the man as he plucks the nearly gone candles from the racks to save himself the bother of carving out the stubs from the racks, as fragile, as transient: our wishes that come from our hearts—starlings. Some sort of poetry is called for.

Harritena will come down the stairs, rest or stop at the first landing, will she see me, no, probably not as she will not be looking, and continue on her way. This is ten years later. She will continue down the steps and will go up to a man holding the hand of a little boy (girl). She will take the man's arm and pat the child on the head. The child will carry my face.

You are my second mistake. Last year there was a Swedish boy who said he would. I know you are already, it is my mistake, this time, you are my mistake. I see my son (daughter). I step in front of the happy family.

Dobra den.

A cold night on Vitosha Boulevard, and back to that cold bed after the night of drinking in the *dola mexhana* under the Balkan Hotel. I remember even drinking some sort of chocolate liqueur. Will you come back?

I will have to leave very early.

And into the dark morning.

I went looking for her apartment in Ulitza 8 Mart but couldn't find it. I have still not found it. I don't think it ever existed and they have changed the map of Sofia so many times with the new blocks, the new complexes; it's a forever new/old city according to the tourist leaflet, Sofia, 1983. *Dobra den.*

The eyes still as luminous, tan. Never have I seen; the rest of her has changed, she has added ten years, I have lost ten years off the top, my face continues up my forehead.

I was looking for you, wrote to you and I knew you said you wanted to become a nun and go to Rome to study with Boris Christoff and I supposed that you had.

I went back and forth to America all that year, spending my patrimony.

The choir came down while the priest gave the sermon. I watched and the choir returned and came down again at communion. I watched. I saw no one I knew and I was not seen by anyone who knew me. I asked or began to ask a man, *azim govori malko Bulgarski,* he waved me away. I saw no one and was seen by no one. I had stood there over an hour and a half. I left the cathdral and walked along Ruski Boulevard to a small garden, sat and knew: years had gone by and part of my past can only exist as words, written down on the page, and any meaning will be contained in the quality of those words.

Yeah, a lot of local color could get shoveled onto the page for this city: ISTANBUL.

From the little boys selling ice water, to the man wearing slippers on his hands, hopping along on the remains of one leg, that leg cut off halfway up the thigh . . . or the, or the . . . though I am more a prisoner of seventeen years ago when here for a couple days I decided I had to go back to Sofia . . . was living over in the old city, down the alley of the shoemakers. Now I am living almost across from the THY bus stop, down from the American Consulate, down from the Pera Palas where there was no room in the inn and I am here in this room, with a noisy elevator that rattles the window, with a door that has a glass upper panel, letting in the hall light all through the night, my legs spread about the night table as I type this. I pick at my underpants and imitate the Turkish men who are always picking at their clothed part as they walk along the street; either the underpants are too tight or they are just making sure IT is still there, since the last time they looked.

Crossing Galata Bridge last night in the dim light a man tapped me gently on the breastbone and walked on. I don't know what it means. Some sort of blessing or curse . . . to think of a curse would be adding . . . a blessing.

I add this city to the list of those I know my way about in, generally, that is, about the streets where tears are ashes clogging my eyes.

To travel alone is interesting but no fun. I thought I was going to hurl myself right into the flesh markets and extract the maximum number of words from the experience . . . the iron gate is still there, the two bored cops are still there. Younger this time, of course.

He's taking his shoes off, he's only looking . . . the hysterical female American voice is explaining to the guard at the Yenni Cami . . . the man with his shoes still on, standing in those shoes at the entranceway as opposed to watching and seeing you are supposed to have the shoes off before you even step on top the entranceway. To walk across the carpets in stocking feet . . . the immediate intimacy with the mosque and then thrust deep into the person the obligation to find a place to kneel and recite the prayers . . . only to face in the required direction . . . to recite the prayers. It is the taking off of the shoes. I am sure a Moslem will smile at my reaction, tsk-tsk another one of them, and this individual will get the walls of Vienna hurled back in reply.

Of course in Hagia Sophia I made note of the portraits of Constantine and Justinian done during the reign of Basil II Bulgaroctonus, the Bulgar Slayer.

Remember the hill of eyeballs and the blinded captured army being paraded before the Bulgarian Tsar. A Balkan tourist bus pulls up in front of Hagia Sophia to pick up a party of German tourists just down for the day.

It is all back there . . . no, trying to discover again, in words, the feeling: lying in bed in Sofia, realizing I was going to Istanbul and could see on a map, how it was all very far away, and every step back now, is like the train slowly moving towards Penn Station: you have been away, but, so, what.

Yes, I have been away. Things have not gotten better, but that has probably been said since the beginning of time. As the body ages the feelings: I have been away. Very far away and I would stay away except

I am said to have a home, now, in the City. Rooms I walk through and that are called home for me, by those who know me. In Istanbul I do not know a single person. Not a single person knows me by name. The hotel clerk knows me by my face but does not remember the room in which I am living. I have not sat and watched Turkish television. I am living in the new city, so-called. Last time I lived over there in the old city, the place where all the then "hip" people used to live and want to live. I walked those streets today and washed them out of my pores in the baths, had them scraped off my flesh.

Back then it was a time of drift. Back then it was a couple days deciding whether to go back to Sofia. Back then there were all the people from the Peace Corps . . . we were all young in those years (punch the jukebox, again) . . . in our early twenties and Istanbul was a place to get drunk and plan to go to Troy; I did not go to Troy preferring to stay in Istanbul with Jim and staying drunk for days it seemed. Then, I had to leave and go on to Greece. And they:

> Jim is in Alaska studying how languages die,
> Don is in Sweden teaching English,
> Anne is living in England, the mother of
> three, cultivating a garden and once in a while some
> prose pages when she can find the time,
> I am in Istanbul.

I walk the dark dismal streets, where Chénier lived, the alleys, pathways about, below and above the Galata Tower. I go down *there,* again, the streets with the shop selling Turkish music cassettes: at least they ain't blaring rock/roll or disco . . . a sense of who they are unlike our Bulgarian friends who disco to the song "Suzanna." Now there is a place that is very far from, very far away, farther than the City, further than Patchogue.

We are now in the Free World. You are not reading an ironic statement. Give yourself five weeks in the People's Republic of Bulgaria. See if, then, you can read irony into that statement. Not to be known or to know a single person. Living in a hotel for Turks and Arabs. Probably the only European. Or at least I think so. All the rest of them are where the guide books tell them to be. I look into the lobby, rather, the entraceway of an apartment building: the small yellow light bulb. Of course I imagine: Barbara, Melinda, Lucja, Lilia (why don't you say you imagine being there along with the kitchen sink . . .).

I make my way about as best as I can. I try not to drop dollar bills all over the place. The moon is nearly full. Early Friday morning they will kill sheep in honor of God holding back the arm of Abraham who was about to stick it to his son . . . what was the son thinking about . . . this son was in Istanbul seventeen years ago and is still living within the same problem. No reason to stay and no reason not to stay. To go back so that, probably I will never be forgiven for this long journey. Why did you go away? You know I cannot share Patchogue with you, or Sofia, Istanbul, Venice, Dublin, so why do you ask and you tell me you hurried back because you knew I was waiting, why did you go away in the first place?

I did not go away. I was sitting in my room and the room has never left me. I am walking along St. Marks Place waiting for the knife to claim me; along Eighth Street or Second Avenue or Fifth Street or any of those other places, streets, not enough space on the pages to list all the possibilities where death or maiming can sway, the cutting off of my life by some kid who couldn't care less, some nigger, spic, some pastry-faced redneck, who don't even got himself a red neck.

Yes, the train is still moving. I am sitting in Istanbul mourning my arrival in the City. To begin again the long complaint, the usual complaint. For a couple hours I have been away from it. In the years since, the tourist industry has cranked up x number of bodies and sent them forth to ruin. Once upon a time blonde hair turned my head—now it turns my stomach because the brain box framed by this hair has laid itself open to every slimy idea loose upon the world and allowed them to set up home within: complete with built-in ice cube maker, carpeted ceilings, pastel plaid scumbags, and an electric drier for asshole.

And if it is another seventeen years before my next visit, a change of mood you will notice, a hint of optimism, seventeen years, another visit, I will be going on fifty-seven, my life nearly at its end, if my parents are to serve as a model, possibly dragging along some awful child who will not want to be here, I could probably sell him or her if there is still a market for white children, so I will be in Patchogue and trying to imagine being in Istanbul, the streets getting ready to receive the blood of the sheep, to see the hard brown eyes under the visors of the riot police and the cold eyes of military patrols that return not with disinterest my close looking at the submachine guns, by then all this will have been a, by then, the dull ache of so many, more, more, of course more, what with seventeen more years, botched chances, and lost opportunities, so called, I will say, to save you the trouble, every end is a beginning, runs the song being sung down by the bridge, as they haul up the corpses . . . an electricity failure just when things were getting interesting.

No one was at Hagia Sophia, of course. There had been no letters in Sofia. No one knows I am here. No one knows where I am. I am not hiding out because I always know where I am: days from, hours from, no, minutes from the City.

This goes back to a time in Dublin. Dick, Susan, and I were talking about the accidents of friendship, how we hoped this would never die. What was this?

That summer, what summer, already ancient history as far as anyone walking around could recall, 1967, before I left for Sofia, after Teresa told me she didn't think she could travel to Yugoslavia, after the break-in at the rooms off Dame Street, a break-in and all they got were some records, a penny collection, leaving typewriter, record player, took the Turkish record, a record of Fugs tunes. The break-in was the end of Dublin for me, the final reason to get the, might as well just go, this was long after Barbara. Susan and Dick still lingered in Dublin, with no place really to go. Then I was the one to be actually going on, getting his shoe on the road and we sat around in those rooms in that building, what building, getting scarce with the details and you being a detail man, an attic room in Fitz-william Square . . . Dick said, I'll see you all in ten years in Istanbul in Hagia Sophia and I said I'll see him there and Susan said she would be there and at this moment of my actually being in Istanbul I can't remember the day when we were supposed to be there and Dick has told me and Susan remembered the promise but Dick said, Where were you, I waited . . .

You did?

I did and no one showed up not even yourself.

If I had remembered the day . . . parts of Hagia Sophia are roped off as repairs are done; Germans are having their pictures taken . . . last time was a grey, rainy day and no one about except Anne and myself and she showing me recently revealed mosaics that had been recovered, I didn't find them this time, I got there too late in the day to go upstairs.

I have not seen Dick since the year after the promise to meet in Istanbul. Susan lives in a district of London where there are few English people, with an Irishman who has kicked his heroin habit except for the odd touch-up, once in a while.

To think Dick was in love with Susan and actually wrote her an original poem! His usual habit was to copy out an old poem and sub the woman's name for the name of the originally intended victim. For Susan he wrote a poem: eyes, canal, vines, trees, you get the picture. I went to the Trinity Ball with Susan; she had eyes for other men. She always has an eye for the young man. For the one man who could abuse her in the best possible fashion. And I am here with the fate of having to go back to the City to mourn my short visit to this city, to mourn my fate in returning to the City, to be captured, again, by the City.

In the Turkish naval museum there is a model, a painting, and relics from the cruiser *Hamidie*—last encountered in the museum for the sailors of the People's Republic of Bulgaria, even a plaque in this museum for the men lost when she was taken out of action, a whole room of plaques for men who have gone, a whole case of mug shots of young men who. The world is made coherent by such details.

Travel narrows one down: | arrival | departure |
eating	sleeping
seeing	not seeing
friendly	unfriendly
loneliness	enjoying being alone

I walk through this city in preparation for the City. I am alone. I do not have to package it, moment by moment, for the other walking with me. There is no one walking with me. It is difficult to do a comedy routine in an empty, save for myself, hotel room. What if laughter started to come out of the sink, rise up through the drain clogged with piss-soaked clumps of hair?

The Galata Bridge moves with the tide and the movement of heavy vehicles. I feel a little queasy when I leave the bridge. The cucumber sellers, the bootleg tape cassettes, the ice water, the grilled fish, the mussels with a slice of lemon . . . a German couple taking a picture of the mosques, the Polaroid portrait maker. Then under the congested inter-section, up the hill, a man with legs trussed up like a chicken, slippers on his hands, pads on his knees, him begging with a cup suspended from neck. He looks at me. I stop a bit down the street, pretend to look into a window of electric fixtures; he looks at me and I feel I have violated him. He is not an object of curiosity.

I feel my face wrinkle, cock shrivel—top of head become a plate of sunburnt flesh.

> The international language in 1269 B.C. was Akkadian.
> The international language in 1984 A.D. is English.

I can feel the City getting ready to pounce and eat me alive, as is said to happen to people who arrive fresh from the sticks: it gobbles you up and if it doesn't spit you out in a couple of days you end up coming out the other end: a tight round pellet of shit, with all the attributes, strengths, weaknesses of a pellet of shit, rabbit, most likely, since the rabbit seems closest to man, don't know if I can swallow all of that—this business of a pellet of shit, this business about a rabbit being like people—too many years of reading, rather, looking at *Playboy,* a round pellet of shit and no place, finally, to call home because the famous bridges have been burnt and no one knows who you are anymore, you don't come from a village in Anatolia, you come from a village on Long Island, near New York City, a village in a county which now has more than a million people—the county, dummy, not the village, not even in America do they have million-citizen villages . . . though you remember Denis D. saying Dublin was the largest village in Ireland, and Dublin got itself more than a million souls, all striving to be saved.

A quick love story: meeting, talking, fucking, some more talking, leave-taking. Can throw in a little bit about the past for each of the bodies. One of them can die or one of them can kill someone and the other has the problem of what to do: Dear John   Dear Mary.

Each person is given one love story. Usually it doesn't coincide with another love story.

That first sight of Melinda in a hall of Patchogue Senior High School has propelled me through, and of course she said she was in love with another. Could probably set it to music. And she was still in love with another a year later, probably another the following year. Was visiting Jesse from Tanzania and met Barbara who was friends with, I don't even want to, again, remember that whole story, and to taste the pleasure of her body, to be touched by pleasure and not to know what to do. So saying: why can't you talk when it was I, struck dumb by the pleasure. Back from EUROPE, again, in Patchogue and Melinda was either at the end of or between so we walked along Main Street and in a dark spot near her street we kissed; I could hear my watch ticking, as I have said, well, that summer, like a

Danish movie that never makes it to the States, I went off to Wisconsin and the following May I came back and I wanted to be taken up by, to be swallowed by a vision. I was demanding and I got a secretarial student. Melinda went through a tough time of it, there was a Danish doctor who did not return her love; she followed him to France and she came back speaking badly of France, she broke her leg in a boating accident and married the first man who was nice to her. He didn't know what to do with Melinda; he installed her in the kitchen. He was a simple sort of fellow, a country bumpkin type, it couldn't have worked out; they were from just different worlds. Melinda had eaten escargot; this guy was a meat-and-potatoes man and so she met NED, who is old enough to be her father, much married, a lover of his own voice, a man who knows a nurse when he sees one, who can feel the age in his blood, and she has good genes and children will be a solace and who ever heard of a woman packing her bags, the bags of her two children and leaving the father of those children, that man who was to make up for her first botched marriage.

(((((Dante and Petrarch were spared this sort of end to their stories)))))
Barbara who I thought to be the older woman turns out to be only a year older.

a little story

I was in an Irish bookstore in New York City and noticed a book by a man named Jonathan. It struck a, is *bell* the word?—Barbara had an older brother who had gone to Trinity; she did not go to university. I forget why and if she told me. I wrote to him at two addresses, a home address supplied by the British Information Service and to the school listed as being where he taught, asking him to forward my name and address to Barbara if indeed she was his sister. A month later a letter arrived from Barbara. She remembered me, but not that clearly—but she did remember me and so we wrote back/forth. She is now married again to a man who works on a Dublin newspaper. She has two children; lives in the Dublin suburb which has an itinerant problem. She, the husband, and daughter came to America during the summer to visit her brother-in-law near Boston. They were in New York for less than a day and Barbara was too shy to telephone. AND you are probably right: I did not run into either one of these women on the train coming into the City. I have not

run into them in Sofia. That was another story. Choirgirls and all, even a
wife in that city, I did not run into them in Istanbul and I will not run into
them in Venice. They are both safely living in the places God carved out
for them, or at any rate, where they are living when I last heard from them
or of either one of them. Wouldn't it be nice on the last day in Istanbul or
on the first day in Venice to run into someone totally unexpected: totally
unprepared for by means of foreshadowing far back in the book, a way to
get it off the hook without having to drag in references to piano wire and
films made for the delight of Der Führer as unlikely as it would be to run
into Barbara in Jamaica station as I change trains for Penn Station.

I think I have to or did I change trains at Babylon. It doesn't matter. I do
not have a suspect political intent in these pages. No one is going to get out
the Long Island Railroad timetables and check, exactly, how long this
journey is supposed to take and how many pages are being rationed per
minute of that voyage back into Second Avenue where the man with shoe
on his head is still entertaining the other drunks down the street from the
pint liquor store where the fat Oriental stands. I am on duty. I have
attempted to even go zen on you and try to let go of the idea of meeting
anyone, or even being conscious of the actual letting go of the desire to
meet someone. I know enough people in New York. Lilia is hot to trot to
Algeria and Tunisia. What more can a man desire . . . glad you asked,
never thought you would be getting around to it—in Istanbul airport I
begin talking with this . . . that's another story and I don't mean to get away
from the point of the story.

The Galata Bridge is dim. Fitted out with shadows and low voltage light
bulbs, not bright like in Paris, yes, the city of lights, I know, an hysterical
shriek: an American female has tripped over a little boy who picks himself
up, dusts himself off and walks away: the American man is saying, it's
okay, dear. I wish this did not happen. Sounds like it was planted on the
bridge for my consumption.

That dark bridge and the faith on display. No knife comes probing out
of the dark looking for a liver or kidney. The orange moon out over the
sea, the lit-up Topkapi, the ferries loading up for the late night crossings to
Asia, not as romantic as it sounds, or it is as romantic as it sounds. Yes, this
is a romantic place. All the places one would sit if one was with someone.
What splendid places for an argument to be hashed and rehashed for years,
begin with bodily irritations, something at supper not agreeing and then
right for the jugular: your life has been a long and consistent slide into

mediocrity, and only you don't know it and only you will never know it because the mediocre are incapable of the slightest self-critical thought, on to the color of the shirt, shade of nail polish, and that watch, that belt, that pen you carry: are you supposed to be the new Goethe? Are you in the running to become the Helen of the Blind because only the blind could find you; my heart is not in it.

The man in the wheelchair who sits near the fishing boats in front of the ferries to Haydarpasha is gone; he was there this morning and afternoon and he was there last night, asleep, with his one leg, that one leg swollen and wrapped in bandages, all these missing legs, I am sure there is a fantasy there: the fingers in Sofia, not missing, and the missing legs in Turkey.

A male city to be sure. Women are present only by their conspicuous absence, in the beer halls off Istiklal Caddesi, thousands upon thousands of men and the only woman is the accordian player who is, for one more time, please, but only a person from Patchogue would note this absence or presence, depending on how you want to cook the dish, as I will observe the absence of men on West Main Street in Patchogue in the middle of the day when the street is filled 'with shopping women.

Skipping about, a last night, sitting in the outdoor tea garden, no, grove of trees, all the trees painted white to chest high, the men are involved in loud *tavla,* dominoes or a game similar, I will not understand with my thirty words of Turkish and most of those numbers, which have to be recited from *bir* to *on* to get the one I'm looking . . . maybe couple more than thirty but not many . . . it is of little matter at this late moment, in the morning as I fly into my fourth language, Italian, and on to Venice: dreamy photographs of canals, bridges, collapsed palaces, German faces blocking the view of a plastic gondola revolving which when wound up sings "O Sole Mio."

Can hear the photo album being riffled for the appropriate picture by which to begin the final assault on Patchogue, fortresses built, cutoff points well established, no one is coming anyway, but just in case: any time now.

And to live in the hope the catastrophe will come within my lifetime . . . this ultimate assault on the down walls, it should be easy, not much to climb over: either they are bent waiting for it up the, or sitting legs apart.

And I would drag to mind the words of Herodotus . . . travel does get us to get out the travel books, the old ones, the old history books . . . back when there was Xerxes going on:

> I was thinking and it came into my mind how pitifully short is human
> life, for all these many thousands of men not one will be alive in a
> hundred years' time

thus this guy was going on back in 480 B.C. as he was watching his army
cross to Hellespont.

If time could hurry itself along a little. I seem to be in mourning most of
the time; to think as I watch this old couple, how short was the appearance
of my own parents on the face of the earth, and myself, now, nearly forty
(actual age at publication will be forty-seven) looking out from a Turkish
airline jet as it works its way up the coast of Italy for Milano, away from and
towards the City, you can always be sure of that. No longer any barbarian
hordes: a vigorous, many-manned powerful force that will rip out throats,
carve off ears, the Turks are coming, rub faces raw along the pavement . . .
I can't get that old one-two one-two—these kids smack you in the kisser
with their designer faces, feeding their faces, their bare shoulders, their
haircuts, the music jerking their heads from side to side, just more images,
more pictures getting fed into the memory bank and it spits back a couple
feelings: take your choice as you will—it doesn't matter much—any will
do . . . it's how we will get you along the pavement . . . into the large public
garden in the center of Milano for a breath of air and looking at the Italian
money which comes with a notice: it is illegal to try to make copies of it.

The machine slows down. No one at the airport to meet me. Telegram
had been sent. Yes, just before the Bayram, just when the telegram should
not be sent. To be surrounded by the soft American voices out for a breath
of air in the gallerias: Oh, you got one of those pretty coins again. In the
train station, *the ship* is no longer on display. This was the model of the Da
Vinci or the Michelangelo, guess someone, so my story would be dated if I
said: *I'll see you at the ship.* I thought of that as a story, met at *the ship* and then
into the large station café for a drink though all the chairs and tables are
outside the glass walls and just an empty space to walk across to the bar, the
cashier off to the left, doesn't look like the setting, to these eyes, out of
which DRAMA can be born. Not wanting to get back, not wanting to
arrive and what will I have to say about Patchogue. Was there a good
story? Lots of course, almost more than I can remember, a series of back
rooms with special trays fitted to the beds for those who planned to open
wrists and lie there, under low-wattage light bulbs blood filling the tanks
to either side of the bed. Back and then what to do for an encore.

To be free of the blonde faces of suicide. No blonde faces any longer in the dirty window of the train as it moves through the night, as they always do move through the night, as is this train from Patchogue, on the way to the City. Shouldn't there be a reference to Augustine's city? There is in the very absence and in all the cities to be built on hills, to be built in valleys or at the end of the road, or on an island where all the good things are to be found with no limit on the number of aspects to what is considered to be good.

I had been on Büyükada and, walking down the narrow streets between the great wooden houses, was struck: ain't it always the case; and not by a taxi thus ending probably on the right note, this narrative or it would have to be ended by an editor, one of those sad friends who took on the task, out of friendship, out of the promise . . . as well kept as my thought once to do a little book of John Currier's—him dead now how many years and not remembered by: who remembers JOHN CURRIER?

Was walking in Büyükada and struck by the thought read in the guide book, there's been something to report from this island since the year 500 and the island is still inhabited, still livable, still pretty to walk around on . . . a new soccer field carved into a cliff just up from the sea, close enough to the sea that a well-placed out of bounds kick would land the ball into the sea—all those years gone and still people could and do live there. Patchogue has only been around for a little more than a hundred years and Suffolk County in which it is situated has been there for maybe three hundred years; people have been here, people as opposed to Indians—you did not get that assumption, I hope, well, it is only since the War, the Second World War, Korea was a police action and Vietnam was just that, Vietnam—has the place filled up and it has within those years made itself unlivable . . . it is a place to go forth into and carved a wide swath with a long blade . . . it is a place where people can kill each other with quiet and efficient pleasure, but to live together, to have one's eyes confronted by the surroundings: you got to be joking . . . only a poet of the Abject School of Poetry could find an object to praise on Long Island, maybe I'm talking about a long apology for wanting to die. That is what Patchogue is the capital of: wanting to die and as soon as possible, please. The card, gentlemen, please.

A fourth language for my ears and again the difficulty of how to count, say please, thank you, give the time of day/night, I want, how much. At least in Bulgarian I can get through all of this with some degree of competence. That little out of the way dead end of the one language on my tongue. However, to learn another language is to learn about impossibility, again, and who needs to get the same cold portion of soggy corn flakes two days in a row?

Italian comes dressed in an interesting package: Saint Siro in bishop's vestments, mitre, gloves, and slippers all about bones, in a glass casket behind an altar in the Duomo in Pavia which was not originally on this path back, have to be flexible, as is said.

DESPERATE?
DESPAIRING? SUICIDAL?
No one to tell your troubles to?
Ring the Samaritans ·
Rome 678 92 27, (4:30–10:30pm)
(24-hour answering service)
In complete confidence
No one need know you called.

IN LOVING MEMORY of young Jean Seberg in her moving interpretation of " Saint Joan". On the occasion of the 5th anniversary of her death. Sincere appreciation to authors and artists of the National Theater, London for outstanding production "Jean Seberg" and to Frances De La Tour, for the brillant revival of the role.

So flexible I have ended up in the Villa Paradiso in Padova. Could one have planned such an ending? Even Ezra Pound didn't get around to writing his paradiso. The old-time failure to cohere, as he would have it and walking this early evening through the district of Venice he loved, Trovasio—I could almost imagine . . . would be pushing it . . . at least felt myself the only person to be thinking of him at the exact moment; his example was being followed, this the fifth time in Venice, came in by train from Padova and directly went to the Lido to swim and surprised at how expensive, how shallow the water is for so far out, the tiny broken clam shells, then, the greed of the Gran Viale S. Maria Elizabeth with the self-service restaurants serving up warmed-over canned ravioli, not even Franco-American brand—you can see what I was up against and then those four New York semites in the Calle Larga XXII Marzo talking about how they beat this guy out of what he thought: he was ripping me off and me from New York City where they got every scam, who do they think they are: this guy with his T-shirt, SAMMY'S WRECKING   If We Don't Have Fun No One Is Having Fun, and a line reproduction of the face of the man wearing the T-shirt planted right where his breasts were budding, and me walking along with string bag full of towel and swimsuit, plastic bag from the supermarket: two half litre cans of Coke, a small can of Pepsi, two small containers of yogurt, the stuff made with the Bulgarian bacteria (when I open it on the train, it is that watery imitation stuff, nothing like *kizalu miyalko,* but then I am just away from both Bulgaria and Turkey), three soft rolls still fresh, cloth bag with Carlos Fuentes's *Terra Nostra,* notebook, red flannel shirt in case it turns cold which it didn't . . . so picture taken of this guy walking and saying: fifth time in this place, that first time on the way to, but didn't know it exactly, of course, first time on the way to Bulgaria, the second time with Lilia leaving Bulgaria, the third time when sent by my father to give me a breath of air, and then there was a fourth time which I can't place a finger on exact date and now this fifth visit, one bookstore, as far as I can see replaced by a dress shop, the Locanda San Stefano has been upgraded to Hotel, though the hotel is just as shabby, but I would have stayed there: old time's sake the oldest fraud possibly. Well, anyway, at Marina's suggestion I am staying in Padova, Italians do it, you avoid all the unpleasant parts of Venice, that long line in the station with the people shouting: do you speak English with drunken kids on the steps of the station, those crosses they carry in the form of knapsacks. Yes, once I did, but never with aluminum frame and I am no longer twenty and looking for a good cheap meal, where are the good rides, too many people on the road and not enough of them have the vocation or maybe they all have the vocation and it was just a false bill of goods, and this bunch is just getting here too, too late.

If there was a Villa Paradiso in Patchogue it would be a sex club dishing up blonde pussy and red pussy and brillo pussy and there would be dicks of all shapes, lengths, widths, angles, cut, uncut. There would be no fun to be had by anybody because fun is not something that can happen in Patchogue if you come from Patchogue. All them wings in heaven cause a draft and everybody wanders around with their dripping noses talking about how if you stick a strand of weeping willow under your pillow you will find a puddle of snot in its place and your cold will be gone by the morning. Here in the Villa Paradiso I sit in a small room, plastic bags hanging from hooks, the large yellow towel drying, the swimsuit over the back of the chair, the Cokes and mineral water cooling on the marble ledge, the sound of pop music from somewhere and the sound of this typing, the warped wheel of the car in which I sit on the Long Island Railroad, almost back to the City. There in the City, to be unbearable, no one will be able to, no one will want to, just a pile of straws for the camel's back-breaking.

I have been away. I have come back. I will go away, again. There is no place for me there in the City. There is no place for me there in Patchogue. There is no place for me in Sofia. There is no place for me in Istanbul, in Venice, in Pavia, in Milano, in Paris, and probably no place for me in Dublin so I am, left with paradise.

Never have I read of a person being with another in paradise. Probably a problem of logistics which in this day of the computer just shouldn't be a problem: work out the space requirements, the individual likes/dislikes, might even write a song and who would dare to disbelieve the truth of a song.

I feel the City closing about me. The arms are very long and very soft. There is a feeling of being welcomed back home, at last, you have come back, didn't we know all along you'd come back, how could you avoid coming back. We know what is there even if we haven't been there, can there be anything there, of course, there can't be anything there, we have known this all along and you keep persisting in your dream of going away and we have allowed you to go away and

LOOK

you come back and have nothing to report except your long list of distempers and disappointments, your failures, your missed chances.

Your longings form the familiar misery you have known all along, so why have you gone away, even in the second place, it is something we really have no interest in understanding but we have to ask these questions to flesh out our role beginning with: how was your trip?

and continuing:

did you have a good trip?

and on with:

did you meet a lot of interesting people?

while we still must ask

was it expensive?

did you think we would find a new way of asking these old questions and

anyway

what is the big deal of going off to Europe? People have gone to the moon, they have sat down among heaps of thigh bones in the middle of Asia and had a jolly good time of it and you expect us to listen to your report of travels to Europe?

And I can only say I have not been away. It was all a frame to investigate the dimensions of living in this room in the Villa Paradiso: the little rooms and beyond a desert across which men and women will be able to walk for thirty-nine and a half days looking at exhibits of photographs just published of the Italian Ethiopian War . . . strings of penises hung up to dry and one gentleman with his penis detached, lying on his back, quite dead he is, the penis lying curled upon his shrunken stomach, for some reason no bloat, must have been a good time had by all, as they say, while, to think our guys, our fine boys, the lads, were only collecting ears in Vietnam and were held up to be monsters of the first order, to think of the horror that has to be hidden away in Patchogue because of what people have read in City papers, all of which is untrue and moreover full of lies . . .

I was not away, not for a moment. I have always been here. I have not left. I am in the City at this very moment as I sit in the Villa Paradiso, where the toilet bowl leaks and the mosquitoes are getting cooked in an electric device fitted into the electric shaver plug and because of the humidity I am aware of body parts I had thought lost to sensation: elbow, knee, both right and left; my nose, my heart, my brain, not the big right toenail because that has only been injured and will remain injured by, for all times, by Frank, a citizen of Patchogue who has moved to Bellport and an unlisted telephone number. He is afraid I will call from the Villa Paradiso and ask him to drive me over to Venice where Melinda is sitting at this moment in Harry's Bar. She could have been sitting in one of the painted salons of Florian's Café on San Marco but she does not, yet, come complete with white poodle. Frank was the driver the night first:love bit the ground and became the great regret of my life, my passion, my heart's, my heart, my excuse, my salad, my potato, *mousaka,* my Pepsi Cola, my English racing bike, my lack of seriousness at this exact moment, when Frank comes to the door and tells me he is unavailable, tonight, and wishes forever more. He is no longer part of this journey and wishes to be forgotten as does the suddenly forming line of those people from the high school Class of 1962, Patchogue Senior High School.

I have held you all close to my heart and now you come wishing me to chisel you out of the marble surrounding the messy organ. What shall I place in your stead?

War is sometimes a good thing. I tried to get this point across in Bulgaria. In Istanbul there was no need to say so. Here in Padova it is

self-evident, to me. One has only to go to the church of the Eremitani with its celebration of the bombing raid back in 1944 which got rid of much of the fresco by Mantegna. What remains is either precious or just enough— but BETTER, it reminds me, nothing endures. Patchogue, Long Island, the whole mess could get swept away in one great hurricane and together with a hurricane the water supply would become fully polluted due to the constant tampering in the last thirty, forty years, there is already plenty of chemical seepage and so, now, just a good hit of saltwater and these people would be coming back into the City where we could await them, armed to the teeth, and make great funeral pyres with their heaped-up corpses, while the stragglers would die in the smoke and lay out a fine carpet for the gulls to wheel over and peck apart. The wild dogs. The bridges would have to go and truly, now, only the dead will know Brooklyn, and only the dead will live with the dead. Ain't it a grand plan and almost a reason to read the newspapers during the months of September and October with the hope there'll be one of those storms down there in the Gulf that will whip itself up the coast, hopefully looking benign and then suddenly   POW
POW
change of direction and not even time really to get the announcements to the citizenry and hardly any high ground for the people to go to. Luckily, Melinda will be in Harry's Bar; Barbara lives in Ireland. The tombs of my parents will be washed away but I carry the picture of their deaths in my heart (sentimental me). Wisconsin, here I come.

   With the final confirmation of the cleansing of what was once Long Island, I will cease to read the newspapers, because who wants to read the dreary Monday morning quarterbacking, backbiting, replay of the moment by moment ecstasy . . . there will be the predictable editorials condemning the spontaneous clapping heard across the country when the words went out: Long Island is no more. Patchogue is no more. How cold and cruel people can be, these pens will complain. They will be answered by more clapping because how else to answer such people. They have not the ears to hear or the eyes to see. They are a vast stomach and no anus for waste removal so it comes up the same way it went down.

   Life goes on and I move about in my room, looking to the streets to walk this evening. I am sure to find one. I will walk down the street and find what I am looking for:
end of story.
End of story. I wish this was the case. It ain't. Story must continue. Train

has not arrived in the City. I'm still after a loose end or am said to be after a loose end. On the train from Venice this afternoon I was looking out at the mist-shaded green fields and was thinking: what is in store for me now that I am/have turning/ed forty.

Should get myself really married. Have a wife who likes to be abused and who likes to abuse. Have two children if possible. Get myself a job that I can allow to slowly fill up all of my waking hours and eventually my dream life. Get a driver's license. Get a car and begin to make payments on it. Start saving money for the kids' education. Have an affair with that blonde pussy now that I can afford the real blonde pussy who likes to go to expensive restaurants and have money spent on her; in return she sucks and fucks with practiced yet tender efficiency. Start paying on the co-op apartment. Make a decision about whether the summer-house will be by the ocean or will be in the mountains: there are arguments to be heard from both parties. Once the summerhouse has been secured begin to worry about what to do with it during the off-season. Plan that European holiday . . . at least a couple while the kid is young enough to go for almost next to nothing because after, we have to be reasonable. Have more work done on the teeth. Have work done on a selected organ of the body which is beginning to show a certain amount of wear and tear. Wife is having an affair and of course it doesn't bother me because I am getting what I want and only hope she is getting what she wants. We should think about moving out of the City . . . this will go on for some time. An old friend visits from college because he saw the mention about my promotion in the college alumni magazine . . . he is wondering if I can loan him some money—I say why not because if worse comes to worse I can write it off the taxes and rather give you the money than give it to the government which only knows how to shove it up some nigger's ass. It's possible, one or even both of the kids have taken a strong dislike to their father and are trying to buy their way into another family; I have offered to pay part of the dowry if they are successful in their negotiations. I must wear a hat because the top of my head is totally bald; the sun gives me headaches. All the members of my mother's family and father's family are now dead and my sister and I are wondering who will be the first to go. I have looked into burial plots and have made some sort of contact with the local church . . . because the church is now reluctant to bury someone who is just showing up for the first time, on this, the day of his funeral. I have seen Lilia in the distance; her hair is grey and she smiles at me. We no longer get together because things have not been good for either one of us and now that we are older and finally can admit it: back at that moment when we stepped down from the train in Venice . . . I felt it this afternoon, in the rain, as I was walking to the toilet, felt how stupid and arrogant and ugly I must have been as we were getting the luggage off the train that April in 1968 . . . and there was so much luggage and I

had to take a piss and Lilia was saying she was afraid to be alone on the platform
and I said, just wait right there with the luggage, it will be okay, we have only to
take a boat and get to Accademia and then there is a little hotel from that time,
but it was more: we were away from Bulgaria and what were we going to do now,
now that we have to, live together and there was no fucking and no sex and we
were just without any words, or words enough and now she has grey hair and I
have none and while we were able to talk for years about the times—as it went
along there came a time when we had to admit—admit what I can't remember
but we did admit something and I have that story but finally I have had to put the
story to the side since I am now a married man with wife, children, job, house,
and responsibility, almost have the grave, where I will lie, paid for, and what can
we talk about. Lilia is counting the years to the date her pension from the United
Nations begins and she can, finally, live.

And each day will be like the next and the one after that will have the
same shape as the one before it and I have shoved myself off a cliff and am
just waiting for the moment of contact with the earth because life follows
fiction and it assumes with the new morning I will not have a new story to
meet when I awake with the sun to get myself back into Venice to look for
the cemetery . . . to remind myself, again, the only lesson a cemetery can
teach: there are no rehearsals for any of this: we go through it alone, only
once.

E PERICOLOSO SPORGERSI
NE PASSE PENCHER AU DEHORS
NICHT HINAUSLEHNEN
IT IS DANGEROUS TO LEAN OUT

I am waiting for a hammer to come along, bang me into the ground.
This has gone on for too long. I wait. It is good to practice waiting. The
skill will come in handy when we go hunting on Long Island to clean the
land of mad dogs and the remnants of those who survived the hurricane.
We will have been warned against falling in love with the intended targets
of our rifles. It can happen, rarely, but it does happen and then. Need I get
very graphic? Going back to that land, ruined in such a short period of
time, that place where the only shadows are the shadows created by the
mountains of shit raised up as monuments to the great open spaces between
the ears of the people. Shadows, in the land of my birth, come complete
with odors of decomposition . . . where in Europe can you find such
advanced shadows . . . in the market in Padova there is a live eel tank.

Tried to feel sentimental about the eels but failed. A sudden capsule of maturity or senility. A herd of grey hairs in my beard. And am struck with the need to get to the end. To write: the end.

To see the final step I have to take, to hear the final station announced, to see the station, to hear the people getting out of their seats, to feel the legs of the man next to me pass against mine, to know in more ways than one: I have arrived, back from the wars, I have returned to where I started out from. I have come back. I have come home. I have gone away. I have returned. To carry flowers, to carry a packet of soil from each of the places I have visited, to set the soil on little dishes and watch tiny houses begin to grow in memory of where I have been: terminal cuteness.

Patchogue is always waiting. It never goes away. I need have no fear.

> Drive Safely
> Washington Memorial Park
> We Can Wait

Nothing will have changed. The rope is warm from many times being used in my absence. The stool is set, the rope fastened about the water pipe running across the ceiling of the bathroom. When I step the one great step a man can still take, there will appear a silhouette from the crowd, down there, in the street, on Second Avenue, and there will be called forth roll upon roll of applause. Another has taken his life into his own hands and seen, with more than just eyes or understood with more than frail understanding: what a waste of time.

A number of stories didn't happen. Ain't that grand. Always time, another time, for another setting forth, another book for the drawer, that drawer crammed full like the sheets upon which I sleep at home, stuffed with farts for a month at a time; finally even I can't stand the accumulation of myself. Ship is setting forth, armies have been defeated. The talks of exile are being perfected but with no place to go into exile to—at a loss where they will be recited, where the lamp will burn low, the music sad and the women will measure the years as alluvial lines ranging out from the corners of their eyes, and the men will gaze at that usual fixed point on the far wall and dream of walls, sunlight, sudden rainstorms and the warmth of her clothed breast, there, standing in the corner of a fallen-into-ruin shed on a property that once belonged to his or her grandmother but was now owned by City People who never left the City because they were too busy counting their money, convinced as they were that every time they counted the money it increased by just that little which was necessary so as to stay ahead of the march of the price of bread.

Just a turning away because YES it is getting close to that time. My watch is neither fast nor slow. Right on time, right on the money. On the button and I can taste her button as the palms of my hand lift her bottom off the sheets and my face into the wetness and my mouth falls to the button, with the wish to find another word for this fleshy morsel.

These nights in Padova, sitting in the Café Pedrocchi, under the wall of glassed-in map of the world, projected down from the North Pole, the whole Western Hemisphere, in such a way, New York is lost in an obscure corner and Long Island, just a blur. The exact necessary way to understand those places. If only it was true in REAL LIFE, that nightmare arriving with the inevitability of the train arriving in Penn Station.

I set forth to Patchogue in May, was it, or it could be June and now I find myself in the early morning chill of October; the leaves getting ready to turn, to fall, and nothing to wait for except the end of the year and the days to begin to lengthen, once again, but before that happens I have to live through my birthday, the anniversary of my potential death day. Halfway through this life. Or more if I look at the performance of my mother and father. Another year. Not getting any younger. This journey will not be made again. I have made it for the last time. I will have to find another somewhere else to get to. I will have to seek out some lowly imaginary fiction, romance. Three years I have postponed this coming to Italy. If I had known, but no way to know and everything, as they say, happens because it is supposed to happen in exactly the way it does happen. We are caught in an awful divine predestination, whether we like it or not and with no stake, fire, dungeon, or rack, who's to say one way or the other for sure, just feels like it to me, feels right to me that I have not come back to Italy until this moment, right on the money landing in the Villa Paradiso which has the same feel as the large house of the Quakers in Dublin, a mansion in Rathmines, where I ended up that first week in Dublin in 1964, the wallpaper peeling, one wall pulling away from the floor, but sleeping in a large warm bed, the covers heaped up all about me because of the chill and I was IN EUROPE, finally, and did not know what was going to happen to me. I was away from Patchogue, but not that far because the shadow of Melinda lurked in the corner. She did not let go that whole year, try as I did, to shake her in Leipzig, Copenhagen, but I am running away from my own comparison, that large house in Dublin and this large house, really, in Padova, of course I don't know where this part of the comparison is going to lead, except it has to end in Penn Station.

This is all getting much too personal. Where is the distance, the cold dreary search for understanding of how we ended up where we did, living on Second Avenue in New York City when all along I have always hoped for, longed for and understood that my true home was in Europe. Now of course the chance to think of myself as a coward and make plans accordingly.

Should lay out as carefully as I can what awaits me in the City. There is always something waiting when you come back from a place like Patchogue. The armor has been stripped away and the spots of flesh where the armor has worn at are newly opened and the heat drops sweat into the wounds; the pain causes a certain distraction which is easier to deal with . . . in these weeks away from Sofia and before the City I have lost the gift of gab. I have had to listen to myself go on, go on filling up the silent space all about me as I sit in the Villa Paradiso under injunctions: you must go to Vicenza, you must see the cemetery, one more time in Venice, you must kill Venice forever, turn it into:

what was Venice like?

Green snakes between crumbling piles of brick.

Ezra Pound has a flowering bush above where he rots.

All the ugly people of Europe and America drift to Venice for a final appearance before heading back to their empty northern hovels, their American suburbs, hurrying in fact because the new season is already underway on the television, brunch is being missed and hey, what about the World Series?

I will fill up my last minutes with such people. I want a suddenly appearing mountain. I want distraction in the form of . . . no, just pure and simple distraction. I am getting old. There are few voices I can listen to without thinking what an interesting lampshade that skin would make.

Nothing dramatic. Not in keeping with the plan of this journey. If something was to happen it would have happened by now. It is too late in the game as the train is in the final plunge for the City. Those few passengers are gathering themselves and their belongings and getting ready to rise and go forth and go forth as must I go forth and be prepared for all the ambushes awaiting me on the journey down from the station to my room and be prepared for, be prepared for that perverse desire to, now, let's get honest with each other . . . wouldn't that be a kick in the head. At these last moments to hurl one's self into a long sacrificial argument and find myself packing and leaving for the Bowery to live out my days because what I have learned on this journey is: to become forty in October is to have no meaning at all. I will walk around the Villa Paradiso on Second Avenue. I will look at the cats. I will look at the books. I will be sitting on the broken-down sofa in the sitting room. I will listen to the cop cars go by down on the avenue. I will watch an ambulance turn and not think who has died but rather who is going home, finally, after a long stay in the hospital. I will try to think sunny days need not always be filled with executions, riots, and myself turning away, for that last time. All those things said and unsaid. To have gone away and come back and be able to think about going away and going to places that do not call up worm-eaten corpses, because have plenty of those right here in my pocket. Always have the corpse of a dream in my pocket. I should make a collection of all my sperm-soaked handkerchiefs so in old age I will really know once upon a time I did have this ability to continue the race and have for my very own a little human reproduction of myself, right there on the floor getting ready to die in his or her own time, as well she or he should plan, because we won't be here forever, as did my parents say before and as they have so wonderfully proven, lying, as they do now, in the sandy soil of Long Island, hopefully to be swept by flood and pestilence.

The Villa Paradiso is very quiet this evening. People have not yet returned from filling their eyes with Venice. There is nothing to bring back from Patchogue. The village doesn't come equipped with postcards. No one has the imagination to package up what there is and reproduce it upon postcards. I have done what I can. You have to go out with camera and hunt down those churches, those water-treatment plants, that Patchogue River; maybe do a sunset as the ferry leaves for Fire Island filled with those last-minute sensation-seekers going over to the beach to see if they have any feelings left, is that the word they are always looking for, *feelings,* though much was lost in the years gone by, always the chance some feeling is still hanging around and with the right chemistry, who knows, why not give it a shot, right, what does a body have to lose and all the rest of the sensitive bullshit.

The plane will call up tears and the station will call up a single tear. Age has dug such ditches across her face and my face, just figures of fun for the young people to point their fingers at.

Patchogue   211

I bring no gifts from this journey. There is nothing I want from the place where I have been. More junk to dust, collecting on shelves and then down to the street, into the rubbish barrels, to reappear in front of some slobbering nigger trying to put together a pint, because this one still got some sense of who he is and he is not a guy who got to go begging nickels off white kids. I bring only myself back. A certain disappointment there. Could have used a nice long list of gifts and enjoyed the exercise of invention.

A long hello and good-bye. No farewells but with a quick get the cover on the box and screw those gold-plated screws down as fast as you can, no second chances, no, just do your job and let's get going. And are you happy? Can there be any more difficult question or a question allowing for any answer under the sun. Moment to moment to moment I wish the wall to close over me. I wish and I wish against and I wish.

It is going on quarter to eight in a September evening in Padova, Italy; in Patchogue at this time of night the televisions are on, the food is working its way down the small intestine and getting ready to plop into the large intestine. Later, I will walk from the Villa Paradiso to the Café Pedrocchi, to sit under the wall covered with a map of the world. The Oasis Bar has been torn down in Patchogue. The vets have moved to higher ground. They are getting ready. No one listens to just a bunch of old drunks. With the Oasis gone, there is no one last place I would seek out in Patchogue. Ben's Bookstore was closed because they had to make room for a new courthouse: who wants to read, is said with a smile and laugh, when you got the beach, television, Felice's Bar, and what is going on every night in the parking lots of Patchogue: better than any old book can match and of course the style is right and exactly on the spark which begins the motor which puts into motion the rack upon which my body has been placed though they will learn nothing from me. No confessions to be made. No absolution sought or offered. Just going about my business. Doing what I can, in my own way to ease the journey from these rooms on Second Avenue. The sun is going to come up or it is not.

I am in the City

I am in the City.

I am sitting in my room. My bags are on the floor in front of me. They have been emptied and the contents heaped on the bed. I have rolled up my sleeves and have tested the razor against the waiting flesh of my wrists. The windows are open. I am back from Patchogue. I am back from Italy. I am back from Istanbul. I am back from Sofia.

I am waiting for the weather report. When it comes over the air I will know what to do. What not to do. The hour will run late and I will have decided to wait another year. I want to see the chaos. I want to hear the screams of shock and disappointment. The train was right on time. Things have improved a little on the Long Island Railroad. The conductor did not have to clobber anyone with his nightstick. On the way downtown I watched the police scrape the remains of something human from the tracks at Twenty-third Street.

The crowds on St. Marks Place were dancing. An old lady was being eaten by these kids from New Jersey. They had cooked her over a fire behind Cooper Union.

The stuff from my suitcase will have to be burned. I can do nothing with it. I cannot stand to have any reminders of where I have been. It is all so painful. To have gone away and not stayed. To have failed, again. Like the other times. This time, a failure, even returning from Patchogue. At least they have the possibility of a great wave rearing up during the hurricane to be announced on tonight's weather. I sit in my room, high up, over the avenue.

I do not know whether I am the urn or the Canova angel carrying the urn into the dark hole in the wall. I have sat on the train as it paused on the bridge coming from Venice to Mestre: the green water, the faded green of a Marine uniform, the distant blue houses, her blue eyes, the sudden turning on of the street lights, a bus speeding by, me sitting in the train for Padova, for the Villa Paradiso, in the rain, to sit, getting the luggage ready to have luggage at my feet in the City, to know I have brought nothing back from this journey, not even the ash of some exotic adventure.

Myself has come back. I am in the City. I have gone to Patchogue. I have been in Patchogue. I have come back from Patchogue.

19 IX 1984, Villa Paradiso, Padova, Italy
28 June 1989, New York City